WHOM SHOULD SHE BELIEVE?

Meryl faced a most fearful decision.

Should she believe her adored fiancé, Edward Willoughby, when the handsome viscount assured her that his beautiful mother was the soul of kindness and generosity?

Or should she believe his blunt-spoken country cousin Jason, when he gave her a veiled warning about that same dazzling winning woman, then refused as a gentleman to say more?

Or should she believe Lady Gloriana herself, when she told Meryl about a secret side of Edward that could only fill a proper young lady such as Meryl with loathing and horror?

Or should she—dared she—believe her own eyes . . . her own heart. . . ?

Barbara Hazard
The Queen Bee

A SIGNET BOOK

NEW AMERICAN LIBRARY

For Loree, with love
—and a promise

NAL BOOKS ARE AVAILABLE AT QUANTITY DISCOUNTS WHEN USED TO
PROMOTE PRODUCTS OR SERVICES. FOR INFORMATION PLEASE WRITE
TO PREMIUM MARKETING DIVISION, NEW AMERICAN LIBRARY,
1633 BROADWAY, NEW YORK, NEW YORK 10019.

SIGNET TRADEMARK REG. U.S.PAT.OFF. AND FOREIGN COUNTRIES
REGISTERED TRADEMARK—MARCA REGISTRADA
HECHO EN CHICAGO, U.S.A.

SIGNET, SIGNET CLASSIC, MENTOR, ONYX, PLUME,
MERIDIAN and NAL BOOKS are published by NAL PENGUIN
INC., 1633 Broadway, New York, New York 10019

First Printing, August, 1988

1 2 3 4 5 6 7 8 9

PRINTED IN THE UNITED STATES OF AMERICA

Prologue

Bath, April 19, 1816

Petite Maman,

No doubt you will find what I am about to tell you hard to believe. I can scarce believe it myself, it was so completely unexpected. For whoever would have imagined, on a casual visit to friends in the provincial spa town that is Bath, so full of the elderly and infirm, that I would find the one ideal woman in the entire world for me? Is it not a miracle, *Maman*? I suppose it serves me right, for I, in my infinite wisdom, have always scoffed at miracles, considered them merely the product of overheated imaginations. I shall never do so again.

Her name is Meryl Lancaster. Such a prosaic name for someone who is all light and loveliness, grace and goodness! She lives here in Bath with an elderly great-aunt, for her parents are dead. I am sure you know the family. She is distantly related to Lord Carson of Dorset. Those Lancasters.

But how to describe her to you? She is tall, with a graceful, slender figure, and when she moves, she reminds me of a flower swaying in the breeze. Fair-complexioned, she has a mass of glorious chestnut hair that waves over her brow in the most delightful way, and she has large hazel eyes a man could drown in. (Are you laughing at me, *Maman*? I do not blame you. Obviously, falling in love also involves a descent into triteness.)

And her voice . . . Ah, it is warm and deep and kind, although when she laughs, it is more melodious than the most beautiful music ever written. For she has, withal, great wit and liveliness, and possesses such a spirit of fun, I call her Merry. You will understand why when

5

you meet her, and I know you will adore her as much as I do.

I met her here at one of the assemblies, by the veriest chance. In fact, I stepped on her gown and ripped it a little. So clumsy of me, and yet she assured me it was no great matter. And then she smiled, and I saw the dimple in her right cheek, next to her lovely, rosy mouth, and I was lost.

Say you forgive me, *Maman*, for my long silence. I meant to write and tell you of Merry before, but I found myself waiting, hoping to be able to announce stupendous news. And now I can. I have asked Merry to be my wife, and she has accepted me. I am sure no man on earth has ever been as happy as your son is right now.

I plan to bring her to London soon so you and Jane may meet the paragon I have won for my bride. And, of course, we rely on you to help plan our wedding. Being motherless, Merry is in great need of advice.

We will break our journey at Cousin Wilma's near Thatcham, and Merry will have her maid with her to play propriety. I am sure, however, that neither one of us will notice she is even there, and I do hope Cousin Wilma will forgive me if I appear a trifle abstracted.

In the meantime, I continue at York House until my Merry is ready to travel, for I have told her to pack all her things. Having been lucky enough to find her, I never intend for her to leave me again, and, of course, we plan an early wedding. The earlier the better.

Maman, why did you never tell me that when I finally fell in love I would feel this way? So joyous and complete, so awed and humbled by the knowledge that my heartfelt love is returned by this one, perfect, incredible woman. It is a miracle indeed.

Remember me to my dear sister. Merry and I will be with you both shortly.

Love,
Teddy

P.S. Merry calls me Edward. It does not sound the least strange on her wonderful lips.

1

MISS Meryl Lancaster stole a look at her fiancé's profile as he glanced out the window of the coach, and once again she experienced that now familiar stirring in the vicinity of her heart. Edward Willoughby, Viscount Trumbull, was one of the handsomest men she had ever seen. Of no more than average height, he still must attract attention with his strong, yet aristocratic features, and his deep-set brilliant blue eyes. Beneath his elegant beaver, his black hair curled in a fashionable cut. It looked shiny and crisp, yet she knew how soft it was to the touch.

She felt a little shy at her thoughts, and her eyes hurried past his broad shoulders and narrow waist, his muscled thighs, to where one of his hands rested on his knee. His hand was long and slender, and was, like his hair, misleading. She had seen those hands in perfect control of a restless, highbred team, but, oh, how gentle they were when he caressed her!

The gentleman being so wholeheartedly admired coughed a little, and she looked up to see him regarding her with one black eyebrow quirked and a dancing light in his blue eyes. Miss Lancaster blushed. Edward Willoughby put his head back and laughed, and she glanced quickly to the opposite seat. Her young maid was quiet, staring out the window of the coach as if she had just entered a world so foreign to her that it fascinated her to the point she could not take her eyes from it. Dear Nora, how understanding she is, Miss Lancaster thought even as she lowered her lashes. For even though the maid was as unobtrusive as a mouse, Meryl Lancaster knew she must not forget she was there. She must guard both her looks and her speech until she and Edward could be alone again.

The viscount picked up her hand in its neat kid glove and raised it to his lips, squeezing it gently as he did so. The stirring inside her spread into a tide of warmth that rose from her toes to the top of the chestnut waves under her green bonnet.

"Are you tired, Merry?" he asked. As she shook her head, he added, "It will not be much longer now. I know it has been tiresome, for Cousin Wilma was a trifle overbearing and boring last evening. How well you handled her, my love! But when we reach Mount Street, my mother will be there to see to your comfort, as will my sister, Jane."

As she smiled at him, he went on, "You will adore my mother, Merry! Everyone does. She is so gay and beautiful, so kind and good. And she is so anxious to meet you! I had a reply to my letter from her just before we left Bath, and she was all impatience to do so. She bade me hurry you up to town, for she claimed that since I loved you, she must love you too. And she said she could not wait to take you in her arms."

He smiled down at her, and Miss Lancaster smiled back, hearing the words he did not speak that told her how he longed to take her in his own arms right now.

"She sounds delightful, Edward," she said in her deep warm voice. "How kind she is, too, for it cannot be an easy thing to have a strange young lady deposited on your doorstep—one, moreover, who intends to marry your only son. Why, for all she knows, I might be a dreadful creature who captured you by devious wiles and who is not at all suitable for the exalted post you have asked me to fill!"

Edward had begun shaking his head halfway through this speech, and now he chuckled. "No, she would never think that, my dear," he said. "*Maman* has the utmost faith in my judgment, for she has always said that I do just as I ought and never forget my consequence or my name. Of course," he added pensively, carefully not looking at her now, "I admit she may be a little prejudiced. Just a little, mind you!''

His fiancée laughed at him, that wonderful cascade of musical notes that he had come to love and that he tried so often to evoke.

"And your sister, will she be pleased, too?" Miss Lancaster asked a moment later.

"I see no reason why she should not be ecstatic," he said. "It will be so wonderful for her to have a sister at last. Although Jane seems happiest in *Maman*'s company and does not appear to care for friends her own age, I know she cannot help but love you almost as much as I do." He paused, and then he leaned closer to whisper, "Almost. She could never love you as much as I do. No one could."

As the maid stirred a little on the opposite seat, reminding them of her presence, only Miss Lancaster's eyes replied. But those large orbs of deep hazel flecked with golden lights and set off by her thick lashes told him clearly that his love was returned tenfold.

It was all so very strange, so very new, Meryl Lancaster thought as the coach rumbled into Staines and the viscount turned away to watch for the inn where he intended to change the team. Never in her most impossible daydreams had she ever thought she would give her heart so quickly. Even when she had been a child, she had known Cinderella was only a fairy tale, and she had never empathized with any of the heroines in the romantic fiction she had read. Love at first sight was only a fantasy, and real life was very different, which she, being an intelligent, practical young woman, understood very well. It was most unlike her to be so precipitate, and in such an important matter that involved her whole future as well.

But when she had first looked up from her seat in the Assembly Rooms at one of the regularly scheduled cotillion balls that were held every Thursday during the Season, and beheld him before her, apologizing for stepping on her gown, she had known her future had been set on an irresistible course.

She was attending that evening with Mr. and Mrs.

George Grant and their two daughters, and when the
stranger had beckoned to Mr. King, the master of
ceremonies, and begged to be introduced to her, she had
known that Edward Willoughby was the only man in the
world for her. And yet she remembered how she had
tried to deny this. She had told herself she must be
cautious, for she knew nothing about him, nothing at
all. He might be a married man, a rake, or a drunkard,
even a thief or a ne'er-do-well hoping to take advantage
of her because she was all alone in the world and
without protection. But when he asked her to dance and
she rose and took his hand, all such cool, considered
reasoning fled away.

She saw he was not much taller than she was herself,
and suddenly that became the most marvelous attribute
he could possibly have. For now she did not have to
look very far up, and she was that much closer to his
shapely, sensuous mouth, his blazing blue eyes. And as
she smiled at him, she was near enough to see the muscle
that moved for a moment in his lean cheek in response.

He had danced with her twice and sat with her party
during tea. On the drive home after the ball, she had
had to endure a lot of teasing in which there was more
than a hint of envy and spite from both Cloris and
Audrey Grant. But this teasing only raised her spirits,
for now she knew she had not been imagining his attrac-
tion for her.

The viscount had not mentioned any further meeting
to her, but when she rose the next morning, she had
dressed carefully in a pretty new gown. And when she
came downstairs to ask her great-aunt her plans for the
day, she found he had sent her a bouquet of spring
flowers, and a small package as well.

Opening it with trembling hands, she discovered a
silver case containing pins and needles. The note that
accompanied the gift told her that since he intended to
be in her company as often as she would permit, it might
be wise for her to carry the case constantly for he had
proven to be such a clumsy fellow.

Fortunately, Great-aunt Elizabeth was going to the

Pump Room that morning with one of her cronies and then on to a card party, and so would not require her services. After she had taken her aunt's fat, elderly pugs for their morning walk, she was free for the remainder of the day. She had sat in the front drawing room with her needlework, and she had not been the least surprised when the viscount sent in his card shortly thereafter and begged her to go for a drive with him.

The days that followed this first expedition had sped by in a haze of happiness. As she learned more about Edward Willoughby and told him of her own life, she had come to trust her first feelings for him. Yes, he was the one. He was good and honorable, always so careful of her. And never once did he overstep the bounds of propriety, although she knew she would have been hard put to stop him if he had tried. But he wooed her in unexceptional style. Even her great-aunt, who had no real love for the male sex, had had to admit he was a pretty-behaved young man. And from Miss Elizabeth Lancaster, that was high praise indeed.

They went for walks, both in Bath and in the surrounding countryside; they arranged to meet at Duffield's library when Meryl went there to change her great-aunt's books; and one lovely day he drove her out to the Mendip Hills for a lavish picnic. And always they talked and laughed together as if they had known each other from childhood, and spoke openly and completely about their pasts as if it were the most important thing in the world that everything about them become known to the other.

When the viscount asked her to marry him after a mere three weeks' acquaintance, Meryl Lancaster had accepted at once. For herself, she knew she would have agreed to it if he had asked her after only a week. And when he took her in his arms, she was quick to put her own arms around him in complete surrender, returning his first passionate kiss with just as much fervor as he gave it.

By now, of course, she knew all about his beautiful mother and his younger sister, Jane, about their town

house on Mount Street in London and his estate in
Hampshire. She knew how he had lost his father when
he was only five, and how brave his mother had been,
bringing up her children alone. She had never
remarried, which the viscount professed a most unusual
thing for a woman with all her attributes. Instead, she
had been content to remain Viscountess Trumbull, and
filled her days seeing to her children's needs and
happiness. Miss Lancaster envied him his mother. She
had never known her own, and her reticent father, so
busy with his books and scholarly pursuits, had spoken
of her but rarely all the time she was growing up. Now
she quite longed to meet the lovely Gloriana, and she
hoped that lady would love her as well as she was
prepared to love her in return.

It was full dark when the viscount's traveling carriage
pulled up in Mount Street at last. Miss Lancaster had
never been to the metropolis before, and she had been a
little disappointed that she could see so little in the dusk.
To have Edward pointing out the various public
buildings, the parks, and the squares when she could not
see them clearly was frustrating, as she had been quick
to tell him. He had laughed at her and promised her a
grand tour of town in the near future.

Meryl looked around eagerly as Edward helped her
down the steps of the carriage. Before her was a tall,
impressive house made of pale granite, with wrought-
iron palings before it, and a set of shallow marble steps
leading up to the front door. Two flambeaux burned in
holders on either side of that door, and she was glad to
see the welcoming lights that told her they were
expected.

And then the front door flew open and a slight, tiny
figure ran down the steps, exclaiming in a high, breathless voice as she did so. The little lady threw herself into
the viscount's arms, to be picked up, spun around, and
thoroughly kissed.

"Oh, my dear, how glad I am to see you at last!" the
lady exclaimed. "It has been such ages, and I declare I
have been in alt for hours, waiting for you!"

The viscount kissed the soft cheek so near to him before he lowered her to the ground. With his arm still tight around her, he said proudly, "May I present Miss Meryl Lancaster, my dear?" Then he chuckled and shook his head as he said, "But, no, that is much too formal for my future bride. This is my Merry, of course."

As the lady smiled a welcome and held out her hand, Merry sank into a curtsy and smiled in return. "I am delighted to meet you, Miss Willoughby," she said. "Edward has told me so much about his dear sister, Jane."

To her surprise, the lady began to laugh, a high trill of complete amusement. "Oh, no, no, you dear, absurd creature!" she exclaimed. "I am not Teddy's sister. I am his mother!"

"His mother?" Merry asked, her eyes widening. "But—but you cannot be his mother! You are much too young for that!"

The lady laughed again and left the shelter of her son's arm to come and take her guest's hands. In the flickering light that came from behind her, she still looked impossibly young to Meryl Lancaster. "Well, it is true I had Teddy on my seventeenth birthday, but I do assure you I am his *Maman*. But you must allow me to introduce myself, since my naughty Teddy has not done so," she went on. She cast a mischievous look at her son where he leaned against the palings, chuckling softly, and said, "I am Lady Trumbull, Gloriana Regina. Such a mouthful for little me, is it not? But both my parents were such tiny things; perhaps they felt if they gave me two long, impressive names, I would grow to fit them? Alas, all their hopes were in vain! I have less than five feet in my dish."

Her lips curved in an irresistible smile, and Merry smiled back. The lady clasped her hands tightly as she said, "What a lovely smile you have, my dear. I do not wonder that my Teddy succumbed to your charms in such a short time. But come! You must be weary from traveling, and in need of refreshment. I have had Mrs.

Wilkie alert the kitchen that supper will be required in half an hour, Teddy, if that will give you both time to freshen up. Do not feel you must change, Miss Lancaster," she went on, skipping a little as she led her guest up the steps to the door. "We are only family tonight."

As they reached the front hall, Merry could hear Edward giving the footmen instructions about the unloading of the baggage and introducing her maid to the butler. She looked at her hostess more carefully now, and although she could see she was nowhere near as young as she had first supposed, it still did not seem possible she was old enough to be Edward's mother. Why, he was twenty-five, and even if she had borne him when she was barely seventeen, that would make her forty-two today. And yet she hardly looked thirty! It was quite a shock. Her camellia-white face was unlined and her neck was as smooth as a girl's. And her black hair, arranged in artless ringlets, showed not a trace of gray.

Merry studied the lady's girlish figure as well. She had small high breasts and a waist her guest was sure she could have spanned with her own hands, and a pair of the smallest, most highly arched feet she had ever seen peeked from beneath the hem of her pretty rose silk gown. Suddenly aware she was staring, Miss Lancaster lowered her eyes in confusion and blushed.

Lady Gloriana seemed to understand, for she clapped her hands and laughed a little. "Yes, it is often remarked, so you need not look so conscious, my dear. You will soon grow accustomed," she said. As she came and took her guest's arm and smiled up at her, she added, "But I think it is mainly because I am so small that people still think of me as a silly young thing. And what a burden it has been to me!" she went on as she led her guest up the broad staircase. "Can you imagine *me* trying so hard to be the stern mama, the all-seeing, all-knowing chatelaine of the house? It has always been very difficult for me to make anyone take me seriously, from the smallest, youngest new maid to my own children when they began to grow up.''

As they reached the landing, she continued, ''But my methods seem to have worked, even so. You see, all I did was love them with all my heart, and expect only the best behavior from them. I think they obeyed me because they could not bear to disappoint me.''

She led Merry along the hallway and opened the door of a pretty bedchamber decorated in blue and white. ''This will be your room, my dear,'' she said. ''One of the maids will bring you hot water to wash with—the dressing room is through that door—and please do not fuss about your appearance. You look charming! We will expect you downstairs shortly.''

Merry nodded and dropped a curtsy, and the lady tripped to the door, where she turned and blew her guest a kiss. As the door closed behind her, Merry sank down on the wide bed. A feeling of relief flooded through her. She had not known what to expect from Edward's mother, and she had tried to be prepared for stiff formality and cold dignity or a barely concealed air of injury, no matter what Edward had told her about the lady's amiability. Instead, she had been given a warm, uninhibited welcome from someone she had been sure would resent her. For every time Edward had spoken of his closeness to his mother, and her love for him, she had worried that the lady would not care to share her son with another. But as it had turned out, she had worried in vain. She could not believe her good fortune!

She rose and removed her bonnet and pelisse as she heard the footmen toiling up the stairs with her trunks. As she went to inspect the dressing room, she thought she could hardly be faulted for making the mistake she had. It was not only Lady Gloriana's appearance that made her seem so young. No, it was her mannerisms as well: that light step with the occasional little skip to it, her breathless high voice, even her exaggerations were those of a much younger woman, almost those of an untried girl. It was truly remarkable.

Merry hoped that Edward's sister would be just like her, for it would be so much fun to have a friend her own age, especially one who was gay and charming and lovable as well.

Later, as she washed her hands and sat down at the dressing table so Nora could brush and rearrange her hair, she wondered why Miss Willoughby had not come to welcome her, too. But perhaps she is out to a party, she thought. Edward had told her how festive London was, the dizzying whirl of balls and receptions and entertainments that were held every night of the Season. He had even spoken of giving a ball and some dinner parties himself, to introduce her to the *ton*. It was all going to be such fun, she thought as Nora arranged a fresh white fichu around her shoulders. But Merry also knew it would only be fun because she would be with her dear Edward. And the reason she could look forward to braving society with such confidence was because she would be beside him, secure in his love.

But when Miss Lancaster went down to supper, she discovered that Miss Jane Willoughby had not gone out as she had supposed. As she entered the drawing room and Edward straightened up from the mantel, where he had been leaning, to come and bring her forward, she saw the young lady seated to one side of the hearth in a large wing chair. She had a look of her mother, and yet at the same time was completely unlike her. True, she had the same black ringlets, the straight little nose, and those intensely blue eyes, but there all resemblance ceased. This lady was tall and sturdy. She had a double chin and heavy arms, and her mouth was only a tiny rosebud between her full, round cheeks.

Merry tried to hide her surprise as Edward introduced her. As she curtsied, she said, "I am so glad to meet you at last, Miss Willoughby! I am sure you have heard by now of my earlier *faux pas*. You see, I thought Lady Gloriana was you when I arrived." She smiled, and the young lady stared at her.

"*Maman* is very young-looking, I know," she said, reluctantly rising to her feet and smoothing the too tight silk gown she wore over her ample curves. Now that she was standing Merry could see she was as tall as her brother.

"Ah, Tiny, I would not blame you in the slightest if you said you were sick to death of it," her mother said, coming to reach up and give her daughter a fond kiss before she held out her arm to Merry. "Come, my dear, we will go to the dining room at once. I am sure you must be famished, the both of you. And although Tiny and I ate earlier, for we had no idea when you would arrive, we will join you and keep you company. You see," she went on as the three of them walked arm in arm to the door, "it will give us a chance to get to know you. I cannot tell you how delighted we both are that you are to make your home with us from now on. We shall have such fun, the three of us!"

"The three of you?" the viscount asked ominously from where he was bringing up the rear.

His mother peeked over her shoulder, a tiny fairylike figure between the two much taller girls, and stuck her tongue out at him. "Pooh, Teddy, my love," she scolded. "You will soon be back at your clubs and your gaming and all the rest of those masculine amusements you so adore. And I cannot think it would amuse you at all to go shopping or to tea parties, or to anything of that nature!"

"No, but I must see Merry sometimes," he said as he came to hold that lady's chair for her and give her a warm, intimate smile.

His mother ran to him and clasped his hand tightly between both of hers as she peered up at him earnestly. "And so you shall, you ridiculous boy! But you must allow your sister and me to enjoy her company as well, isn't that so, dearest Tiny?"

"I wish you would not call me that, *Maman*. I have asked you not to before, if you remember," the girl said as she sat down across from their guest. Merry thought her blue eyes looked sullen as she added in a constricted voice, "I am not tiny anymore."

"Well, no," her mother agreed. "I keep forgetting

you are all of twenty-three now, and grown-up indeed.
But to me, you will always be my dearest Tiny.''

She turned to Merry then and explained, ''You see,
Jane was the smallest, wee baby! The doctors were so
worried she would not live! And so she became Tiny. Of
course, she takes after her father. He was such a tall,
well-set-up man. It really is too bad that Teddy was not
the one to do so. But no matter. I am content with my
little man and my statuesque daughter.''

She bit her lip for a minute, and then she said
seriously, ''I do beg your pardon, Jane, and I will try to
do better, I promise!'' As she went and took her seat,
she mused, ''I wonder now why I called you Jane? I
thought I liked it at the time, and it is my dear sister's
name, but now I consider it plain. Why, do you
suppose, did I never think of Melisandra or Elizabeth or
Margaretta? Such lovely, long, grown-up names, are
they not?''

Everyone was smiling now, even the reserved
daughter of the house. ''Oh, *Maman*,'' she chided as
she passed Merry one of the covered dishes that had
been set out so they could serve themselves, ''you are
ridiculous! I should hate to be named Melisandra, for
you would have been sure to shorten it to Melly or Sansy
or some such thing.''

Merry thought Lady Gloriana looked a little disappointed, but in a flash her eyes lit up and she smiled at
them all impartially. ''No, I cannot claim I would never
have done such a thing,'' she confessed. ''It would be
just like me to saddle you with the most impossible pet
name!''

She turned to her guest then and began to question
her about her family and her life, begging her pardon
for her curiosity even before she began. Merry answered
as best she could, in between bites of the delicious
repast. She was hungry, for they had not lingered for
more than a light luncheon on the road in their haste to
reach town.

She was glad when Edward came to her rescue.
''Enough, *Maman*! Let Merry eat,'' he ordered, a fond

smile taking the sting from his words. "You will have some weeks to get to know her before our wedding can be arranged. Oh, and that's another thing: Merry's great-aunt gave her permission for the banns to be published immediately. I shall see to that tomorrow. And I don't see why we cannot be wed by the first week of June, do you?"

"As soon as that?" his mother asked, her blue eyes round. "Why, we will be rushed off our feet if you insist on it, my dear. But of course you do not realize how much work there is to arranging a wedding. And I am determined that your darling Merry shall have the finest wedding ever seen in London! But to do that, we must shop and shop and shop, and there will be alterations— perhaps a ball—all the festivities that young brides love."

Her son shook his head at her as he helped himself to more of the game pie. "But the shopping is what you look forward to, isn't it, *Maman*? Admit you have always adored it."

Lady Gloriana sat up straighter and tried to look stern, although to Merry, she just looked adorable. "I will confess a fondness for shopping," she said. Then, turning to her guest, she said, "You must forgive me for saying so, Merry, but you must not look provincial here in town. I am sure that is a most suitable gown for Bath and the country, probably considered all the crack there, but it just will not do here. And no matter what Teddy says, you are not going to be a dowd! No, you are going to be attired in the finest, most becoming gowns and ensembles we can find. But men do not understand these things."

Merry looked down at her neat green traveling dress. It was new, and one of the nicest she had ever owned, and she was a little surprised that it would not do.

She looked up to see Jane Willoughby regarding her with a cynical twist to her little mouth. "It would be best if you agreed with *Maman*, Miss Lancaster," she said. "She will find a way to persuade you to her views in the end, you see. She always does."

"Won't you please call me Meryl or Merry?" she asked a little shyly. "I would be so pleased if you did."

For a moment, Miss Willoughby hesitated, but then she nodded, and Merry took a deep breath. It appeared that Edward's sister needed careful cultivation. She was nowhere near as welcoming as her mother, but perhaps she was not of such a mercurial nature? Then too, she might resent someone coming between her and her brother after all these years.

Merry was recalled to the others as Lady Gloriana said, "And that's another thing, Teddy. Do you think it a good idea to post the banns before Merry even has a chance to meet some people in society?"

The viscount put down his fork, a little frown between his brows. "Whatever can you mean, *Maman*?" he asked.

"But you cannot have thought, and although it pains me to have to point it out to you, my son, you are being more than a little selfish. Surely you would not deny Merry the chance for some fun and frolic and gaiety before she settles down to the staid life of a fiancée. Why, she has never even made her comeout, enjoyed the giddy things any young girl looks forward to!"

Merry turned to look at Edward's face. His frown was very pronounced now, but before she could speak up and deny she wanted any such thing, Lady Gloriana went on, "Why not let me put it about that Merry is visiting me, at least for a few weeks. That way she will grow more accustomed and be more comfortable in the *ton*. And then, when your engagement is announced, no one will think a thing of it, not as lovely as she is. I shall say she is the daughter of an old childhood friend of mine. And consider too, darling Teddy, that any appearance of unseemly haste can only give rise to ugly conjectures. You know the tattle-mongers! You would not subject your intended to anything so distasteful, now, would you?"

"No, of course I would not," Edward said hotly. "But if we delay, our wedding cannot take place in June as I planned."

Merry saw a little look of impatience on his mother's face, but it was gone so quickly, she was sure she must have imagined it. But perhaps Lady Gloriana did not care to be contradicted?

"But of course it can, you impossible boy," she said lightly. "How silly you are, Teddy! While we are shopping for clothes for the Season, we can also be ordering bride's clothes. And the banns need only be posted for three consecutive Sundays. You shall be married at the end of June, the final gala occasion of the Season. It will be a triumph, and so suitable!"

Merry Lancaster ate her supper quietly, although she was as disappointed as she was sure Edward was at the delay. It was not that she did not appreciate his mother's concern for her reputation and well-being, but she did so yearn to belong to him fully and completely. She stole a glance at his handsome face, not knowing that her expressive eyes told him her thoughts as plainly as if she had spoken them. His own eyes kissed her as he said, "We shall see how she goes on, *Maman*. But I will agree not to make the announcement just yet."

The conversation became more general then, not only at the table but in the drawing room later. At last, Merry could hardly contain her yawns. She was weary from traveling and she could not wait to go to bed.

It seemed an age before Lady Gloriana looked up at the mantel clock and jumped to her feet. "But do look at the time," she exclaimed. "You must forgive me, dear Merry, for keeping you from your bed. Come along, Tiny," she ordered. "We must allow these love-birds a chance to say good night in private."

Her daughter rose obediently, her eyes lowered as she came to stand beside her mother and tower over her. Merry could feel herself blushing as she curtsied, but Edward hugged his mother and kissed her cheek. "Dear, dearest *Maman*," he said, his blue eyes twinkling. "You are the most wonderful, understanding woman in the entire world."

Lady Gloriana looked amused. "As if you would have let me whisk her upstairs before you had done so,

Teddy," she said. But as she walked to the door, her daughter striding along beside her, she added, "However, do not keep the poor child from her rest for long, or you will incur my most severe displeasure! I already think of Merry as my new daughter, and I intend to take the greatest care of her."

"And, besides, you plan an early shopping trip tomorrow, is that not so, *Maman*?" the viscount called after her.

The lady did not deign to answer, but her lilting trill of laughter was a confession in itself.

Edward Willoughby turned back to Merry and took her in his arms. "At last," he breathed as he lowered his head a little to kiss her. Merry put her arms around his neck and buried her hands in his thick black curls. His kiss was urgent, passionate, hungry, and she reveled in it and in the warm familiar tide that swept over her as it always did when he embraced her.

As he lifted his head at last and his hands caressed her back and her waist, he said, his voice shaking a little, "How hard it will be to sleep tonight, my love, knowing you are only a few doors away." And then he drew back so he could look deep into her eyes, and a little anxious look came into his own. "I hope I do not shock you, my dearest, but I want you so much," he said earnestly.

"No, no, you do not shock me, Edward," she whispered, running her hand lightly down one of his hard lean cheeks. "But I must say you surprise me."

"How so?" he murmured as he captured that hand and held it to his heart.

Merry leaned back in his arms. "Well," she said demurely, "we slept only a few doors apart last evening, if you remember, and it did not seem to disturb you then. Why would it do so now?"

He chuckled and shook his head. "But we were staying with Cousin Wilma, my dear, and I defy any man, no matter how much in love he might be, to have passionate thoughts in that pristine, spinster environment. It would be almost a desecration of all the lady holds dear, I assure you it would!"

Merry smiled up at him, her eyes full of love and laughter. Then she leaned closer and whispered, "I will find it hard to sleep too, my dear, even as tired as I am."

At that, he kissed her again with great warmth and tenderness. And he raised his head most reluctantly when they both heard the butler's footsteps, his little cough, in the hall.

As they drew apart, he said, "We will talk tomorrow. *Maman* always naps in the afternoon. I will take you driving then and show you the London you could not see when we arrived. And now I think I had better let you go while I am still able," he told her, putting his arm tight around her to lead her to the door. "Besides, if I do not, no doubt *Maman* will be back here with a switch to beat me for keeping you from your sleep. She may be little, but she is invincible, my love."

They went up the stairs together, and when they reached Merry's door, the viscount could not resist kissing her once again.

"Teddy! Good heavens, you are even worse than I thought!" his mother exclaimed. The pair sprang apart looking guilty as Lady Gloriana ran down the hall. She was wearing a diaphanous wrapper of deep blue, a charming confection of lace and satin that swirled around her tiny feet. In one hand she held a glass of warm milk. "I have just come to bring Merry something to help her sleep," she explained as she reached them. "Now run along, Teddy, do!"

The viscount drew back and bowed in defeat as his mother pushed Merry through the open bedroom door before her.

"Men!" she said, her voice amused as she went to place the milk on the bedside stand. "They are all of them so impatient, so impulsive."

She turned then and held out her arms, and Merry went into them as naturally as if she had done it every night of her life. Lady Gloriana stood on tiptoe to kiss her cheek. "I had to make sure you had everything you needed, my dear," she said. "I think it is so sad you never knew your own mother, but if you would not dislike it, dear Merry, I would be so happy to try to take her place.''

Merry's throat was tight with unshed tears and she could not speak, so she only nodded. Lady Gloriana saw some of those selfsame tears in her eyes, and she reached up to pat her face. ''Dear girl,'' she said softly, ''it is all right. You'll see. And I am sure we will be the happiest family in England, for I shall see to it myself!''

2

MISS Meryl Lancaster overslept the following morning, worn out by emotion and excitement. For a moment, when she first woke, she could not remember where she was, but then Edward's handsome face came to her mind, and she smiled. She was here with him in London . . . She would never be alone again! And besides her dear love, she now had a sister and a mother, the lovely Lady Gloriana who was so caring and concerned. Had anyone ever been so lucky? she wondered as she rang the bell and threw back the covers to get up.

It took her quite a while to dress, for she wanted to look her best for the elegant lady who was Edward's mother. Finally she chose a gold gown that was trimmed with knots of darker gold ribbon, and had Nora arrange her hair in a soft chignon. The gown seemed to turn her green eyes golden as well, and she was pleased with her appearance as she hurried down the stairs. Durfee, Edward's butler, smiled at her before he escorted her to the breakfast room.

As she entered, she saw that Edward and his mother had almost finished their repast, and she apologized for being late. Her fiancé rose to drop a soft kiss on her hair before he helped her to a chair and went to select her breakfast himself from the array of silver dishes on the sideboard.

"You must not apologize, dear girl, for you are no ordinary guest, oh no!" Lady Gloriana said, pouring herself another cup of coffee. "There is no need for haste, after all, and the rest did you good. And I am sure Madame Céleste will not care that we are late to our appointment when she sees the amount we intend to order."

Merry nodded as she tucked into the food Edward had brought her. It all looked so good, the shirred eggs, country ham and sausage, the piping hot scones and deep red cherry preserves. As she ate, she noticed that although Edward appeared to have eaten as large a breakfast as she was busy consuming, his mother still only toyed with a thin half-slice of toast unadorned by either butter or preserves.

"Your sister has already eaten?" she inquired, smiling at Edward as he settled back in his chair to admire her, his morning post forgotten.

"Dear Tiny, er, Jane has decided she would rather not come shopping with us," Lady Gloriana explained. "She says she has some letters to write, but in truth, she does not care for shopping. And she claims she has more than enough gowns to last her for several Seasons."

The lady sighed and frowned a little before she made a conscious effort to throw off her abstraction by asking Merry how she had slept.

Merry studied her carefully but unobtrusively in the clear morning sunlight that streamed through the break-fast-room windows as she replied. In that unforgiving light, she saw a few things she had not noticed the previous evening. The lady had several delicate lines around her deep blue eyes, and her skin was nowhere near as youthful and elastic as it had appeared in candle-light. Yet even with this evidence of her age, she still seemed impossibly young, with her slight figure garbed in a delicate morning gown of soft blue. It had a lace collar and tight sleeves that emphasized the fragility of her arms and little hands, and her hair was arranged in a cascade of soft, shining black curls. Somehow she made Merry feel very large and awkwardly robust, a great gawky thing in her provincial gown.

"As soon as you have finished, Merry dear, we shall be on our way," this lady was saying now. "Teddy, dear boy, can we drop you anywhere?"

"Thank you, *Maman*, but I think not," he said. "I have some business in the City, but remember, Merry, I shall be here later to take you for your grand tour of London."

"How famous!" Lady Gloriana said. "I wonder if Tiny would care to join you?"

She tilted her head to one side as if deep in thought, but after only a moment she burst into a trill of laughter and clapped her hands in delight. "Oh, my dears," she said when she could finally speak, "if you could have seen your faces! Such disappointment and chagrin! It was too, too funny. Of course I was teasing you."

"*Maman*, you are incorrigible, and very naughty besides," her fond son said as he rose from the table and picked up his post. Then he came to Merry's side and lifted her hand to kiss it. His eyes never left her face as he did so, and she stared back at him, helpless with her love.

"Til this afternoon, my dear," he said softly. "*Au revoir*."

After he had left the room, Merry was surprised to see Lady Gloriana frowning down at her plate and looking pensive. "Is there anything wrong, ma'am?" she asked in sudden concern.

The viscountess looked up and tried to smile. It was a rueful and not completely successful attempt. "No, no, my dear," she said, reaching out to pat Merry's hand. "It is just that for all my lack of size, I find I am still a great stupid. To think I am upset because Teddy did not kiss me good-bye. But I cannot remember a time when he has ever left me without doing so."

Merry started, and she clasped the lady's hand, her heart going out to her. But when she would have spoken, Lady Gloriana laughed a little. "Now you must not be concerned! It is just that I see I shall have to learn to take second place to you, as well I should. And I do assure you I am not one of those horrid *clinging* mothers, Merry, for I am no such thing! I have always encouraged my children to have their own friends, their own amusements. And even though they are so close to me, that is by their choice alone. There is nothing more depressing and despicable than a woman who insists she must always come first, be the be-all and end-all for everyone around her. And that I am not guilty of, nor ever shall be!''

She shook her head, looking almost severe, and Merry smiled at her. ''As if anyone would ever think it of you, ma'am,'' she said. ''I am sure they think you as wonderful as—as I do myself,'' she added shyly.

Lady Gloriana brightened at once, her pretty smile returning as she patted her lips with her napkin and rose from the table. ''Thank you, darling Merry,'' she said. ''And now, if you have quite finished breakfast, shall we be off? We have a great deal to do today, a very great deal indeed!''

As the two were being driven to Madame Céleste's shop on Bond Street a few minutes later, Merry looked around eagerly. London was so large, so busy! It seemed the entire population must be abroad this bright spring day, all driving or walking, or, in the case of footmen and other servants, running. There was an almost palpable air of restless energy here in the capital, as if the inhabitants were vastly different from their easygoing compatriots in the country. Merry sensed that life in London was lived at a higher pitch, for it was here that great decisions were made and men's lives changed by trade agreements, military strategy, and the building of the empire. London was the hub of every Englishman's universe. How exciting to be part of it!

It was apparent to her as the carriage continued on its way that they were in the fashionable part of town just by the way people were dressed, the impressive buildings, the grandeur of Berkeley Square. By her side, Lady Gloriana ignored the passing scene to chatter gaily of the clothes they must acquire and all the accessories that would be needed. Merry only heard her with half an ear until that lady said, ''And we must see the hairdresser as well, Merry. Why, it would be fatal to delay, for there is an important *ton* party this evening—and your first appearance. But believe me, my dear, you cannot make that appearance with the great mane of hair you possess at present. It is not at all the thing.''

Merry reached up to touch the shining waves of chestnut that Edward had told her he loved so much. ''But—but I do not think I want to have my hair cut, ma'am,'' she said a little hesitantly.

''Whyever not?'' Lady Gloriana demanded, looking puzzled. ''The style now is for short ringlets and curls such as I wear. Only governesses or abigails have long, heavy hair done up in buns.''

''But Edward loves my hair the way it is,'' Merry tried to explain. ''I do not think he would approve.''

Lady Gloriana smiled. ''Oh, my dear child,'' she said, shaking a playful finger at her. ''Men know nothing about fashion. And if you do not have it cropped, Teddy will begin to wonder what there is about you that is not quite right. Men are so imperceptive! Do trust me, Merry. I assure you that even if he should notice the change—and it is highly probable that he will not—he will soon come to love it.''

Before Merry could reply, the carriage stopped in front of what apepared to be a private home. There was not even a discreet brass plaque to tell any passerby that that arbiter of fashion, Madame Céleste, did business here. Obviously, such an advertisement would be beneath this artiste's touch.

Lady Gloriana tripped up the steps, an apprehensive Miss Lancaster in tow. An hour later, that same Miss Lancaster was completely bewildered and overwhelmed. A number of gowns had been bespoke, in a rainbow of colors, including one for the party this evening that Madame just happened to have made up.

Merry thought all the gowns very beautiful, although she could not care for some of the low necklines that showed more of her fair skin than she was accustomed to baring. But when she protested, or asked for a concealing frill of lace or ribbon, Lady Gloriana only laughed, while Madame looked horrified that any of her creations should be so desecrated.

''Darling Merry, what a little country mouse you

are!" Lady Gloriana exclaimed. "Now, at my age, I cannot wear such things anymore, lest I look like mutton dressed as lamb, but a young lady is expected to. Of course, if this were truly your first Season we would have had to have been more circumspect and dress you only in modest pastels. Isn't that so, Madame?"

The thin, ugly Frenchwoman with her improbable golden hair sniffed and stiffened. "*Mais, oui*, m'lady," she said as she snapped her fingers to her assistant to bring another bolt of material forward. "But I never dress *jeunes filles*. I consider them boring, and therefore unworthy of my talent."

Lady Gloriana smiled and nodded. "There, you see, Merry?" she asked. "But since Teddy told me you are twenty, you do not have to be banished by Madame. Yes, we will take the deep blue too, and the crimson ball gown."

Merry spoke up again then. She had not ventured many opinions, since Edward's mother and the modiste had not seemed to require them from her, but now she could not remain silent. "I do not care for the crimson gown," she said carefully. "Nor the deep rose one you chose earlier. I never wear those colors, for they are so blatant, so jarring with my complexion and my hair."

She was glad to see Madame nod in agreement, although Lady Gloriana shook her head as she burst into speech. "But of course they do, my dear, and that is why you must have them," she said. "They will make you noticed at once. You do not realize it, Merry, but there are so many lovely girls—such beauties some of them are, too—that care must be taken to make you stand out, become singular. It is true that you look well in almost every shade of green or gold, and that blue is becoming too, but to really attract attention, you must make a startling appearance!"

Merry longed to ask why this was necessary, since she was an engaged girl and Edward had tumbled into love with her without the use of such stratagems. Surely, there was no need for her to employ them now. And she would so much rather not attract anyone's attention but her dear Edward's.

Lady Gloriana seemed to sense her misgivings, for she rose from her little gilt chair to run to her in an impulsive way and kneel at her feet. Taking both her hands in hers, she said softly, "My dear child, please trust me! I only want the best for you and Teddy. And perhaps you are not aware that he is considered quite a beau here, a veritable pink of the *ton*, in fact. In his company you must be more than just prettily dressed, you must be as stunning as he is himself."

Her deep-blue eyes pleaded her cause, and Merry was forced to smile and nod. But still, later she insisted on ordering an ecru evening gown that was trimmed with pearls and dark-brown ribbons. Lady Gloriana looked doubtful at this choice, but Madame nodded approval of her taste.

When they left the shop, they discovered they had spent so much time there that they were only able to acquire a pair of sandals, a reticule, and a handsome Norwich shawl to complete her toilette that evening. Because, of course, there was still the hairdresser to see.

Lady Gloriana explained to this worthy gentleman exactly what she had in mind as he took the pins from Merry's hair and brushed it smooth.

"But please do not cut it too short, sir," Merry begged as he picked up his shears. Mr. Wilson smiled and nodded. He was a slight little man with gray hair, and to Merry he looked more like an apothecary's clerk than the famous hairdresser he was. His smile had reassured her, but still, she had to close her eyes as he began to snip. It seemed no time at all before he was arranging what was left of her hair with the help of the curling tongs, and her long chestnut tresses lay in heaps on the floor around her feet. And when he was done at last and pronounced himself satisfied, Merry was not at all sure she liked the arrangement. Her hair was so much shorter, although nowhere near as short as Lady Gloriana had wished, and it was now a mass of tight ringlets that covered her head and hung in artless clusters to her neck.

"You look charming, my dear," Lady Gloriana told her as they gathered their things and went down to the waiting carriage. "It is not quite as sophisticated as I had hoped, but it is a vast improvement. I cannot wait to show Jane!"

"And Edward?" Merry asked, studying her reflection in the carriage window before she took the footman's arm and climbed to her seat.

Lady Gloriana chuckled. "But of course, Teddy, too," she said. "But do not quite eat him if he should not notice a thing different about you, darling Merry," she warned.

The warning was unnecessary. After Lady Gloriana left her to take her afternoon rest, Merry had changed quickly into one of her old familiar driving gowns. When she ran down the stairs, she found Edward waiting for her in the hall, and he noticed the difference at once.

"But what on earth have you done to your hair, Merry?" he asked in a stunned voice.

She did not think he seemed pleased, for there was a little frown between his brows. She made herself smile at him. "Lady Gloriana said I needed a smart new look, Edward," she told him as she turned around so he might admire her new coiffure from all angles. "Is it not stunning?"

Suddenly the viscount became aware of the interested footmen and his butler, and he led her out to his tilbury after only a curt bow. But after they had taken their seats and he had dismissed his groom, Merry said hotly, "You don't like it! Oh, dear, I should have stood firm, but your mama insisted. And she has been so kind to me, just like my own mother, advising and directing me. She said I would look like a governess if my hair was not in the current mode, and she also said she could not bear it if I were to appear a dowd. But—but, Edward, if you do not care for it, I am sorry I took her advice."

Her voice was constricted and her head was turned

away a little, and the viscount felt like a beast for upsetting her. "I suppose it is only that I was not expecting it," he said, giving her a fond smile. When she would not look at him and he saw her twisting her hands together in her lap, he commanded softly, "Look at me, my love, do!"

Her large hazel eyes turned to his, and the misery in them made him add lightly, "It was only that I have been having the most wonderful dreams of that night when I could take down your hair and run my fingers through all its glorious length. But you are right. It is very smart, and you do me proud. Forgive me for being so selfish."

Merry smiled now, her color slightly heightened as she contemplated the scene he had made her see. She, at her dressing table late at night, while he stood close behind her. And both of them quite, quite alone, and married at last.

"Dare I ask what you are thinking now, my dear?" he inquired, one corner of his handsome mouth twitching a little.

"No, much better not," she said, trying to look reproving. "You will tell me instead, if you please, what that very imposing building is over there. Have you forgotten you are to be my guide to London today, sir? But I shall not let you forget it, oh, no!"

He chuckled and complied, and harmony was restored. For over an hour he showed her the glories of the city. They drove through Hyde Park and then to Buckingham House before they proceeded through the Mall to Somerset House and the Thames. He paused there so she might admire all the many vessels sailing with the tide downriver to the Channel and the sea. Merry took deep breaths of the fresh briny air as she watched the gulls that floated so effortlessly over the water.

And then there was the massive and impressive bulk of Westminster Abbey to admire. The viscount promised her a tour of it on another day when they would have more time to do it justice. But when they reached Green Park, Merry was surprised to find his groom waiting for them, to walk the horses while they strolled across the soft stretches of grass that were so unusual here in the heart of a great metropolis. Edward even found a clump of primroses and picked them for her, telling her she was so dear and lovely, she put the flowers to shame. Merry was sorry when they had to return to Mount Street at last. Just to be alone with him, to be able to exchange smiles, touch his hand, and steal a kiss, was nothing less than bliss. But she did not demure when he mentioned the lateness of the hour, for she knew she must take a great deal of care with her toilette this evening. After dinner, they were all going on to a soiree at the Duke and Duchess of Rutland's in Berkeley Square, and it was here that she would be introduced to everyone who was anyone in society. She resolved to do both Edward and his mother proud.

At teatime, neither Lady Gloriana nor Jane appeared. Merry was sorry Edward's sister had not joined them, for she was anxious to begin making her better acquaintance. When she asked after the ladies, Edward told her his mother never took tea, and he didn't have the slightest idea what Jane was up to.

"But surely your mother cannot be resting all this time, my dear," Merry said as she passed him the plate of tea sandwiches.

"I have no idea what she does," he told her as he searched among them for a particular favorite. "I only know that *Maman* is never seen between two and seven. She claims she needs to recruit her strength for the evening's festivities. I suppose it is not to be wondered at, for she is such a fragile little thing." Then he leaned closer and said, "I am not only delighted by her absence, dearest Merry, but by Jane's defection as well. You see, I had not hoped to be alone with you still. But as much as I love Jane and *Maman*, it is wonderful not to have to share you."

Merry blew him a kiss across the tea table and blushed at the sudden gleam in his dark-blue eyes.

When she dressed for dinner later in her new gown of

sea-green muslin and matching satin sandals, she thought she looked very well. Nora exclaimed over the gown and her new coiffuer as well, as she fastened on the string of pearls Merry had inherited from her mother. Merry herself draped the Norwich shawl gracefully over her arms and took up her reticule and gloves before she turned slowly before the pier glass.

But when she came downstairs, Merry realized that even if she did have a decided air of fashion now, she could never compare to the Lady Gloriana. As she accepted that lady's fulsome compliments on her turnout, she admired her sophisticated silk gown. Long-sleeved and cut high to the neck, it was an almost unadorned sweep of dark blue to match her eyes, with only a narrow satin braid trimming to relieve its starkness. Somehow, it made her own sea-green muslin, with its three deep flounces and tiny puffed sleeves, seem fussy and girlish. The lady wore sapphires and diamonds as well, in her hair, around her neck, and at her wrists, and when she moved, they sparkled in the light of the candles. Beside her, Jane Willoughby seemed even larger than she was in an elaborate gown of palest blue.

Edward was quick to compliment all his ladies before he took his mother in to dinner. Walking behind him, Merry stole a glance at his sister's face. She was staring straight ahead and striding along as if she were completely alone. Merry wondered at the petulant twist of her mouth, the high color in her round cheeks.

The Duke and Duchess of Rutland welcomed the Willoughby party sometime later, and professed their delight that Miss Meryl Lancaster was also honoring their party. Merry stared around in awe. The large drawing room of the duke's town house was already crowded with more people than she had ever seen at any party in Bath. She was quick to notice the low-cut gowns and short ringlets the other young ladies who were present sported, and she was glad Lady Gloriana had insisted on her transformation. Now she could be comfortable, knowing she herself was of the first stare.

Once again, she found herself paired with Jane
Willoughby, both of them trailing in the wake of the
viscount and his mother. Lady Gloriana paused often as
they strolled about the room, to introduce Merry to her
friends and to other young people. Merry noticed that
Jane had very little to say for herself and never spoke
unless directly addressed. Surely, besides being so very
large and awkward-looking, she was very diffident. But
perhaps, even as used as she must be to perfect squeezes
like this, she was shy. Merry told herself she must try to
bring her out and encourage her.

Eventually, Edward relinquished his mother to a
short, very thin gentleman wearing a startling puce-and-
gold waistcoat, who was fervent in his admiration for
the lady he called Lady Glory. He was soon joined by
another man his age who had heavy beetle brows and
what appeared to be a permanent frown, and a much
younger man whom both elder gentlemen eyed with
undisguised loathing.

Miss Jane Willoughby excused herself to Merry
abruptly, to follow her mother as her escorts took her to
a chair. The viscount was then free to offer his arm to
Merry, explaining in a stage whisper that his duties for
the evening were over, now that *Maman* was safe with
her usual court.

"They are so funny, all of them," Merry whispered
back. "The way they glare at one another! Why, if
looks could kill, not a one of them would be breathing
now."

Edward smiled at her. "How true, my dear! The two
older gentlemen have been *Maman*'s cicisbeos for more
years than I can remember. The shorter of the two is
Jeremy Overton, Marquess of Saterly. He has buried
three wives and claims nothing would bring him such
rapture as installing *Maman* as his fourth
marchioness." He chuckled. "But I suspect the marquess knows there is small chance he will succeed."

"What of the others, Edward?" Merry asked as she
accepted a glass of champagne from a footman's tray.

"The other older gentleman is Mr. Nigel Brethers. He

is the crustiest old bachelor you could ever imagine, and he hates Lord Saterly. The two of them watch each other like hawks, where *Maman* is concerned, fearful the other will steal a march on them. The young man, Reggie Horton, is a complete chucklehead. He is just my age, but he has formed a *tendre* for *Maman*. He is such a mooncalf he does not realize how ridiculous he appears, to be madly in love with a woman old enough to be his mother. I have tried to get *Maman* to discourage him, but she only laughs at me and says there is no need to stifle his pretensions or wound him in any way. She claims his eye will light on some lovely young thing any day now, and she will be forgotten in the twinkling of a bedpost." He frowned a little. "But still, I cannot like it. I don't care what kind of cake Reggie makes of himself, but I don't like to see my mother made to look foolish. And I think his adoration for her does that, for it is so very unbecoming."

Merry pressed his arm. "But no doubt she is right, Edward," she told him. "And it is just like her to be kind to him, no matter how it may reflect on herself. She is all goodness!"

The viscount smiled at her. "You like her, don't you, Merry?" he asked.

"Oh, I quite love her already," she told him. "How wonderful she has been to me, how very understanding! She has even offered to take the place of the mother I lost so many years ago. How could I not love her when she is so selfless, so happy to share you with me?"

They were interrupted then by two of Edward's friends, begging an introduction, so he could not reply. But Merry saw the gratitude in his eyes. And when she saw how proud he was to make her known to his friends, she was glad she was not wearing one of her old gowns and had had her hair cut after all. Lady Gloriana had been right to insist she must do Edward proud. He was so stunning in his formal evening wear. He had the straight, shapely leg that knee breeches and silk stockings demanded, and his frilled shirt was immaculate under his dark, long-tailed evening coat.

Above white collar points, his handsome face and crisp black curls set him apart from other, less fortunate men. She knew she was a very lucky young lady.

The soiree was a lengthy affair, but Merry did not notice in the excitement of meeting so many new people, dancing with Edward and his friends and being introduced to some young ladies as well.

She was sitting with a Miss Mary Griffin, a vivacious blonde who had acquired quite a court around her, when she chanced to remember Edward's sister. She looked around. Jane Willoughby was still with her mother, sitting a little to one side as Lady Gloriana laughed and teased her own little court. Merry wondered that she would care to remain there, that she should make no effort to join others her own age. She decided she must ask Edward about his sister soon. She did not think Jane was at all happy, and she wondered why that should be so.

She forgot her, however, when Miss Griffin invited her to walk in Hyde Park with her the following afternoon. At once, two of the young gentlemen present demanded to be included as well, and Miss Griffin agreed to their escort if Miss Lancaster would consent to come too. Merry did not know how to refuse the invitation, and Edward had turned away for a moment to greet some friends. As she was forced to accept, she had to remind herself to smile.

"And I insist we must have Lady Amelia Rogers and her elder brother as well," Miss Griffin declared.

"But why are you so insistent on Lady Amelia?" Mr. Anthony Best inquired. He was a tall young man with skin as soft and smooth as a girl's, and a truly magnificent nose that quite overshadowed the rest of his face.

Miss Griffin giggled. "It is because of her dark hair," she explained. "Just think what a stunning party we will make, two blondes, two redheads, and two brunettes!"

Struck by a sudden thought, Merry spoke up. "Could we not ask Viscount Trumbull and his sister instead?" she asked. "They are dark, too, and since I am staying with the Willoughbys, it would be so very appropriate.''

Miss Griffin considered her request. She had long fancied herself more than a little in love with Teddy Willoughby, and had toyed with the possibility of bringing him to the sticking point this Season. But she was more than seven, and she could see that this new young lady who was staying with his mother had captured his interest to an alarming degree. Why, the viscount had never looked at *her* with such a warm light in his eyes, and he had never danced attendance on *her* as he was doing for Miss Meryl Lancaster tonight. Miss Griffin decided he must be punished for his defection from her ranks of admirers. She cast about in her mind for an excuse to exclude him and his sister. And then her face brightened.

"Well, we can ask Jane Willoughby, Miss Lancaster, but I do not think she will come," she said. "She never joins us on our romps. And she is not at all prime for a lark, is she, Tony? I myself suspect she is blue."

"Never say so!" Sir Frederick White, he of the bright-red hair, exclaimed. "Oh, much better not to invite her, then, lest she begin to spout poetry or some such thing. Assure you, Miss Lancaster, you would not care for that at all. And neither would I," he added, determined to be honest. "No patience with these poetry coves or their admirers, don't you know? All airs and graces, and nothin' but regular jaw-me-deads!"

Edward Willoughby returned to their circle then, and Merry did not think he seemed at all pleased when he was told of the proposed outing. And she wondered at it when Miss Griffin told him so pertly that there was no sense in his asking if he might join them, for the numbers were all made up.

3

MERRY Lancaster was very busy in the following days. There was not only more shopping to do, and sightseeing and parties, but she was soon caught up in a group of gay young friends, all anxious to include her in their revels. The viscount did not approve. In fact, on the short drive back to Mount Street after the Rutland soiree, he had taken Merry to account for getting involved with Miss Griffin and her set, calling Freddie White an odious little bounce, and Tony Best, a bobbing block. And as for Miss Griffin herself, he said he had always considered her a peagoose who had more hair than wit.

Merry had listened to him, considerably startled at his vehemence, but it was Lady Gloriana who had finally brought his diatribe to a close. Leaning forward to rap his knee where he sat across from her, she had said, "Give over, Teddy, do! I will not allow you to pull a crow with Merry over such a silly thing. And you know very well there's not an ounce of harm in any of those young people. Surely you do not believe Merry is in any danger in their company? Such passion must be the result of jealousy, and it makes you look absurd. And if you remember, it was just for this purpose that we decided not to announce your engagement until Merry could make some friends and learn to be at ease in the *ton*. Do let the child have some larks and enjoy herself!"

The viscount had agreed somewhat curtly that perhaps his mother was right. But for the first time, Merry had been disappointed in the brevity of his goodnight kiss and the lack of time she was given to explain. After begging her pardon for his behavior, he had said it was late, flicked her chin with a careless finger, and told her to run off to bed.

The following afternoon, however, when she came in from her walk, Durfee had taken her aside to tell her—in a voice that implied they were conspirators in some daring deed—that the viscount wished to see her in the small back salon. He had escorted her there himself, tapped on the door, and bowed, a distinct twinkle in his faded blue eyes.

The minute Merry entered the salon, Edward's arms came around her to hold her tight, and he kicked the door shut with one booted foot. "Edward? What on earth?" she asked.

"I had to see you alone," he told her, his voice husky. "Do tell me, my love, did you enjoy your walk in the park?"

Merry leaned back in his arms and studied his face. Had he asked to see her so he could scold her again? Was he still angry? Reassured by the mischief she saw deep in those dark-blue eyes, she said, "It was very pleasant. Miss Griffin . . . all of them were so friendly and full of fun."

"Really?" he asked, one finger coming up to trace the skin at the neck of her gown. Immediately, warmth grew where he touched her.

Merry closed her eyes. "Yes," she said weakly. "But you know I would so much rather have been with you, Edward. Truly."

He lowered his head and covered her cheek with a dozen tiny kisses, his lips lingering as if to savor her.

Forcing herself to put sensation aside, Merry whispered, "But, Edward, should we be here alone, with the door shut? I do not think Lady Gloriana would—"

"No, no doubt *Maman* would not approve," he said calmly. "But it was important for me to see you. I had to apologize for the way I acted last night, admit it was only because I love you so much that it made me jealous and abrupt. Besides, we have so little time to talk now, just the two of us."

As his hands were busy running up and down her arms, Merry chuckled a little. "Talk, my love?" she asked, trying to sound incredulous.

"Well, among other things," he told her with the air of a man determined to be honest. "For I can see how it will be already. You will be running here and there with your new friends, or busy with my mother or Jane, and if we get to exchange a minute's worth of private conversation a day, it will surprise me. And, my darling Merry, that is a state of affairs I will not stand for."

She nestled closer in his arms. "I wish it did not have to be like that, too," she said. "But your mother is only trying to assure my comfort and my reputation, you know. It is so good of her."

He did not answer. Instead, he put his lips on hers and kissed her, a long, lingering kiss that left her knees weak and her body warm and trembling and eager.

When he raised his head at last, she was gasping. He picked her up in his arms then and carried her to a large chair by the fireplace, to settle down in it with her on his lap.

"But, Edward," Merry said as she cuddled closer and put her head on his chest so she could hear the steady beating of his heart, "what if one of the servants comes in?"

"No one is going to come in," he told her, sounding firm. "*Maman* is, as usual, secluded in her room, Jane is visiting one of our cousins, and Durfee has been told we are not to be disturbed—for anything. Not even a fire, earthquake, or flood."

"But how bad you are!" she exclaimed, although she felt nothing but happiness and complete contentment in spite of her scolding words. "You have ruined my reputation with your butler without even a qualm or so much as a by-your-leave."

"Not quite without a qualm," he admitted. "I thought long and hard before I acted. But no one will know but Durfee, and he will stand our friend. I can tell he thinks it romantic, and he is delighted! No doubt he is already making plans for my heir."

Merry blushed and his arms tightened again. He lifted her chin with one finger until they were staring deep into each other's eyes. "And it is romantic, isn't it, Merry?" he asked, his voice rough. "Oh, not quite like swimming a dangerous moat to storm a castle wall, or jousting to win my lady's favor, but romantic enough for staid old London town."

As he had been speaking, his lips had been drawing ever nearer, and as they took possession of hers again, she realized his question had only been rhetorical.

They sat together in the big chair for some time, kissing and whispering together, sometimes laughing and joking, sometimes lost in the pure joy of being together, and alone. It was with the greatest reluctance that the viscount finally rose and set her on her feet as they heard voices in the hall.

"It grows late, my love," he said. "Time we parted. And that voice we heard was Jane's, if I am not mistaken. Now she is home, she might well take it into her head to pop in to see how you go on, and you must be in your room. I will leave first, to make sure the coast is clear. Follow me in a few minutes. For, Merry, love you as fervently as I do, I have no intention of either of us skulking through the halls or diving behind the draperies like actors in a bad farce."

Merry had to cover her giggles at the thought of the elegant beau that was Edward Willoughby forced to such stratagems. But she was also uneasy. It had been wonderful, exciting—and very, very dangerous. She did not feel she drew a deep breath until Edward opened the door to the hall, inspected it quickly, and just as quickly waved to her and withdrew.

As she sat quietly in the small salon, smoothing her gown and her ruffled curls, she realized that it was not so much Jane she worried about, as it was the servants. How they loved a juicy on-dit! And how quickly such a one as this would spread through the servants' hall clear out to the stables. Pray Durfee would be discreet!

For even though she admitted Edward made her feel a complete wanton, helpless with her desire for him, she could not risk a scandal. Their marriage must not take place under a cloud. Not even a cloud of servants' gossip.

As she went up the stairs a little later, she was thankful that they had appeared to have escaped notice. And she was not at all concerned that Jane Willoughby would "pop in to see how she did." She had made it very plain to Merry, even in this short a time, that although she would always be civil, she had no desire to be truly friendly. Merry decided she would not give up. After all, she and Jane were going to be family, were they not?

But although she managed to prevail on the lady to go out with her occasionally the following days, she could not feel the expeditions had been much of a success, no matter how hard she tried to gain her confidence. Jane Willoughby seldom spoke, and then only in response to a direct question. And although she was perfectly agreeable now to walk or drive, accompany Merry to Hookham's library, or join her for tea or some sightseeing, she volunteered nothing about herself and seemed just as content when she remained home alone.

When questioned, Edward had said he did not know what was the matter with her. And when Merry pressed him, he told her that although Jane had been the happiest, most outgoing little girl imaginable, somehow she had changed when she turned seventeen. "*Maman* says it is only a stage she is going through, and we must be patient," he admitted. "But I wish she would talk to me, confide in me as she used to do, for I can see as well as you can, Merry, that she is not happy now. But when I try to discover why, she tells me not to be so silly, that everything is fine and she is quite content. She is a puzzle."

Merry would have liked to have asked Lady Gloriana about her daughter, but although they were growing closer every day, she hesitated to pose such a personal question. As it turned out, it was Lady Gloriana herself who brought the subject up.

The three ladies had been sitting together at the

breakfast table, and when Jane excused herself from accompanying them that morning, her mother had frowned. And when she left the room shortly thereafter, she had sighed.

Catching sight of her guest's questioning look, she had said, "Yes, Merry, I am sure it is obvious how very concerned about Tiny I am. I have noticed you trying to make friends with her, and I do appreciate it. But as you have seen, it is no use at all. I fear Tiny is in a massive sulk, and it is all my fault!"

"Your fault, ma'am?" Merry asked, knitting her brows.

"Why, yes," Lady Gloriana told her. "You see, just before Teddy brought you to London, I taxed Tiny about her weight and her attitude. She is so very heavy! It is most unbecoming in a young woman. And as I pointed out to her, as gently as I could, what gentleman would ever propose to such an ungainly, sullen creature? And surely my Tiny must hope to marry someday! But she refuses to listen to me, or to diet. Why, you saw what she ate this morning! Porridge swimming in cream and sugar, sirloin and eggs, four scones dripping with butter and jam. She is eating this way because she is angry with me, and so defies me. It makes me so miserable!"

Her speech ended in a soft wail and Merry got up to hug her and comfort her. "But, my dear ma'am," she said, "surely Jane can see that becoming fatter and fatter only hurts her, not you." She thought for a moment, and then she said shyly, "Let me see what I can do. Perhaps if I gain her confidence, get her to be my friend, she will listen to me."

Lady Gloriana hugged her back before she wiped her eyes on her napkin. "You are so good and kind, dear Merry," she said. "Teddy is a very fortunate man. But enough! I refuse to be in the mopes on this beautiful spring day. Run and fetch your bonnet, my dear, and we will go and see if we can't find the perfect hat for your new walking dress."

It seemed to Merry Lancaster that every day brought

more bandboxes, parcels, and bundles to the house on
Mount Street, as her new clothes were delivered. And
sometimes, when she saw the finished gowns hanging in
the large armoire in her room, she would frown a little,
for she was still not at all sure they really became her.
That vivid-crimson gown with all the ruffles and
beading, for example. It seemed overornate and made
her feel like Christmas beef. She knew if Lady Gloriana
had not insisted on it, she would have refused it with a
shudder. She was tall, and she had never been
comfortable in elaborate, fussy clothes, or thought she
looked at all well in them.

And sometimes, when she came downstairs, she
would see a puzzled look in Edward's eyes, even while
he was complimenting her on a new pelisse, a dashing
feathered hat, or a formal ball gown. Perhaps he did not
think she looked well, either? But she knew what an
innocent she was when it came to matters of fashion.
And surely Lady Gloriana, with all her sophistication
and expertise, knew what was correct.

But for all the new clothes she was acquiring, Lady
Gloriana seemed to have forgotten all about her bride
clothes, and Merry herself did not like to remind her.
She knew the tiny lady was doing too much for her
already. Sometimes Edward's mother did not even join
them for dinner if there was no party to attend that
particular evening. She would send her excuses, saying
she meant to have a tray in her room, and Merry would
feel guilty that she was such a charge on her. On those
evenings, Merry tried to include Edward's sister in the
conversation, but more often than not, Jane would go
right to the piano after dinner to play softly, leaving
Merry and her brother to converse alone. And since
Merry was delighted to have the chance to do so, she did
not object. He had not asked to see her alone in the
house again, for she had begged him not to. When she
thought about it later, away from his compelling
presence, her blood had run cold at the risks they had
taken. But now she saw even less of Edward than she
had in Bath, even though they were living in the same

house. As his mother had predicted, he was soon caught up in a press of business, involved with his friends and his clubs. She mentioned this to him almost wistfully one evening as Jane sat playing some Beethoven études.

He raised her hand and kissed it. "Are you telling me you miss me, Merry?" he asked, a note of disbelief in his voice.

"But you must know I do!" she said hotly.

"Then why are you always so busy yourself?" he asked seriously. "When I inquire for you, more often than not I find that you have gone for a drive, or shopping, or to a tea party, or you are paying calls. Or I discover Freddie or Tony are here, and you are busy entertaining them."

"But you could join us, Edward, and, oh, how I wish you would!" she said, her large hazel eyes pleading for his understanding. "I would so much rather be with you."

He squeezed her hand, rubbing his thumb over the soft skin until she blushed a little. "And I with you, my dear," he said softly. "How much longer do you think it will be before you are comfortable in the *ton* and we can announce our engagement?" he asked. "I am finding it so very hard to wait for you."

Before she could tell him that as far as she was concerned, he might announce it tomorrow; he added, a dark look coming over his face, "And then I can send those trumped-up April squires about their business. Silly chubs that they are, to be dancing attendance on you when you are mine."

Merry tried to smile at him, but his expression reminded her of a look she had seen on his face that morning. He had been standing in the hall, glaring at an innocent posy of flowers that had just been delivered for her, when she came down the stairs to breakfast. The stern lines of disapproval on his handsome face had made him look almost sinister, and she had felt her heart quicken in dismay. But how could she stop Freddie or Tony from sending her flowers? How could she tell any of her new beaux that she wished them all at

Land's End rather than forever on her doorstep? And Lady Gloriana thought them such a triumph for her, too!

At breakfast, she had only laughed at her son's highly vocal displeasure. "Could anything be more absurd, dear Merry?" she had asked as soon as Edward had left them, still tight-lipped and stern-eyed. Miserable, because he had not even inquired her engagements that day or attempted to make any plans to see her, Merry had stared down into her coffeecup.

"One would almost think darling Teddy believed you had tumbled into love with another. But can he seriously think you would exchange him for any of your new beaux? He is ridiculous, and I shall tell him so myself! He is not to make you miserable with his jealous starts, his possessiveness. A man like that makes a miserable husband, so full of suspicions and distrust. If Teddy does not take care, you might well begin to think twice about this engagement, and that I could not bear!"

Merry had looked up to see the lady leaning forward, her face full of concern, and she had been quick to reassure her that such a thing would never, ever, come to pass, for she loved Edward truly and forever.

But now she remembered how he had looked this morning and how he had behaved toward her lately, and her little smile faded away. Surely he knew how much she loved him. Surely he was acting in a very shabby way, just as his mother had claimed. And so, instead of telling him that she was finding it very hard to wait for their wedding as well, she said, "I doubt we can even begin to think of announcing it, at least until the ball your mother is planning for me is over. And you know that is not to take place until May twenty-fifth, which is two weeks away."

"Perhaps we should announce our engagement at the ball," he persisted.

Merry shook her head. "I do not think Lady Gloriana would hear of it, Edward," she said. "You know how she is calling it my come-out. I don't think a girl comes out and announces her future wedding at the same time. It sounds a trifle havey-cavey, does it not?''

The viscount released her hand and moved away from her a little. ''I begin to think you are not as eager as I am for our wedding,'' he said stiffly. ''Perhaps you wish to cry off?''

''Oh, Edward, no, no!'' she cried, forgetting his sister was even in the room. ''How can you be so cruel? How can you say such cutting things to me? You know I consider myself pledged to you, that I have felt that way ever since the day you asked me to marry you. Why, I love you dearly!''

The viscount stared deep into her hazel eyes. They were filled with chagrin, and as he watched, they filled up with tears as well. He put his arm around her and pulled her close, to cradle her head on his chest and murmur to her, ''Sssh, ssh, darling. I would not distress you for the world. It is just that somehow, things have changed between us. And I do not care for that change. Why can't it be like it was back in Bath, do you suppose?''

Merry had composed herself now, but before she could answer, they both heard Jane's little cough as she finished her piece, and they drew apart.

''Please excuse me, Merry, Teddy,'' Jane said in a gruff voice as she rose and straightened her music, carefully not looking at them. ''I find I am tired this evening and would go to bed early.''

Edward got up and went to put his arm around his sister and hug her. ''What you really mean, my dear dissembler, is that you are bored playing gooseberry to a pair of lovebirds, but I can understand your reticence in speaking of it. We will let you run along, but for heaven's sakes, Jane, take a good book up with you. If you go to bed at nine, you will be up before the birds.''

Merry was blushing now, but Jane laughed. It was the first time Merry had ever heard her laugh or seen her heavy face light up with mischief. ''It would serve you right if I decided to sit here til midnight and never took my eyes from you, Teddy,'' she told him. Then, catching sight of Merry's rosy face, she added, "There is no need to look so conscious. Of course you want to be alone. I, er, I myself can think of nothing more delightful for two people in love. The wonder of it is that you have endured my company so long."

Merry would have spoken, but Jane only waved her hand as she left the room with quick, impatient steps.

In only a few minutes, Merry forgot all about her. Edward took her in his arms again and kissed and caressed her until she was lost in that wonderful, warm feeling of being surrounded by his touch, his lips, his love. As his hands brushed her breasts and she sighed against his eager mouth, she heard a high, breathless voice exclaim, "My dears! Now I understand why Jane was so distraught!"

Pushing Edward away, Merry straightened up and adjusted her gown as Lady Gloriana ran into the room. She was dressed in one of her floating wrappers, this one a symphony of various shades of dusty rose. As she took a seat nearby, it settled into flattering folds around her slender form. Merry felt large and hot and disheveled, and somehow ashamed—even though Edward remained close beside her and kept a tight grasp on her hand.

"For some reason I was restless tonight," his mother told them. "I was about to come down when I heard Tiny passing in the hall. I went out to her and saw how upset she was. And now I see why. What naughty children you both are to make her so sad! Although I do assure you, she did not say a word about it. Tiny was never a tattle-monger."

"Why, we did nothing while she was here, *Maman*," the viscount declared, pressing Merry's hand to reassure her. "Yet you say Jane was upset? I do not understand. She was fine when she left us."

"Nor do I understand," Merry said. "She even teased us and laughed at us."

Lady Gloriana looked from one to the other before she compressed her lips. "Teddy, I must ask you to excuse Merry and me for a few minutes," she said.

"There is something I wish to say to her privately. Please wait in the library. I will send for you shortly."

Edward Willoughby stared at his mother for a long moment before he rose. "But of course I am at your service, *Maman*," he said formally. Then he turned to his fiancée, "I shall see you in a little while, Merry."

His look was warm with his love, but Merry did not notice, for she was staring at Lady Gloriana. She had never heard that stiff tone in her voice before, and she wondered why she appeared so angry.

The lady waited in silence until her son had closed the door behind him and they were quite alone. Then she sighed as she came to take the seat on the sofa that he had vacated only moments before. As she took Merry's hands in hers and peered up into her face, Merry held her breath.

"My dear girl, there is something I must tell you. It is for your own good, but, oh, I wish I did not have to say it!" she began. She paused for a moment, and then she went on in a rush, "You see, it was your behavior, and Teddy's, that upset Jane. Of course she hid it from you, but how do you think it makes her feel, as fat and unattractive as she is, to see you both so happy and in love, touching each other and whispering together? It was very unmannerly of *you* especially, and I would never have thought you capable of it."

She shook her head sadly, and Merry felt the blood rush to her face again. "I—I do beg your pardon, ma'am," she managed to get out.

Lady Gloriana squeezed her hands. "I am sure that it was just that you didn't think, darling girl," she said, her voice much kinder now. "But until your marriage, you must behave with more decorum. I am sure your own mother would have taught you the proper behavior, if she had but lived, poor lady! And since you have been kind enough to allow me to try to take her place, in whatever small way I can, I feel it is my duty to tell you these things. I do hope you understand?"

Merry nodded, her throat so constricted now she was not capable of further speech. How terrible this was!

How shameful! And when she thought of the narrow escape they had had that afternoon, alone in the small back salon, her skin crawled under her gown. Thank heavens his mother had never found out about that, elegant lady that she was.

"There are a few other things as well," Lady Gloriana was saying now. "I have hesitated to mention them, but I have come to see that not to do so would be cowardly. And even if your feelings for me change after I speak, I must accept that risk. At least I will know I have done my best. And if anything, *anything* at all, were to happen to estrange you and my son, I would feel guilty the rest of my life. You know how fervently I desire this marriage, my dear."

"Yes, I do know it," Merry forced herself to say through stiff, dry lips. "What is it you would tell me, ma'am?"

"Well, it is not only Jane who is upset. I am sure you must have noticed Teddy's startling change of manner?"

She waited until Merry nodded again before she went on, "I do not think you realize how difficult all this is for him. And that is quite understandable. You had no brothers, and you have grown to maturity in a feminine establishment. How could it be otherwise? But you forget that Teddy is all a man, my dear, with a man's passions and needs, and he wants you. And for you to kiss and caress him so often . . . Why, it is agony for him, poor boy. I do suggest you curtail any more love-making for the present, Merry. It makes you look like a cruel tease."

"Oh, no, no!" Merry exclaimed. "Not a cruel tease, dear ma'am!"

"Just like one," Lady Gloriana said firmly. "I have wondered at it, and I know Teddy has, too, but he is too much the gentleman to mention it to you."

"But it is Edward himself who initiates any—anything of that nature," Merry found herself saying. "You must believe I am not so bold as to—to—"

Fortunately, Lady Gloriana interrupted. "Yes, I am sure he does," she said. "He may be a gentleman, but he is, as I have told you, also a man. My dear Merry, it has been ever thus. It is the woman's responsibility to decide how a relationship shall be conducted, which liberties may be taken and which denied. He is waiting for you to set the limits. Until you do, well . . ." She held her little hands out, palms upward.

Before Merry could say a word, Lady Gloriana sat up straighter and continued, "And that is one of the reasons I wanted you to go about with others, meet other men. For living in this house, so close to Teddy, leads to all kinds of temptations, as I am sure you have already discovered."

She paused and gave Merry a serious, considering look, and Merry could not help but wonder if that fatal hour of blissful privacy had really gone unnoticed, after all.

"Please, my dear, until your wedding, try to behave with more discretion," she went on. "Try not to be alone with Teddy any more than you can help, and do your best to keep him at arm's length."

Merry forced herself to nod, even though it was very hard to agree to such a plan. She loved Edward; she needed to be with him, to be able to talk to him, kiss him. For a moment, a strong feeling of resentment and rebellion rose in her breast. Why was love, even passion, such a bad thing? And if it were, why were they delaying their wedding?

Lady Gloriana smiled at her, and she quelled her tumultuous thoughts. "Since I am opening my budget, dear Merry, there is one other matter as well. I have to say I have been astounded at your playful, sportive behavior in company. It is not at all the thing. I know other people are wondering at it as well. Why, last night at the theater, your laughter could be heard over everyone else's. Old Mrs. Bartholemew and her party gave our box such looks, I almost sank! And then for you to wave to Miss Griffin, when she was situated quite on the other side of the house, made you look so

peculiar! I noticed Teddy giving you some speculative
glances, too, and he has every right to be upset when
you make an exhibition of yourself by carrying on so.
You see, London is not at all like the provinces. Here,
good taste and a strict observance of the rules of correct
behavior are all. Any young lady is expected to behave
with modesty and serene manners. She must not laugh
loudly or be overly gay, and she certainly must not show
any undue enthusiasm, as you are so apt to do. But I am
sure you will soon become accustomed, now that I have
given you the hint. Do strive for an air of quiet good
taste, even one of bored sophistication. That way you
will not call attention to yourself, as you have been
doing since your arrival.''

Merry put both her hands to her hot cheeks. To think
she was guilty of such a lapse! To think the viscountess
had been cringing at her manners, that Edward thought
her provincial, and rude, and gauche! "Oh, dear,'' she
whispered. "I—I never suspected. I—I didn't know.''

Lady Gloriana put her arms around her and hugged
her close. "Dearest girl, how could you know?'' she
asked, her voice warm and kind. "But you do see how
important it is for you to learn how to go on, before you
and Teddy are affianced?''

Merry nodded. "I shall try to do better,'' she
promised the little lady beside her. "Truly, I will.''

Lady Gloriana kissed her before she rose. "I am sure
you will, my dear, just as I am sure you will carry all
before you and be a complete success in society. And
bless you, darling Merry, for taking it all in such good
spirit. You cannot imagine how terrified I have been,
thinking that if I spoke openly to you, it might cause a
rift in our relationship. And that I would find very hard
to bear, for you are such a dear girl! I think of you quite
as one of my own, indeed I do, and I look forward to
the day when you will be my daughter in truth.''

She skipped a little as she went to the bellpull. "And
now, no more gloomy lectures, I promise you. I shall
have Durfee bid Teddy rejoin us, and we will all have a
comfortable coze until the tea tray is brought in.''

Merry rose and curtsied. "If you please, ma'am," she said with quiet dignity, "I would like to excuse myself— go to my room. You have given me a lot to consider, and perhaps a little solitary reflection now might not be amiss. Besides, I really don't think I can face Edward just yet, not right after you have shown me all my horrid faults."

Somewhat to her surprise and relief, Lady Gloriana did not try to get her to change her mind. "I am sure you are very wise, Merry," she said. "I will tell Teddy that you felt the headache coming on and have gone to bed. Besides, it will give me a chance to speak to him alone. You may be sure I have a few home truths for my son as well. You are not the only one to have to bear with a lecture. But before you go, Merry, please say that you are not angry with me. I could not bear it if you were angry!"

Merry made herself go and kiss the tiny viscountess, and smile, even though she felt a steady ache of discomfort under her heart. "No, of course I am not angry, ma'am," she made herself say. "I am glad you told me. I know how difficult it must have been for you to do so, and I—I appreciate your concern and your care. I am sure not even my own mother could have been so good."

Lady Gloriana's face lit up. "Now, don't you worry about Teddy," she said. "You may trust me to explain everything to him so we may all go on much more comfortably in the future!"

4

MERRY never did learn what Lady Gloriana said to Edward, for when she came downstairs the following morning, she discovered he had already left the house. And although she waited and watched for him, she did not see him all day. He did not come in to tea, and when they met just before dinner, he was cool, his smile for her a mere formality.

The Willoughbys were entertaining guests that evening, and Merry tried to tell herself that it was because of their presence that Edward ignored her all evening. But perhaps it was not fair to say he ignored her, she told herself as she sat down between Jane and one of her cousins in the drawing room after a sumptuous repast. It might be that she was too sensitive, taking a slight where none was intended. For, after all, he had spoken to her occasionally and introduced her to those people she did not know. And surely, as host, he must see to his company first.

Lady Gloriana made a charming hostess for her son. Always concerned for her guests' comfort, smiling and serene, she moved through the evening with her usual impeccable manners and grace. She made sure the shyest, youngest guest was drawn into a lively conversation, and the eldest had a comfortable chair near the fire. And she gave politics, possets, and play-going her equal and close attention. Merry admired her completely and reminded herself of her plan to emulate her.

She had given herself quite a talking to after she had left the viscountess the evening before. And after, of course, she had shed more than a few tears of mortification, that she had been behaving in such a common way.

Why, no better than a little dairy maid who didn't know how to comport herself, she thought as she pounded her pillows in frustration. But eventually, she had dried her eyes and then she had made herself a fierce promise to become the kind of woman Edward deserved. She would be quiet, ladylike, proper, for she knew he was worth any effort of hers. And never again would she allow her fun-loving nature to betray her into telling a joke, laughing immoderately, or calling attention to herself in any way, no matter how difficult such a course would be for her. She had a warm and naturally gregarious nature, and primness and reticence were completely foreign to her. But still, she had made a start toward her goal this evening, and much later as the guests were leaving and she saw Lady Gloriana's little nod and her warm smile of approval, she knew she had been successful. Still, she had to wonder why such an achievement did not make her happier, why the party had seemed so dull and long.

Everyone else present considered it the complete success all Lady Gloriana's parties were, no matter how diverse the company. And this evening, it was diverse, ranging from some of the Willoughbys' relatives who were currently in town and a few young people who were friends of the viscount's to Lady Gloriana's elderly beaux.

But although Lord Saterly and Mr. Brethers had been included, the viscount had drawn the line at his mother's youngest admirer. Merry had marveled at the skill with which the viscountess had managed the two who had been included. She had not spoken to one a second longer than she did to the other, and even when a few terse rumblings had been exchanged between them, she had smoothed their ruffled feathers and separated them with a minimum of effort. Merry had to wonder if she would ever have such social finesse.

Lord Saterly himself had made a point of coming to talk to Merry, supposedly to ask her how she liked London. But he had hardly settled down beside her before the conversation turned to his favorite subject:

the Lady Gloriana Regina Willoughby. "How very lucky you are, Miss Lancaster, to stay with the divine Lady Glory," he told her, his eyes lighting up as he admired their hostess. "She is an angel, a divine nymph! And she is everything a man could desire to worship and adore."

Merry agreed with him, although she found his sighs and lovelorn airs more than a little ridiculous. Jeremy Overton was a man in his early sixties. He was very short and thin, and when he stood beside Edward's mother, they looked almost doll-like together.

Now the gentleman lowered his quizzing glass and sighed again. "It will come as no surprise to you, my dear young lady, to learn that I have been trying to persuade the glorious Gloriana to marriage for some years now. She, however, declares she cannot leave her children. She is so devoted to them, she puts her own wishes and comforts aside. Such nobleness should only be applauded, however much I myself deplore and regret it."

"But the viscount and his sister are grown now," some little devil prompted Merry to remark.

As Saterly swung around to stare at her, she hastened to elaborate. "What I mean is, they are hardly children anymore, and surely they are capable of taking care of themselves, are they not?" she asked, the picture of innocence.

The marquess's eyes lit up. "Do you think so indeed?" he asked eagerly. Then his little frown returned. "It is true that Lord Trumbull has no need of a mama anymore, but I know for a fact that Gloriana will never grant me the wish of my heart until her daughter is safely settled in life. And that, I fear, my dear Miss Lancaster, may not be for a very, very long time."

Merry followed his gaze to where Jane was sitting a little apart from the others. Tonight she was wearing a bright-pink gown that did nothing for her heavy arms, her ample curves. And she looked sullen again, for she was making no effort to join in the general conversation. Merry did not know whether she most wanted to go and shake her in exasperation, or put her arms around her and sympathize with her. As she watched, the viscountess came up to whisper something in her daughter's ear. Merry saw Jane's face redden, although she nodded and rose. Standing beside her mother, she looked twice as tall and ungainly. And her bright-pink gown looked garish beside the older lady's soft blossom silk.

Lord Saterly sighed again and Merry excused herself. Fond as she was of Lady Gloriana, she had no intention of sitting and talking about her all evening, or listening to her being praised to the skies.

As she walked toward Jane, she searched the room for Edward. Yes, there he was, over by the mantel with a small group of gentlemen. As she stared at him, he raised his eyes and they exchanged glances across the crowded room. For a moment, all the conversation and quiet laughter died away for Merry until she felt there was no one present but the two of them. And, oh, how much she wished that were so, for then she could run to his arms, kiss him! Her gaze faltered as she remembered that she must not think of doing such a thing again. When she looked back, she saw that Edward had turned away.

It was a very long and tiresome evening for her. She had found Jane talking to Mr. Brethers, but tonight Merry did not find the way that gentleman's beetled brows rose and fell with his words at all amusing. And his abbreviated way of speaking, the way his eyes followed his hostess's slender form, was just as tiresome as Lord Saterly's effusive, flowery compliments had been.

When the guests finally took their leave, the viscount excused himself almost at once, making no attempt to see her alone so he might give her the good-night kiss she had come to expect. Instead, he kissed his mother and Jane. But although Merry waited eagerly, he only bowed and kissed her hand as he said he hoped she would sleep well.

Lady Gloriana linked arms with the two girls as she

urged them to the stairs. "I declare I must have your assistance, my dears, after such a tiresome evening," she said even as she skipped a little. "Is there anything to equal relatives for making a wonderful party dull? For example, I am sure there was no need for Cousin Maria to come in a hackney, or talk about her economies all evening, especially when I know her late husband cut up warm and left her a considerable fortune. And Jane's great-uncle Horace . . . well! No conversation, no clothes sense, and the man is as fat as a flawn!"

"But he is a kind man, *Maman*," Jane said from her other side. "I am sure he tries very hard not to be dull."

"Then he must try harder, for it is obvious further effort is necessary!" the viscountess exclaimed as they reached the landing. "But never mind, Merry, my pet, you shall not have to see a one of them again until the ball, and in that squeeze, I daresay you won't have to exchange more than a few words with any of them."

Although Lady Gloriana seemed eager to continue to discuss the evening she was castigating, both Jane and Merry excused themselves to go to bed. Seeing that the discontented look was back on Jane's face, Merry asked her if she would care to join her for an early-morning ride. Secretly, she hoped she might catch Edward engaged in the same occupation and thus have a chance to speak to him. She knew he often took a quick canter before a great many other gentlemen saw fit to rise from their beds.

Jane agreed, without any marked degree of enthusiasm, although her mother clapped her hands and declared it a wonderful scheme. "And I shall have Farewell order the horses for eight, my dears, so there is no need to trouble yourselves," she said as she kissed them both good night.

Miss Farewell was Lady Gloriana's maid, and Merry wondered how she would communicate the order, for never once since her arrival had she heard the woman speak a single word. Although she was quick to curtsy when she was encountered in the hall or spoken to, she only nodded or shook her head in response. She was a tall, strong-looking woman of Welsh descent, and Lady Gloriana had explained that the Welsh were noted for their reticence. Merry would have disliked having the woman as her maid, but the viscountess did not appear to mind. And it was true that Farewell turned her out in marvelous fashion and seemed tireless about the concerns and wishes of her mistress.

When Merry woke the next morning, she discovered that a steady rain was falling, so a possible meeting with Edward in the park was not to be. She canceled the order for the horses and set herself to a day of quiet, indoor occupations. She ate breakfast alone, and when she could discover no one in the lower rooms but servants, busy cleaning up after the party, she went back to her own room to write some letters to her friends in Bath. Later, that afternoon, she wandered down to the library to look for a book to read.

At least that is what she told herself she was doing, although she knew, deep inside, she was still hoping to run into her fiancé. She felt she had to talk to him without further delay, for his behavior of the previous evening was still troubling her. But Edward was nowhere to be found. Instead, she surprised Jane curled up in a large wing chair eating sweetmeats and reading.

"I won't disturb you, Jane," Merry said as she came into the library. "I just wanted to see if there wasn't a book I would like to read. Such a quiet, dreary day, is it not?"

Jane selected another candy. "I like days like this in town," she said almost absentmindedly. "They are so peaceful. And even though they do tend to drag toward evening, I find them refreshing." As Merry studied the shelves, she added, "Do not run away. Sit down and keep me company, please."

It was the first time she had ever sounded friendly, and encouraged, Merry smiled at her as she selected a large volume containing etchings and an account of the Grand Tour.

"Yes, I suppose they make a nice change once in a

while," she said, taking a seat across the hearth from Jane. "Bath was so quiet compared to the hurly-burly of London. Sometimes, even, I miss it a little."

She opened her book, but surprisingly, Jane began to question her about her past, her great-aunt, and how she had spent her days in that sedate spa town. Merry told her all about the Pump Room, the walks and drives to be enjoyed, the fine libraries, and the occasional balls and receptions that were held in the Assembly Rooms. "And then there are clubs to join—glees and sketching groups. It did not seem quiet to me until I had London to compare it to," she admitted. "Of course, I also had to attend Great-aunt Elizabeth, wait on her and fetch her medicines, and walk her pugs."

Jane grimaced. "That doesn't sound very exciting," she said.

"No. I hated the pugs especially," Merry confessed, delighted at their new rapport. "Their names were Caesar and Brutus, and two fatter, uglier little morsels of dogdom you have never seen. Brutus absolutely adored nipping an unwary ankle and Caesar had a nasty habit of yapping at the most inappropriate times. And they smelled so bad. Ugh!"

She was delighted to see Jane smile. "So, how on earth did you meet my brother?" she asked next. "And did your aunt truly like him, even though he was going to take you away?"

Merry told her how they had met, and about their whirlwind courtship. Just thinking of it again made her eyes sparkle, and a delicate color came into her face.

But when she recalled herself to the library, it was to see that Jane was looking despondent again. "It sounds wonderful," she said abruptly. "I envy you."

Merry would have asked her more about herself then, but Jane put an end to the conversation by dipping into the box of candy again and opening her book. Soon, she was lost in the pages.

The two sat in silence until a footman came in to attend the fire and light several branches of candles. Merry's eyes strayed to the gleaming expanse of cherry that was Edward's desk. She wondered where he was, what he was doing, and how long it would be before she could see him alone again. For even though she had taken Lady Gloriana's lecture very much to heart, she knew she must see Edward on occasion, or she would not be at all happy.

Fortunately, he came in just as the tea tray was brought in, and the three of them sat and chatted about the previous evening and the parties still to come. "I see that we are stay-at-homes again this evening," Edward remarked as he took a piece of spice cake. "I think I will go on to Brooks's after dinner. Two evenings at Mount Street in a row is unheard of during the Season."

"Yet you think nothing of condemning Merry and me to that fate," Jane teased him. She seemed happier now that her brother had joined them, and several times during their repast she made a small joke and grew quite animated. Merry wondered at it. She was never this way when her mother was present or in company, but Edward seemed to be able to draw her into the conversation and set her at her ease.

"If it does not rain tomorrow, perhaps I shall take you ladies riding," the viscount said, smiling impartially to them both.

Merry nodded and smiled back at him, and a muscle moved for a moment in his cheek before he turned to his sister to see if she agreed.

Jane looked from one to the other, obviously hesitant to intrude until Merry begged her to say she would come. At that, she agreed, and a time was set.

Dinner was a quiet affair. Lady Gloriana seemed a little abstracted, Miss Willoughby was once again her usual silent self, and Merry was on her best and most refined behavior. It was left to the viscount to carry the bulk of the conversation, which he did with his usual aplomb.

But as the ladies were crossing the front hall later, to adjourn to the drawing room for the evening, the knocker sounded. Lady Gloriana looked at the hall clock standing against the wall. "Now, who can that be at this hour?'' she wondered as she shepherded the girls before her. "Never mind. Durfee will tell us presently. Perhaps dear Teddy has asked one of his cronies to take him up in his carriage," she added.

But only a moment later, the elderly butler knocked to tell them that Mr. Jason Willoughby had called, and begged to see them.

Merry heard Jane's sharp little intake of breath and turned to see that her face had grown quite pale and she was twisting her hands in her lap. As Lady Gloriana turned to her daughter as well, a mask of indifference came over Jane's face and those restless hands stilled.

"It is quite all right, *Maman*," the girl said gruffly. "Do not refuse Jason on my account."

Lady Gloriana nodded to the butler, but she still looked troubled. A moment later, a tall, broad-shouldered and loose-limbed gentleman dressed in traveling clothes entered the room. He was followed closely by the viscount.

"Just see who I discovered cluttering up the hall, *Maman*," Edward said with a chuckle. "Can you believe it? Cousin Jason deserting the country for all the evils of London? We must roast him for that."

"You are already doing so, halfling," the visitor tossed over his shoulder as his keen gray eyes inspected the room. One eyebrow rose when he spotted Merry, but he made his bow first to Lady Gloriana. "Dear, dear Aunt," he said, "how delightful to see that you have not lost your youthful looks as yet!"

There was nothing in his compliment to remark, but still Merry wondered at the slight sneer she imagined she heard in his careless words. As he moved toward her and Jane, she studied him more closely. A few years older than his cousins, he had the same dark hair. But unlike their curls, his hair was as smooth as a raven's wing, and his complexion was swarthy. He was also much taller than any of them. Merry judged him to be well over six feet in his stocking feet. His face was made up of strong rugged planes, as if it had been hewn from rough stone by an apprentice sculptor, and his mouth

was set in a stern, uncompromising line. As he held out
his hand to Jane, he said, "Well, cuz, I trust I find you
in good health?"

Jane nodded as she gave him a tremulous smile. He
turned then to Edward, a questioning look in his gray
eyes. The viscount came forward.

"May I present my fiancé, Miss Meryl Lancaster,
Jason?" he asked.

His tall cousin bowed to her. "Your fiancé, my
boy?" he asked, sounding surprised. "But I have not
heard of your engagement. Surely this happened only
recently?"

"Very recently, indeed," Lady Gloriana contributed.
"So recently, in fact, that we have not announced it as
yet, and it is not generally known, even in the family.
But do sit down, Jason, and tell us what brings you to
town, and how your mother and all your family are."

The gentleman strolled to the mantel to lounge
against it. "I have been sitting in a rocking coach for
some hours, and I prefer to stand, thank you," he said.
"As for my reasons for coming to town, that is only
some estate business, Aunt, and of no interest to
anybody but me," he added, in his abrupt way. "My
mother has been sickly of late, but is much improved
now. And I am happy to say that my brothers and
sisters are all well. You would not know Gerald, Teddy.
He bids fair to top my inches, he is shooting up in such
an alarming way. But I have been most remiss. Allow
me to congratulate you, sir, and to offer my best wishes
to the bride as well."

His sudden engaging smile lightened his expression
and made him look almost handsome, and Merry smiled
back at him in quick response.

"And when is the happy occasion to take place, Miss
Lancaster?" he asked.

"It—it has not quite been decided," Merry said,
trying hard not to look at Edward, standing nearby.
"Sometime before the Season is over, I believe."

"We are letting darling Merry have a chance to
become accustomed to the *ton* before we pitch her into

the frenzy of a wedding," Lady Gloriana added, with a fond smile for her daughter-in-law-to-be.

"I am sure you are, ma'am," Jason Willoughby said, his smile gone and his voice expressionless again. "But where did you meet this lovely lady, cuz?" he asked, turning his shoulder a little.

Merry had the strangest feeling he was trying to exclude Lady Gloriana from the conversation, and she wondered at it. As the two men talked and laughed, she stole another look at Jane. Although supposedly busy with her needlework, that young lady often studied the rugged face of their visitor. And once Merry caught her peeking quickly at her mother to see if she had been noticed. There was some undercurrent here that Merry knew nothing about. She wondered what it could be.

Mr. Willoughby stayed with them until Edward's carriage was announced. Then he took his leave of all the ladies with careless address, saying he would do himself the honor of calling on them at a more conventional time. For of course, he added, he was eager to hear all his aunt's news so he might relate it to his mother when he returned to the country.

"Dear Jason, how often have I asked you not to call me Aunt?" Lady Gloriana said with a little laugh as she reached up to take his arm and walk with him to the door. Merry noticed she barely came up to his chest. "I am no such thing, and you know it," she went on. "The late viscount was only your father's second cousin. How that makes us related I have no idea, but surely I cannot be your aunt."

"But it seems so appropriate a title for a lady of your years, ma'am, so respectful," the gentleman replied. "Lady Gloriana is much too formal for even distant kin, is it not?"

"Then why don't you call me *Tante*," she persisted. "It would be so apropos when my own dear children call me *Maman*."

"Yes, I am aware they have always done so," he remarked. "Somehow *Maman* is nowhere near as definitive a word to the English as Mama, is it? Your servant, Aunt.''

He turned and bowed to Merry and Jane then before he waved his hand and left the room. He was followed closely by Edward.

As the door shut behind them, Merry stared at Lady Gloriana's back. She was standing very still and staring at that door, and for some reason, her shoulders seemed squared and stiff. But when Merry wondered if she were angry at the man who had brought so much strange tension into the room, she turned to show a smiling face even as she shook her head.

"Jason, what a bear he is," she said lightly as she took her seat again. "You should know that his estate marches with ours in Hampshire, Merry. We have known him all his life. He is the quintessential country squire, is he not, Jane?"

She paused, but Jane was intent on threading her needle and did not reply. "He is interested only in his acres and his crops, and he is a man who would be bored to tears at an evening spent at a *ton* party. His father died several years after my husband did, and as the eldest son, he naturally took over the estate as soon as he was grown. I must say that although he is a strange, abrupt man, he does very well caring for his mother and all those children that followed him. Unfortunately, she is a woman afflicted with moods of despondency, and she has a tendency to imagine she is constantly ill. But perhaps having all those babies, one right after the other, would make any woman despondent and concerned for her health. And I can never keep them straight. Tiny, how many sisters and brothers does Jason have?''

"Five living," her daughter said, her voice even.

"I wonder what did bring him to town?" Lady Gloriana persisted. "He so rarely comes here. I was absolutely astounded when his name was announced! But I do hope he will not be forever on our doorstep. He is not an easy man to entertain, although I suppose, as

relatives, we are honor-bound to invite him to dinner
some evening soon. What a shame he did not come
sooner, so we might have included him with the others
last night and thus have fulfilled our obligation."

There was a moment's silence, and then she cried,
"Good heavens! You don't suppose he was waiting for
me to ask him to stay here with us, do you? Dear, dear!
I wonder if he came directly to Mount Street and all his
baggage was outside on his coach? I never thought to
ask his accommodations, but I really would not care to
have him here."

"I doubt he would have agreed to it, even if you had
tendered the invitation, *Maman*," Jane said, her dark-
blue eyes steady on her mother's lovely, concerned face.
"You know very well we have not been friendly with his
branch of the family. At least not for some time now."

"Oh, don't put it that way, dearest Tiny," her
mother said, rising to come and kiss her daughter.
"Surely you know how hard I have tried, time and time
again, to draw him into our circle, but he remains so
aloof and sarcastic! He has such an abrasive
personality, I am sure even Merry must have remarked
it."

Merry hardly knew what to reply, but when she saw
the lady was waiting for her answer, she made herself
say, "There was something about him that was
different, that is true, ma'am, but what a handsome
smile he has!"

"When he remembers to use it," Lady Gloriana
agreed. "But let us forget Jason the bear, girls. Tell me,
what are you both planning to wear to Lady Roper's
ball tomorrow evening?"

Merry was very late for her ride with Edward and
Jane the following morning, and she was almost crying
with frustration when she ran down the stairs at last.
She had heard the two of them talking as they passed
her door some time before, but when she would have
joined them, Lady Gloriana had made a surprise visit to
her room. She was horrified at the comfortable old

habit Merry had donned for the early-morning ride, especially, as she said, she was to have the viscount's distinguished escort. Nothing would do but to change it for a more fashionable one that had just been delivered. And then the viscountess had not cared for the way Nora had dressed her hair, nor the tilt of her riding hat. It was quite twenty minutes after the time set before Merry could escape. She found Edward and Jane walking their horses slowly up and down the street, a groom engaged in walking her mount as well.

Merry saw Edward's severe expression at once, and she knew he was displeased. He was a punctual man at all times. Indeed, they had often laughed together how about how well they would suit, for Merry herself was always before time to her appointments.

"I do beg your pardon, Jane, Edward," she said after the groom had helped her to the saddle and she had settled her skirts and gathered up the reins. "Lady Gloriana insisted I change my habit, and it made me late. I hope I am not quite in your black books?"

Jane assured her it did not matter in the slightest, but she thought Edward's remarks to the same effect a little curt.

They rode in single file until the park was reached, and Merry searched her mind for what she could say to him to bring back the smiles and the tender looks she had come to associate with him whenever he looked at her. But even when they were able to ride three abreast along Rotten Row, she never had the chance. The viscount urged his horse to a canter, and both girls followed suit. And somehow, Merry found herself riding on the outside, with Jane between her and her fiancé. Still, she prepared to enjoy herself. The park was not crowded at this early hour, and the bright spring day was fresh and enticing. And after the steady rain of yesterday, every blade of grass, every new leaf, seemed a more verdant green.

At last, they slowed their mounts to a sedate trot. Merry was delighted, for although she knew herself to be a fairly good horsewoman, she knew she could never

compare to Edward's sister. Jane sat her horse as if she
had been born in the saddle, and it was one of the few
places where she appeared to advantage. Her gelding
was so large, she herself looked smaller than she was.

Now the three of them talked about a number of
casual subjects. For once, Jane's sullen moods were in
abeyance, and she laughed and joked with her brother
as if she didn't have a care in the world.

Just before they decided to return home, they saw a
horseman cantering toward them, and Edward raised
his crop. "Why, it's Jason!" he exclaimed. "I might
have known he would be abroad early. He keeps
country hours wherever he is."

Mr. Willoughby reined in at his signal and greeted
them all. He seemed more relaxed this morning, too, as
he turned his mount so he could join them. Of necessity,
they rode in pairs now, and Merry found herself beside
Edward at last.

When she heard the others talking behind them, she
said softly, "How glad I am for this opportunity,
Edward. It seems ages since I have had a private word
with you."

The viscount turned his head to study her in her smart
new habit. "You have something you wish to discuss,
Merry?" he asked.

He sounded so formal, so distant, that Merry was
confused. Still, she made herself smile at him. "No,
nothing of importance, my dear," she said as lightly as
she could. "But since the other night in the drawing
room, when your mother came in and surprised us, I
have barely seen you."

"But surely you knew I was only trying to abide by
the rules you set, Merry," he said, still not smiling.

"What rules?" she asked, bewildered.

He stared straight ahead, refusing to look at her as he
said, "*Maman* told me you wanted me to keep my
distance. I had not realized my attentions were
disturbing you. I only wish you had had the courage to
tell me so yourself, instead of forcing my mother to be

your emissary. Giving her such a distasteful chore was hardly fair to her.''

"You must have misunderstood her, Edward," Merry said firmly. "I never said anything of the kind! Why, it was the viscountess herself who suggested we be more discreet, told me to be careful not to be alone with you until we can be married. I would never, ever say something like that, for it would be a lie. You know how I adore being with you, how I have always welcomed your kisses.''

"But that is to call *Maman* a liar, Merry," he said swiftly.

"No, no, I did not mean that," she said just as quickly. "Perhaps you did misunderstand, or perhaps she thought to help me. Yes, that must be it. She is so good!''

Edward looked over his shoulder and saw his sister and his cousin riding close behind. "We cannot discuss this now," he said.

Merry listened carefully, but she could not be sure he believed her, for his voice was no warmer than it had been before. And he had not called her his dear, nor told her how much he adored her kisses, too. Suddenly she felt heavy, leaden. What was happening to them? Where had their warm rapport, their firm commitment to each other gone?

As they rode in silence now, she felt a bleak stab of bewilderment. Why were things so different here in town? And then a tiny flicker of doubt caused her to wonder if she had been too precipitate, after all. Perhaps Edward was showing her his true nature at last, and the man she had believed herself to be in love with was only a pretense, an act. For it was all too true that he had changed drastically since their arrival. Yet she had been able to excuse his moods, his jealousy, even his anger. Only a few minutes alone with him were enough to steady her trust in him, and in his love. But now that he seemed determined to keep his distance, that reinforcement was gone.

She turned her head to stare at him, and the yearning expression she thought she could detect in his dark-blue eyes made her bold. "I must speak to you alone, Edward. Perhaps we could go for a drive this afternoon?" she asked. She could see the park gates ahead, and she knew that when they reached them, their intimacy would be at an end.

He shook his head, but she thought he looked disappointed. "I'm afraid that will not be possible, Merry," he said. "I have engagements this afternoon, appointments I cannot cancel. But perhaps tomorrow? Yes, let us plan a drive to Twickenham then, if the weather is fine. We will take a picnic lunch, just like we did that day in Bath."

With this, Merry had to be content, and she nodded. A moment later they reined in to take their leave of Jason Willoughby. Merry saw that Jane was smiling, her color a little heightened as that gentleman bade them farewell.

And she was still smiling when they reached Mount Street again. Edward thanked them both formally for their company, and Jane laughed at him as she prepared to climb the steps. Merry went inside with a lighter heart, too, for Edward had held her hand for several moments and given it a warm, reassuring squeeze before he let her go.

5

THAT evening, for the Roper ball, Merry wore the ecru evening gown she had chosen herself. And when she came down to join the others, she felt much more herself, yet still fashionable. Edward's warm compliment and smiling nod told her he thought so too. So when Lady Gloriana, resplendent in emerald silk, twitted her gently and called her their country mouse, Merry only smiled. Tonight she was able to ignore the teasing, especially since Jane, dressed in emerald to match her mother, also told her how becoming her gown was.

The ball was a perfect squeeze. The widowed and wealthy Lady Roper, a fat, ebullient woman long past her girlhood, had invited as many guests as she could possibly fit into her large house in Portman Square. Merry glowed with happiness as she danced the first set with Edward, but only moments after it concluded, she found herself face to face with an eager Sir Frederick White.

Since her arrival in town, the baronet had tumbled into love with Miss Lancaster. She was so attractive, her smile so enticing, and her spirits as merry as her name, how could any man not love her? he asked himself. And her slight reluctance to be in his company, her occasional refusal to drive or walk, had only seemed to whet his appetite for her and intrigue him further. Now he bowed low as he asked her to honor him with the next dance.

Merry glanced sideways as she felt Edward stiffening. But then he seemed to make a conscious effort to relax as he gave her hand to the young man with the flaming red hair.

Merry was surprised to see Mr. Jason Willoughby leading Edward's sister into the same set. She had not thought he would be present. Surely Lady Gloriana had said *ton* parties bored him? But although she was glad Jane had a partner at last, and one who was tall and broad enough to compliment her, she forgot them as she fended off Sir Frederick's drawled compliments and ignored his more outrageous remarks.

After their dance, they joined the group that surrounded Mary Griffin, and were greeted with cries of delight. Still, Merry was not sorry when Jason Willoughby bowed to her after a short intermission and rather abruptly asked her to dance.

It was a waltz, and for a moment Merry felt a pang that she and Edward were not dancing it together. She loved to waltz with him, feel his hand at her waist, be able to look into his eyes and see his love for her there as she followed his lead to the intoxicating beat of the music.

Jason Willoughby waltzed creditably, if not with the élan and expertise her fiancé brought to dancing. But she reminded herself that his cousin was as much a country mouse as she was, even as she smiled at him.

"We had not looked for you this evening, sir," she said as they turned.

His dark brows rose. "I see that my aunt has been telling you of my preference for the country, Miss Lancaster," he said. "But I do come to town occasionally, and surely it cannot be bragging to tell you I know a great many people in the *ton*. That I do not prefer their sybaritic existence is certainly my own affair."

Merry thought he sounded stiff, and she hastened to say lest he think they had been criticizing him, "But of course! I myself was brought up in the country, and this is my first trip to London. And when I first arrived in town, I was sure I would not be able to sleep a wink for the noise. Yet I have heard people say that although they never hear a thing in town, not even the crier, a cock crow at dawn ends their slumbers most effectively whenever they leave it."

He smiled a little at that. "Yes, and then they tell you how hard it was for them to get to sleep, do they not? All those noisy insects whirring about, owls hooting, even the wind disturbs them. Incomprehensible, don't you agree?"

She chuckled before she asked, "Do you make a long stay in London this time, sir?"

"Not very long. I do not like to leave my mother to deal with estate problems. She is not a well woman," he said, as his face darkened.

Merry was about to commiserate with him when he added with a visible effort, "But enough of that! May I say again that Edward is a truly lucky man?"

"Why, thank you, sir," she replied.

"And if I may be so bold, Miss Lancaster, as one of the family, so to speak, may I suggest you do not delay your wedding for much longer?"

Merry looked confused. Surely this was a very singular remark, even from a relative. "I—I don't understand," she said. "Why do you say that?"

He shrugged. "As a gentleman, I cannot tell you. But you seem an intelligent young lady. You will discover why for yourself, sooner or later. I only said what I did because I hope it will be sooner, for your sake and my cousin's. Sometimes, to wait for later is to risk more than just time."

"Well, I thank you for your advice, sir, even though it appears to be a riddle," Merry said. She thought Mr. Willoughby strange, but somehow she knew that he meant her no harm, that he had indeed spoken out of kindness and not from a desire to meddle in what did not concern him.

When the waltz was over, she asked him to escort her to Lady Gloriana and Jane. As they approached the ladies, she heard his quiet little snort of disgust, and she looked up at him in inquiry.

He nodded toward the tiny lady in emerald, seated between her two elderly beaux, with the young Mr. Horton dancing attendance as well. "I see my aunt has captured a hapless youth's heart," he said harshly.

"But that is no surprise to me. No man can ever be too old or too young and unsuitable for the lady."

"She does not encourage him, you know," Merry said, quick to defend Edward's mother. "It is only her kind heart that keeps her from dashing all his hopes. I have heard her say that any day now, he will discover a girl his own age, and forget her before the cat has time to lick her ear."

Mr. Willoughby did not look convinced, and she felt required to add, "And she is so beautiful, is she not? So gracious and kind? It is no wonder she is so much admired."

They had reached the lady's sofa just then, and Jason Willoughby was not required to agree or disagree with this fervent praise. He seated Merry next to the lady they had been discussing, and after a few common-places, strolled away.

Lady Gloriana raised her fan and winked at Merry behind it. "Somehow, my dear, I do not think Teddy will be the least bit jealous that you danced with his cousin," she whispered. "How could even he resent such a bear?"

Mr. Horton demanded her attention then, and as her two elderly beaux snorted in unison, Lady Gloriana turned away. Merry began to talk to Jane, and she noticed how that lady watched the broad retreating back of her cousin as he made his way through the throng. Merry was sure now that Jane was attracted to Jason Willoughby, although she was also sure that gentleman had no idea of her interest.

It was much later in the evening, after the supper dance with Edward, that Merry found herself in Sir Frederick's company again. But instead of leading her to the floor as the orchestra began to play, he begged her to sit out the dance with him. "Somethin' to say to you—can't wait—a surprise!" he said, taking her arm and steering her toward the door. Merry really did not care to go apart with him, but Lady Roper's house was so crowded, she did not expect she was in any danger of an intimate tête-à-tête.

But here she did Sir Frederick a disservice. Freddie had been on the town quite long enough to know almost by instinct where he could find a secluded alcove, a quiet salon on the back of the house, even a convenient balcony. And it was to one of the balconies facing the gardens that he led her now.

Merry tried to hold back as he opened the long door, but he would not release her hand and she did not feel she could make a scene, not when she was trying so hard this evening to subdue her high spirits and appear sophisticated and the perfect lady. So she allowed Freddie to pull her out on the balcony and close the door behind them.

He turned to face her and said eagerly, "Now, isn't this grand? Alone at last!"

"I want to return to the ballroom, Freddie. Right now!" she told him, trying to pull her hand free.

He clasped it tightly in both of his. "Not yet! Somethin' to say to you. And it's such a perfect spot!" he exclaimed. "Reminds me of that gent on the balcony in the old play, you know the one. . . ?"

He paused, but Merry just looked confused, and he went on, "The chappie that kept dronin' on about the moon and the sun, and wantin' to be the glove on her hand, or some such nonsense. Silly thing, couldn't make heads nor tails of it! But I understand the ladies think it very romantic."

As he had been speaking, Merry's brow had cleared and her ever-ready sense of humor overcame her distrust of the situation. "I believe you must be referring to Will Shakespeare's *Romeo and Juliet*, Freddie," she said, trying not to giggle.

"The very one," he said. "Well, here I am, Merry. Your Romeo!"

Miss Lancaster's face grew cold. "But you have it all wrong," she told him. "It wasn't a balcony. She was at a window. And he wasn't with her. He was down in her father's orchard. Besides, I am not Juliet, and I certainly don't want you to be Romeo!"

Freddie cast a doubtful glance two stories down to

Lady Roper's garden. It seemed very far to him. "Can't go down there, m'dear," he protested. "Can't have thought! Have to yell to make m'self heard."

Merry did not have time to insist they return to the party again, for Freddie, finding poetry didn't work and feeling as if he had been led off the scent somehow, took her in his arms and rained hot kisses all over her face. Merry could not stop him, for he was much stronger than she was. Suddenly, she remembered her feet, and she kicked him as hard as she could. As he released her, uttering a sharp yelp of pain, she pushed him away. "Stop this at once!" she exclaimed, her hazel eyes flashing fire.

"But, darlin' girl, I have been longin' to kiss you this age," he said, coming toward her again with his arms outstretched.

"Stop right where you are," Merry commanded. "I do not want you to kiss me. How dare you assume I would?"

"But—but, Merry, my love," he said, looking a little bewildered now. "Can it be that I have loved in vain? Can it be that you do not return my regard? Can it be that you have not been longin' for me to declare myself?"

"It can," Miss Lancaster said baldly. Freddie's face flushed.

"Now, now, dearest," he said more quietly, almost, she thought, as if he were calming a skittish mare, "you must have known how I have come to adore you."

He edged closer and then he dropped to one knee before her. "Perhaps I did not make myself clear?" he asked, his brow lightening. "Yes, yes, that must be it! But know I am proposin' marriage," he said, as if proud of his perception. "One of your quality would never be offered a slip on the shoulder, dear Merry. I am surprised that you doubted my intent for an instant, although I suppose girlish modesty—or perhaps you were startled?—but rest assured, I offer you the protection of my name."

He sounded so pleased with himself for his insight

and refinement that Merry found herself wanting badly to giggle. She was not afraid of Freddie, he was such a ridiculous man!

She was about to tell him again that she did not return his regard when the balcony door was thrown open and she saw a glowering Viscount Trumbull standing there. He looked like an incensed bull, and she almost fancied she could see wisps of steam escaping from his ears. Without a word, he strode forward and grasped the collar of Sir Frederick's evening coat, to haul him to his feet.

"Here now, I say, m'lord!" the startled baronet exclaimed. "Watch what you're about! It's bad *ton* to interrupt a man when he's proposin' to a lady, to say nothin' of ruinin' the set of a brand-new coat."

The viscount released him, but only so he might make two fists that quickly connected first with Freddie's left eye and then the right side of his jaw. Once again, Freddie found himself on the floor of the balcony, this time, however, in a most undignified sprawl.

"Oh, Edward, no, no," Merry cried, running forward to grasp his arm.

"No? You say *no*?" he asked through clenched teeth. "I'll teach this cawker to keep his distance from you. You there! Get up!" he ordered, turning to the hapless young man lying at his feet.

One eye closed, Freddie massaged his aching jaw, but he showed no inclination to obey this order. He might not be needlewitted, but even he could see he was much safer where he was.

Edward shook off Merry's hand and bent down to haul his opponent up, if need be. But before he could go further in ruining the set of a stunning evening coat, someone else joined them on what was becoming a very crowded balcony.

"Easy, halfling," Jason Willoughby said as he grasped his cousin's shoulder. "There's no sense in this, you know. You can't have a mill at Lady Roper's ball unless you want Miss Lancaster's name on every tattle-mongering tongue."

Edward stopped struggling then, although his blue eyes still glittered with anger. His cousin waited until he nodded curtly, before he released him and said, "You can't even call him out. A man has a right to propose to the lady of his choice, I believe."

"You're right," Freddie said eagerly as he struggled to his feet at last, now that he felt it was safe to do so. "Can't have thought, m'lord. Know Merry's a guest in your house, but my intentions were honorable, don't you know. Perfectly unexceptional. In fact," he added as he anxiously smoothed his wrinkled lapels, "don't know why you're makin' such an argle-bargle of it. It's not like I'm a loose screw, no, sir! And after all, as I assured Miss Lancaster, I was proposin' holy matrimony."

As he eyed the viscount's hands curling into fists again, he added, his voice rising, "Tell him so, Merry! The man's unreasonable!"

Before Merry could come to his rescue, the viscount said in a cold, deadly voice, "I do not believe it can be considered unreasonable of me to defend my fiancée from such rude advances as yours, however, sir."

Freddie's reddening jaw dropped. "Your fiancée?" he gasped. "Well, but—but—how was I to know?" Peering intently at the viscount through his one functional eye, he asked anxiously, "Hasn't been puffed off in the papers yet, has it?"

Edward Willoughby shook his head, and his rival whistled in relief. "That's all right, then," he said in an easier voice. "Must admit, don't keep up with the papers as I should, and I hardly ever read the Court News. And that's another thing! It stands to reason that since I don't, I couldn't be called to account, even if it *had* been announced."

Merry unclenched her own fists and said in a constricted voice, "Please go away, Freddie. Now. Right now."

"Is it true, though?" he asked, turning to her. "Are you engaged? To him?"

"Yes. She is," the viscount said firmly.

Merry nodded as well, and Freddie drew himself up to his full height and squared his shoulders. "Well, it seems to me, if anyone's made a cawker of himself, it's you, m'lord," he said. "For if you was engaged, the fair thing to do would be to tell the other chaps, not let them come a-courtin'. Never knew you to be such a flat."

Merry could see Edward's eyes beginning to glitter again, and she hastened to say, "There were reasons we could not—but it is too bad! And I beg you to forgive us, Freddie, please!"

The two Willoughbys stood stiffly as Freddie bowed and said he supposed he would have to. "Can't call a man out for gettin' engaged before you," he said slowly. "At least I don't think you can . . ."

"No, no, you are quite right," Merry told him, pushing him toward the door leading inside. "But you must leave us now. We have a great deal to discuss."

Freddie opened the door before he turned and bowed. "Give you good evenin', Miss Lancaster, Mr. Willoughby, m'lord," he said in his best and grandest manner. Then he bowed again. "Oh. Must allow me to wish you both happy, of course."

As soon as he was finally gone, Jason Willoughby chuckled in genuine amusement. "Silly chub! It's clear he's had too much champagne, trying to get his courage up to the sticking point," he said carelessly. "Not that I don't think he's got a point, mind! You should have announced your engagement as soon as you reached town. And Teddy, until you do, you will be forced to endure more of these occasions. Your Merry is much too lovely a lady not to have the beaux buzzing around her."

He paused, but when Edward did not reply, he turned to Merry. "I will take my leave, Miss Lancaster, since I am as obviously *de trop* as Freddie. But remember what I told you. There comes a time to believe in your dreams and press on, no matter what, er, arguments are advanced to make you delay."

After he bowed and left them, Merry turned to see the viscount staring at her as if he had never seen her before. She reached out and took his hands. "Please do not look at me like that, Edward," she begged. "I had no idea Freddie felt that way about me, nor that he was going to bring me out here to propose to me."

"Really?" Edward asked, his voice leaden. "And yet I cannot believe that even someone of White's extremely limited intelligence would have persevered unless he had not had some encouragement."

Merry opened her mouth to dispute this, but he went on as he removed her hands to offer her his arm, "Come! We cannot talk here. And people will be wondering why you have been absent from the ballroom for such a long time. At least *I* have a great care for the reputation of my future wife, even if she does not herself."

Seeing that Merry still would have spoken, he added harshly, "No, no more now! We will discuss this tomorrow."

Suddenly, Merry was as angry as she had ever been in her life. Without thinking of the crowded room they had just stepped into, she stopped dead to say, "I wish to go home—*now*!"

The viscount noticed how her hazel eyes gleamed almost golden in her fury, and since he did not suffer from Sir Frederick's handicap, he understood that now was not the time to either chastise her or attempt to soothe her.

"If you do not call for the carriage at once, I will walk right out the front door and make my way to Mount Street on foot," she went on quickly.

Edward led her a little apart from a pair of suddenly interested dowagers before he said, "There is no need for such threats, Merry. If you wish to leave the ball, you shall. Allow me only to go and tell *Maman* and Jane that I will send the carriage back for them. Wait here."

But when the viscount returned a few minutes later, both Lady Gloriana and his sister accompanied him. For the first time, Merry felt bitter disappointment at the sight of his mother. Why couldn't Lady Gloriana have waited? Why did she have to go home with them now?

But as she explained to them that she had a bad headache, trying to keep both her face and her voice noncommittal, Merry realized that it was probably just as well Lady Gloriana and Jane were coming. There was no sense talking to Edward now, not when she was so angry and distraught and he was so jealous and unreasonable. Perhaps a good night's sleep would clear the air.

When the four reached Mount Street, Merry was quick to excuse herself, declining all offers of pastilles to burn or a special posset for her headache.

As she said good night, she saw Jane's little frown, Lady Gloriana's sympathetic face, and she tried to pretend that everything was perfectly normal. She even curtsied to Edward, but she was relieved that he made no attempt to kiss so much as her hand as he wished her a good night.

Jane Willoughby looked from her brother's stormy, set face to her mother's concerned one, and she begged to be excused as well. Neither one of them noticed her as she followed Merry up the stairs.

"Teddy? My darling Teddy, come into the library and let me pour you a brandy," Lady Gloriana said quietly, taking his arm.

The viscount patted her hand before he drew away, saying, just as quietly, "Please excuse me, *Maman*. I must be alone now."

For a moment, he thought his mother would protest, and he was relieved when she said, "But of course. I understand, my dear, and I will not intrude. But remember that I am here for you if you need me, just as I am ready to assist Merry any way I can. And don't worry, darling boy," she whispered as she reached up to hug him and kiss his cheek, "it will work out for the best, you'll see."

As he poured the brandy his mother had wanted to get him, Edward Willoughby went over the evening's events. At first, he attempted to fan his anger, justify his actions, but that cock wouldn't fight. He knew he had been unreasonable and ridiculous as well.

But ever since he had brought Merry to London, he had been uneasy, distraught. He had been jealous not only when she was with other men, and he had had to picture her smiling at them and dancing in their arms, but even when she was just engaged with a party of her new friends. And yet he trusted Merry, he believed that she loved him. How incomprehensible his behavior was, therefore. Could it be that he was the type of man who was so consumed with jealousy that he wanted to lock his love away from the world, share her with no one else? No, no, that could not be!

Yet perhaps his uneasiness could be justified, he thought. In some strange way, he felt that he was losing Merry, that she was going farther and farther away from him all the time. When she had begged him not to arrange any more secret meetings in the house, he had not only been disappointed, he had wondered at it, and her motives. But she had explained—and logically, too, he told himself as he sipped the golden liqueur—why such trysts were dangerous. But although he had agreed, he had regretted abandoning them. How he had missed talking and laughing with her, taking her in his arms and kissing her until her soft, rosy mouth became swollen with passion. For now, it seemed he never saw her alone. She was out, she was busy with his mother, she was just not available. And so he had gone back to his own pursuits, his clubs and friends and all the masculine activities that had formerly made up his life.

The viscount threw himself down in a large armchair near the fireplace to brood into the dying coals. He remembered anew what his mother had told him the night she had interrupted them in the drawing room, and he had returned to discover Merry gone to bed without even waiting to bid him good night. His mother had pursed her lips at such discourtesy, but how kindly she had tried to explain it. The viscount's blue eyes grew keen as he recalled the scene. At first he had tried to

deny that what she was telling him was true, but he had
grown silent under the weight of her words. Merry was
shy and unsure, she had said; besides, she felt
awkwardly placed here in this house. And so she wanted
him to keep his distance until she felt more the thing,
although she had confessed to her hostess that she did
not know how to tell him so herself. And, Lady
Gloriana had said with a shake of her head, she feared
Merry was really enjoying her new friends and all her
activities apart from him. Even now Edward
Willoughby could hear her words.

"It is just as I have told you before, Teddy," she had
said, holding tight to his hand to comfort him, "Merry
is very young and naïve for a girl of twenty. But we must
remember that she has led an extremely sheltered life
with that elderly aunt in Bath. You must be gentle with
her, my son, and very patient. After some time, she will
be more at ease. It is only that she is unsophisticated and
a little gauche. I do not think that she is really flighty,
mind. I think she is just reveling in her popularity here
in town and torn between wanting it to continue and
marrying you. But if you allow her her little fling,
treating her more distantly, Teddy, I am sure all will end
well at last."

The viscount put his glass down on the table beside
him and rose to add more coal to the fire. He had not
only tried to follow his mother's advice, he had been
sure he had succeeded in curbing his jealousy and
passion as well, until he had found that silly ass Freddie
White kneeling at his Merry's feet this evening.

As he settled back in his chair again, his black brows
formed a solid bar across his handsome, frowning face.
How dare Merry allow such a thing? How dare she?

And then he shook his head, and a rueful little smile
of self-perception replaced his frown. How very arrogant he was, to be sure! Edward James Saint-Marystone
Willoughby, Viscount Trumbull, was just as much of an
ass as ever Freddie White had been!

And yet he had never thought of himself as an
arrogant man. He realized he was fortunate, born to

wealth and privilege as he was, but he did not think he
had ever abused his good fortune. And although he still
regretted he had never really known his large, handsome
father, he knew he had his mother to thank for the man
he had become. How easy it would have been for her, a
young widow, to make him into a mama's boy, telling
him how wonderful and precious he was, he thought as
he sipped his brandy again. But she had refrained from
that. Instead, she had insisted he spend most of his time
with his nanny and governess and later the superior
tutor she had provided for him. And she had
encouraged him to engage in sport, insisted the tutor
teach him to ride and hunt and fish. Not for her son
dawdling afternoons spent at her footstool in the
drawing room! She had not even insisted on the
customary portrait of her with her children, because, as
she had told him later, "I knew it would mope both you
and Tiny to death, Teddy, and I could not bear to have
you suffer so!" Instead, she had sat for her portrait
alone, considerate as she was. And when it had been
time for him to go to school, she had not flinched,
although he had seen the tears in her eyes the day he had
left.

When he had gone to Oxford later, she had made sure
she was either absent or very busy entertaining during
his long vacations. That way, the agent could take him
in hand without distractions, to see to the most important part of his education: that of being capable of
handling his estates wisely and well. She had even
turned a blind eye to his first mistress, his first
unsuitable friends, even his first gambling debts. But
although she had pretended to go her own way,
cultivating her own friends and amusements, he knew
how much she loved him. She would never intrude,
however, just as she had refrained from doing so
tonight. He might not have had a father's love and
guidance, but thanks to his mother, he had had an
exemplary life.

He ran a hand over his dark curly hair and sighed. He
had always considered himself an uncomplicated man,

with no dark side to his nature, no hidden weaknesses. His childhood and youth had had few clouds, and he had enjoyed his life in town and on his estate ever since he had reached his majority. Until now. Until he had met Merry Lancaster, wooed her, won her, and carried her off to London. Yet how could that be? They had been so happy in Bath. But tonight . . . ah, tonight!

He rose to pace the room, the frown he had worn earlier returning. Thinking with clarity now, he knew very well that Merry would never encourage Freddie White even if she were unattached, and yet he had as good as accused her of it. No wonder she had been furious! He must beg her pardon most humbly tomorrow.

But then he seemed to hear his cousin Jason's voice, telling him that until he announced their engagement, Merry would never be free of other men's attentions. And then he recalled that he had already announced that engagement this very night, and for the first time in several hours he smiled broadly. Knowing what a rattlepate the man was, the viscount was sure Freddie must have bruited the news about the ballroom, and that by the time the last weary partygoer had wended his way home, it had become common knowledge. By tomorrow, those of the *ton* who had not attended the ball would hear the news, and in only a week's time, those presently in the country as well would be informed through their correspondence. His formal announcement, inserted in the papers first thing tomorrow morning, would be almost anticlimactic. Still, he hesitated, not wanting to press Merry before she was ready. And there was another factor too: his mother.

He knew she believed Merry should have more time to become accustomed to society and to enjoy the Season. But in thinking it over after his soul-searching tonight, the viscount did not feel Merry could possibly be enjoying it the way things stood, no matter what his mother claimed. And Lord knows, he wasn't! It seemed to him they had been at odds almost from the time they had arrived in town.

No, their betrothal would become public tomorrow, although if Merry insisted on it, they could still have a long engagement. As he went to his desk to write a note to her, telling her his intent, he smiled. He would be able to see a great deal more of her as her acknowledged fiancé, and no one would think a thing of it if he insisted on privacy. And when they were alone, he was sure he could convince her that their early marriage was something greatly to be desired. Why, he could start tomorrow on their picnic to Twickenham! For no matter how Merry behaved under his mother's eye, or in public, when they were alone she was his dear love again. Perhaps a June wedding was not impossible, after all.

After he finished his note and sealed it, he banked the fire and went to bed at last, running up the stairs two at a time with the air of a man who has just solved a weighty problem and all his former moodiness gone. He paused only to throw a kiss to Merry as he passed her door. Everything would be all right now. He was sure of it.

The viscount was up early the next morning. Surprisingly, he did not seem to feel the lack of a good night's sleep, for he was whistling as he made his way to the breakfast room. And when Durfee smiled and nodded as he gave him Merry's note to deliver, the viscount grinned at him.

He found his mother before him, toying with her usual piece of dry toast and looking paler than he liked to see her.

As he kissed her before helping himself to the dishes on the sideboard, he said, "I did not expect to see you, *Maman*, not after you cut such a dash at the ball."

Lady Gloriana stirred her coffee. "I was worried about you, darling Teddy," she said. "Do tell me what happened last night that upset both you and Merry so, I beg you. I have been imagining the direst things!"

The viscount sat down across from her and ignored his heaping plate as he told her briefly what had occurred.

"Oh, dear," Lady Gloriana whispered, her hand to her mouth. "How very unfortunate! But, Teddy, I am sure dear Merry did not realize what she was doing, or what Sir Frederick had in mind. You must not blame her, you must not! She is such a baby! But when she has been about town a bit more, you'll see. She is the most agreeable girl, so eager to learn and to please. And she is so lovable."

The viscount nodded, his mouth full of ham, and she went on, "And I am so glad that you do not appear to be angry with her for her indiscretion to the point you want to break off the engagement. Why, that would be the most—"

Having disposed of his ham, the viscount interrupted her. "Far from it, *Maman*. I know Merry. She did nothing wrong. But since I told Freddie we were about to be married, you do see I must get the announcement to the papers this morning. As soon as I finish breakfast, I am off to do so. Idiot that he is, I'm sure by now he has spread the news far and wide."

He was surprised to see his mother crumbling her toast and frowning a little. When he asked her what was troubling her, she sighed and said, "Oh, Teddy, I wish it did not have to be like this! It is almost as if you have been *forced* into the announcement. I am sure I could find some way to diffuse the gossip. Of course! No doubt Sir Frederick was foxed last night and did not perfectly understand. Just see how that would answer!"

She stared at him hopefully, and then she said, "Besides—and you must forgive me, dear Teddy—I do not think you and Merry are as happy as an engaged couple should be. There have been so many misunderstandings, so many quarrels! And as close as I am to Merry now, I cannot like my beloved son to marry where he does not love. Perhaps you should think further about this before you act?"

The viscount was frowning now, his breakfast forgotten. Of course *Maman* was right. There had been a lot of misunderstandings. But even so, he knew he would never love another woman the way he loved

Merry. And he was sure she loved him, too. In his mind's eye, he saw her lovely smile, the dimple flashing in her cheek, her glowing hazel eyes. He remembered her soft lips and how shy yet eager they had been when he first proposed to her in Bath, and he knew he didn't need to think about it for a moment longer.

He laughed as he rose from the table. "How like you to be so concerned, so loving, *Maman*," he said. "But there is no need to fret. I have not been coerced to this move. Oh, perhaps Freddie inadvertently hastened it up a bit, but there was never a doubt in my mind that I would marry Merry someday. And now that day is not as far in the future as I had feared."

He saw that the little frown was still there between his mother's brows, and he added, "You must not doubt me, *Maman*! I shall see to it myself that Merry is less green from now on. And as her acknowledged fiancé, there will be no more beaux, no more misunderstandings, no more contretemps of any kind. Trust me. Marriage to Merry Lancaster is the wish of my heart."

As he blew her a kiss and walked to the door, he added, "I have left her a note. Well, it is more of a letter, really. I had so much to say to her, to explain. And yesterday, we planned to drive to Twickenham, just the two of us. I gave orders to Mrs. Wilkie to see a basket of food is prepared and told Durfee to select a bottle of wine for us as well. And perhaps tonight we might dine *en famille* to celebrate? I shall tell him to ice some champagne so we can all drink to my future happiness. Mine, and Merry's, of course."

After he left the breakfast room, Lady Gloriana sat quietly, staring out at the lovely spring day. But her son's words did not appear to have reassured her, for she was frowning still.

A short time later, she returned to her room. She told her maid that she was not feeling well, and so intended to spend the day secluded. And she gave orders that she was not to be disturbed, for any reason.

6

LADY Gloriana was not the only inmate of the house on Mount Street who did not sleep well after the ball. Miss Meryl Lancaster had paced her room for some time, her fictitious headache fast becoming a reality. In fact, if Merry had thought to open her door around three in the morning, the viscount might have delivered his message in person, for he was only just then making his way to bed. But Merry did not open the door, so she did not see the kiss he blew her, nor his warm, loving glance.

The almost sleepless night caused her to wake very late, and it was after ten before she rang for her chocolate. And when Nora came in a few minutes later, she found her mistress sitting up in bed and staring out at the sunny day with a look on her face that would have been more appropriate for someone watching a dismal storm.

As soon as Merry saw the bulky letter on the tray and recognized Edward's handwriting, she dismissed her maid, telling her she would ring when she needed her. Nora was smiling as she left the room.

For several minutes, Merry only stared at her letter. At last she took a deep breath as if to steel herself, and broke the seal. She had no idea why Edward would write such a tome unless he were crying off, and suddenly, in spite of her anger of the night before, she knew she would not be able to bear it if that was what he had done.

But her set expression and compressed lips did not survive the first paragraph. The letter was not a very good example of the viscount's usually fluid, graceful style, for he had poured out his feelings and his love

without regard for proper English, the correct use of
punctuation, or a lucid continuity. And yet Merry knew
she would keep it always. As she read his last fervent
words, she was blushing, and she kissed his signature
before she put the letter against her cheek and leaned
back against her pillows with a sigh of happiness.

He had begged her pardon first, as he said he had had
to do so often since their arrival in town. He told her
that he loved her so much he could not bear to have
another man anywhere near her, never mind actually
proposing to her. And although he could understand
why Freddie adored her—for who would not?—that did
not make him a whit more sympathetic to his plight.
Then he told her that since he had already announced
their engagement to one of the biggest gibble-gabbers in
town, he would see that it was placed in the papers this
very morning, thus setting an official seal on the whole
affair. He begged her to forgive him for doing so
without speaking to her first, but he said he hoped his
darling Merry would understand why it had been
necessary. There followed several paragraphs about the
joy this would bring to him, and, he hoped, to her, and
of all the years of love and happiness they could look
forward too, beginning this very day. At the end, he
reminded her of their drive to the country and told her
he would be waiting for her, however impatiently, in the
hall at noon.

Merry read the whole letter again, more slowly this
time, to savor every word. But when she heard the hall
clock striking the hour, she threw back her covers and
rang her bell. This was one occasion she would not be
late! And since she wanted to look her best for Edward,
it behooved her to bustle about. She told Nora to bring
her some coffee and a roll, as well as a can of hot water,
and then she went to her armoire to inspect her
wardrobe. Rather impatiently, she pushed aside one
smart London gown after another, and she did not smile
until she saw the pale-green dimity she had worn the day
Edward had proposed to her in Bath. Yes, of course!
She would wear it again, and the broad-brimmed chip-

straw hat with the matching ribbons as well. Perhaps he would remember that other happy day, and be pleased that she had remembered, too. And since they were going into the country, there would be no one to remark her lack of style.

It was not quite twelve when Miss Farewell, carrying a tray to Lady Gloriana, saw Merry leave her room. For a moment, the maid stared at her, admiring her glowing cheeks and her little smile of complete happiness, and as she bobbed a curtsy, she smiled too. Miss Lancaster was so young and lovely, and her joy was transparent. Farewell knew the reason very well, and she was glad for the girl, and for the viscount as well. As Merry nodded to her and picked up her skirts to run down the stairs, the maid's smile faded. Suddenly, she had remembered the difficult afternoon she herself must spend.

True to his word, Edward was waiting for Merry at the bottom of the flight. As he took her hand and bowed over it, Merry smiled at him. "Darling," he murmured, his deep-blue eyes intent on her face. "Shall we be off?"

Not trusting herself to speak just then, she only nodded. And her cheeks were very rosy indeed when they reached the viscount's tilbury and pair at last. For not only had Durfee given them the satisfied, benevolent smile of the successful accomplice, but the two footmen had grinned at her as well. And even Edward's groom had winked at her, before he remembered himself. It seemed that any formal announcement had been redundant.

She busied herself settling her skirts as Edward dismissed the groom and gave his team the office to start, but she was still blushing as they drove down the street.

"Feeling shy, my love?" he asked, a little smile playing over his lips. "But why should that be? After all, we have been engaged this age."

"I know, it is silly of me," Merry confessed. "But Durfee, everyone, was so knowing. And although they might have had suspicions before, now it is all out in the open." She thought his sideways glance seemed worried, and she patted his arm lightly. "I shall soon grow accustomed, Edward. And I am so happy about it I cannot tell you."

The viscount's brow lightened, but he did not speak until they reached the King's Road and the outskirts of town, where he could relax his vigilance over the team, now that conditions were less crowded.

"And so am I happy, my dear," he told her, resuming their conversation then. "I only wish we had not waited for so long."

"Thank you for your letter," Merry said, suddenly shy again. "It was beautiful. I shall keep it always."

"I cannot say I will never write you a love letter again, Merry, but I rather think that from now on, I would prefer to tell you of my love in person," he said with a devilish grin.

Merry smiled back at him. She felt as if everything in her world had come right again, that nothing bad would ever happen to either of them, now that they were finally, and truly, engaged. And as they drove toward the little hamlet that was Twickenham, which was situated on the Thames, she hoped Edward would insist on an early wedding. These past weeks in London had seemed an age to her.

It was a golden, once-in-a-lifetime afternoon. They ate their picnic lunch on a rug the viscount spread out on the banks of the slow-moving river. He had chosen an isolated spot near a small stand of trees, and as if the gods were smiling on them, no one came to disturb their idyll. The food was delicious and the wine refreshing, not that either of them noticed what they were eating or drinking. And when they were through and the remains packed away, Edward took her in his arms and kissed her. His lips were warm from the sun, and at first, tender and undemanding. But when she put her own arms around him and pressed closer to him, and her hands tangled in his black curls, he kissed her more passionately. The faint sounds of the river and some

mewing gulls faded away. To Merry there was nothing
—and nobody—in the world but themselves.

When he lowered her to the soft rug and lay down
beside her, she closed her eyes. And then she wondered why she wanted to cry, when she was so very
happy.

A few moment later, the viscount raised his head and
leaned on one elbow, so he might admire her lovely face
and the way her breasts rose and fell in the dimity gown
he remembered so well.

He wanted her so, it took all his self-control to lighten
this potentially dangerous situation by saying, "I
wonder what we shall do when winter comes, my love?
We seem to spend so very much of our time alone,
outdoors."

Merry's dimple appeared as she grinned up at him,
feeling warm and lazy and adored. "But, Edward, by
then we will be married," she said.

He bent to kiss the tip of her nose. "So we shall," he
agreed. "Just picture a cold January night with snow
falling outside and the two of us tucked up in bed before
a glowing fire. Mmmm."

"Mmmm, indeed," Merry said dreamily.

"I hope you will consent to a June wedding,
though," he teased her. "After all, there is no need to
wait for the snow to fall, don't you agree?"

"I couldn't agree more," she said fervently, and he
smiled. "I have always dreamed of being a June bride."

"Have you, really?" he asked, tickling her cheek with
a blade of grass he had plucked.

Merry chuckled and grasped his hand. "No, not
really, Edward," she said, determined to be honest.
"That was a bouncer! But I do want our marriage to
take place as soon as possible, if I may be so immodest
as to tell you so."

"You must see to your wedding gown, then, without
delay," he said. "And tomorrow I will myself see to the
banns. But stay! We can, of course, be married in Westminster Abbey, or St. Paul's, but perhaps you would

prefer a country wedding? There is a lovely little village church in Trumbull.''

Merry did not have to consider this for more than a minute. "Oh, could we be married there, Edward?" she asked, sitting up in her eagerness. "The London cathedrals are so grand. And you know I have always felt a wedding to be a private thing. I do not want any pomp, anything overly elaborate. I would much prefer to go to church, hand in hand, for a quiet ceremony."

The viscount agreed at once, although he said no doubt his mother would be disappointed. "But only see how it will answer," he added when he saw Merry's doubtful look. "A quiet ceremony will not take anywhere near the time to plan that a smart London wedding would. And between us, I am sure we will be able to roll *Maman* up, horse, foot, and guns!"

They did not leave the riverbank until a little breeze came up and they could tell by the sun that the afternoon was far advanced. They had talked of their wedding, the viscount's estate . . . a thousand things. And Merry had laughed until her sides ached at all the improbable places in the world Edward was sure she would like to visit on her wedding journey. But just before they went back to the patient horses, which had been grazing happily on the new grass, Edward suddenly took hold of her hand.

"You have bewitched me, my dear," he said, shaking his head as he reached into his pocket. "I meant to give this to you earlier."

He handed her a narrow velvet box, and she opened it carefully, to gasp when she saw the delicate diamond necklace and ear bobs it held.

But when she began to protest such extravagance, the viscount only laughed at her, saying that this was a mere token, since he had not had time to really look that morning, yet still had wanted to give her something to remember this very special day. And then he said he had his eye on a very handsome topaz set and an emerald pendant to match her eyes until she shook her head at him.

And after he had taken his seat in the tilbury beside her and backed the team, he said, "But that reminds me that I must ask *Maman* for the family jewels. They are yours now, or at least they will be when we are married."

Somehow Merry felt uncomfortable, and she was quick to beg him not to deprive Lady Gloriana of any of her jewelry. She was told in a firm voice that she must not be so silly, for the late viscount had bought any number of baubles for his wife alone, as he himself intended to do, and that the family jewels always belonged to the current viscountess. And when he reminded her, with a sideways grin, that someday she herself would be giving them up to their son's bride, she laughed and acquiesced.

That evening, Merry wore her sea-green muslin. When she entered the drawing room, her fair skin was a little flushed from the sun and from her awareness that she was wearing the diamonds Edward had just given her. She was also wearing one perfect white rose, selected from the many bouquets he had had placed in her room while they had been absent.

As she came forward a little shyly, Lady Gloriana ran to put her arms around her and draw her face down for a kiss. "My dear child, how very happy I am!" she exclaimed. "What a wonderful evening this is, to be sure!"

As Merry kissed her back, she thought the viscountess did not look her usual, beautiful self. There was a shadow of strain in her eyes and around her mouth. She was quick to ask how she did, therefore, but Lady Gloriana only laughed and said she had suffered nothing worse than a slight indisposition, no doubt due to her folly in eating a lobster patty at midnight. But then Jane was there to kiss her and call her "sister," with a warm smile on her face, and Merry forgot her future mama-in-law in her delight.

That evening, Merry noticed that Jane seemed happier than she had ever known her to be. She did not know that it was because Jason Willoughby had called that afternoon. Since Edward and Merry were out, and Lady Gloriana was incommunicado in her room, Jane had had the pleasure of entertaining him alone. With only a little coaxing, she had managed to get him to tell her what had happened last evening, and she laughed so heartily when he described the balcony scene and repeated Freddie's remarks that he chuckled himself again, remembering. But he was not chuckling when he asked her how her mother was taking the news.

"I have not seen her today, Jason," she told him. "She is not feeling well, and when *Maman* is indisposed, she cannot bear to have company or be fussed over."

She thought his dark, rugged face wore a satisfied look for a fleeting moment, and she wondered at it. And she wondered as well why he hesitated then, as if he were about to tell her something else, before he changed the subject.

As he was leaving and made bold by the tête-à-tête they had enjoyed, she had asked him to join them for dinner. Mr. Willoughby had been forced to refuse, due to a prior commitment. She was as disappointed as he professed himself to be, but when he said he hoped he would see them all in the park the following morning, her spirits revived.

Now, only the immediate family sat around the dining-room table to discuss the quiet wedding in the country that Merry wanted, and who should be invited to attend it.

As the viscount had expected, his mother pouted at the thought of such a simple affair, and she had several objections to it. First, she said that such a shabby genteel wedding was sure to raise eyebrows among the *ton*, especially after dearest Teddy's unique way of announcing his engagement.

"Why, I myself saw Sir Frederick afterward, as he was leaving, and he was sporting the beginning of a spectacular black eye. His jaw was discolored as well," she concluded. "Of course at the time, I did not associate his condition with either Merry or with you, Teddy, but you may be sure that by now society has jumped to the logical conclusion, if indeed, Sir Frederick did not go so far as to reveal your brawl with him to one and all."

Her son raised his champagne glass to his fiancée before he replied. "But neither Merry nor I care what society may think, *Maman*," he said easily.

Merry unloosened the fingers she found she had clasped so tightly together in her lap beneath the table.

"No, and that is very commendable," his mother agreed. "But not only will even a simple wedding be difficult to arrange on such short notice, there are sure to be those who will be upset that they were not invited, and others in the family who will not be able to attend because they will not have time to arrange their affairs and travel to Hampshire. I quite understand and sympathize with your desire for a June wedding, but I cannot like giving offense to our relatives and friends. It will put us in such an awkward position! And I hardly like dearest Merry to begin her married life under a cloud."

Edward was frowning now and Merry took a deep breath. "Perhaps we could solve that problem by not inviting anyone, ma'am?" she asked, a little diffidently.

Lady Gloriana's dark-blue eyes opened wide. "Not invite anyone, Merry? Anyone at all?" she asked, sounding stunned.

Now the viscount laughed as he stretched out his hand to Merry and took hers in his warm grasp. "But of course! We shall say the ceremony was private. A great many people marry that way, after all. And it will simplify matters no end, will it not, *Maman*? For who can be offended if no one is included? Besides, it will save us the bother of having them all cluttering up Trumbull Hall and making a long stay." Before his mother could speak, he added, looking at his fiancée alone, "The more I think of it, the more I like it. We will choose a day, and then we will go hand in hand to church, just as you wished, my dear."

"I do hope Tiny and I will be allowed to come," his mother said in a broken little voice as she covered her face with her napkin.

Both Merry and the Viscount turned to her in concern, she had sounded so upset. But in a moment, she lowered the napkin to show them her dancing eyes and broad smile. "Oh, I should not tease you so! But the pair of you are so gullible, I could not resist," she told them between her chuckles.

"*Maman, Maman,*" Edward said, shaking his finger at her. "You are very bad. Of course you will be there, and Jane, too."

"Indeed, I hope Jane will be my maid of honor," Merry said, smiling across the table at her.

"Yes, do say you will attend us, dear sister," Edward begged. When his sister smiled and said she would be delighted, he said slowly, "I think, if it would not upset you, *Maman*, that I will ask Jason to stand up with me. I have always felt close to him, and he is, after all, already in the vicinity."

"I do not know why you think I would object to any choice of yours, Teddy," his mother said. "This is your wedding, yours and Merry's. Naturally, I shall do my best to see that it goes just as you both wish."

Both her son and Merry gave her a warm smile, and the conversation turned to the coming ball. The viscount told his mother that she might give as elaborate an affair as she chose, and Lady Gloriana was full of plans, declaring she would make it the fete of the Season, in honor of the bridal. It was only when her daughter pointed out that less than a week was not enough time to redecorate the ballroom in silver-and-white brocade that she resigned herself to masses of flowers, the decorations she had already planned, and special favors for the guests to commemorate the evening.

Those few days before the ball sped by. Both Merry and Jane were caught up in the preparations, for with Lady Gloriana still adhering to her afternoons resting alone, of necessity they were forced to make decisions, oversee the cleaning and the decorating, and handle all the myriad details that such a festive evening entailed. And Merry had had to order her wedding gown, and one for Jane as well. The viscountess had gone with the two of them to Madame Céleste's, but for once, her advice was not heeded. Merry had strong opinions about what she wanted to wear on her wedding day, and since the ceremony was to be so quiet, and in the country, Lady Gloriana's preference for a deep-gold brocade, embroidered with seed pearls and heavy with lace, was easy to reject. The viscountess had sighed a little in her disappointment and said that neither Merry nor Jane knew how lucky they were.

"You are both so tall, so regal-looking," she had said. "Why, you can carry a gown like that, show it off to advantage, and how I envy you! For I am so very small, my choice is limited to plain ensembles, lest I appear overwhelmed."

But in spite of her compliments, Merry finally chose a simple gown of ivory silk. It was high-waisted, with long tight sleeves, and the only concession to the current rage was a train that Madame assured Miss Lancaster could be replaced or removed later. And after one look at Jane's height and ample curves, the modiste suggested a similar gown for her, to be made up in deep blue. Both girls were to wear matching bonnets of pleated silk, Merry's to be adorned with a mass of ivory roses and veiling.

The afternoon of the ball, Merry left the remaining details in the hands of the viscountess's capable housekeeper and went to her room to wait for Mr. Wilson, the hairdresser. Lady Gloriana had declared Nora incompetent to arrange a coiffure for such an important evening. Merry could not help feeling uneasy. Because she had not taken her advice about her wedding gown, she had agreed to wear Lady Gloriana's choice to the ball. But now, as she saw the crimson silk again, so covered with beading and with its extremely low neckline, she frowned a little. No doubt it was all the crack,

but every time she had had it on, she had felt over-
dressed, uncomfortable. She realized it was a feeling she
associated with the viscountess. Lady Gloriana was so
tiny and graceful that she could not help but make
Merry feel large and awkward and gauche in her
presence. And very, very young.

Now Merry bathed and had Nora wash her hair as
Mr. Wilson had requested. She was seated at her
dressing table while the maid toweled it dry when the
hairdresser was announced.

He was all business, for which Merry was grateful.
She had never had a man in her bedroom before, not
even one who looked like an apothecary's clerk, and she
was feeling a little awkward. Briskly, he combed her
hair out before he spread a large towel over her
shoulders. When he uncorked a small bottle he carried
in his bag, the smell of it made Merry wrinkle her nose
and exclaim.

"Whatever can that be, Mr. Wilson?" she asked. "It
smells awful."

Wilson bowed. "It is a special preparation, Miss
Lancaster," he told her, pouring a little on her damp
hair and combing it through. "It is meant to brighten
the hair, make it shine. Lady Gloriana asked me
specifically to bring some for you today, since this
evening is such an important occasion."

Merry bit her lip and tried not to inhale too deeply. "I
hope it will not smell so vile when my hair dries," she
said anxiously.

The little hairdresser laughed and shook his head.
"No, indeed, miss," he assured her. "All that will be
left will be a new look for you."

It was over an hour later before he had her hair
arranged to his satisfaction. He had dressed it high in
something he called an Apollo's knot on the crown of
her head. From this elaborate confection, some curls
dangled over her forehead, and formed clusters at her
neck. It seemed somehow theatrical to Merry, but in the
end, it was not the coiffure itself that upset her. When
Nora brought in the candles and lit them after Mr.

Wilson had bowed and taken his leave, she saw that her chestnut hair had turned a much brighter red. She did not like it, and she wondered, with a little quiver in her stomach, if Edward would approve.

But the full glory of her hair was not apparent until Nora had lowered the crimson gown over her shoulders and hooked it up. The bright-orange tints of her hair clashed with its brilliance, and for a moment, Merry was tempted to change it, Lady Gloriana or no. Only the fact that it was growing late deterred her.

She was almost ready to go downstairs when she heard a knock on her door. At her nod, Nora went to open it, and in the pier glass Merry saw Edward standing in the doorway, holding a leather box. Her heart sank as his warm smile turned into a disbelieving frown.

Without asking permission, he stepped into the room. As the maid gasped, he was reminded of her presence, and without taking his eyes from Merry, he ordered her curtly to wait outside.

Nora looked to her mistress for instructions, and Merry said as calmly as she could, "It is all right, Nora. Do as the viscount says, please."

Edward continued to stare at his fiancée until the door closed quietly. Then he came forward and said, "What in the name of all that's holy have you done to yourself, Merry? You look just like a common actress!"

Merry flushed bright red, which added nothing to her appearance as he went on, "And your hair! Have you *dyed* it?"

"Mr. Wilson said it was only a special preparation, Edward," she whispered from a suddenly dry throat. "I am upset too! And I know the gown is very ornate, fussy, but your mother asked me to wear it. She said I would be the envy of every woman in the room."

"I rather doubt that, but I can assure you you will certainly be the only topic of conversation all evening," he told her swiftly, putting the box he carried down on her dressing table. "The gown is bad enough! It is true I know little about feminine fashion, but I do know I do not care to have my fiancée make such a spectacle of herself. All that heavy beading, to say nothing of that extremely vulgar neckline. But, as bad as the gown is, it pales in comparison to your hair. I cannot imagine why you let the hairdresser do such a thing! You had such lovely hair, so warm and rich a color. Now you look no better than some opera dancer, or Miss Mary Griffin.''

"Mary Griffin?" she asked, perplexed.

Still he did not smile. "Why, yes," he said. "It is common knowledge that Miss Griffin has mouse-brown hair and she dyes it blond.''

"How on earth could you know that?" Merry demanded.

"Everyone knows," he told her. "And even though I was not one of the, er, fortunate gentlemen in the park that day, I was told about it by two impeccable sources. There was quite a wind that day, you see—certainly it could not be called a breeze!—and Miss Griffin's gown was blown right up to her waist for a very revealing minute.''

As Merry's flush deepened, he went on, "There was so much talk about it, so many snide caricatures, that she was forced to forgo the remainder of that Season. Even now, it has not been forgotten. On occasion, she is still referred to by a very crude nickname . . . But never mind her! It is you that I am concerned about. And what a good thing I came in, to bring you the Trumbull pearls to wear this evening.''

He gestured to the box he had brought and then he said, "But I hardly think any more adornment could add to what is already a very theatrical appearance.''

Merry took a deep breath. Edward did not sound angry, he only sounded upset and disappointed, and since she agreed with him on all counts, she could feel nothing but the same emotions.

But before she could say so, he added, "You must excuse me, Merry. Our guests will be arriving soon.''

He saw the pain in her expressive hazel eyes, and he tried to say more lightly, "There, now, don't fret! I am sure you look stunning, and it is only for one evening, after all. We shall contrive to muddle through somehow.''

He blew her a kiss and left the room. Merry remained standing where he had left her, as Nora hurried in again. As she stared at her reflection in the glass, she remembered Edward's understated elegance this evening. The perfectly tailored evening coat with its long tails, the crisp immaculate white linen, and the simple stickpin. That pale-gray brocade vest and subdued knee breeches and silk stockings. He had been every inch the noble gentleman, and she looked like a common bit o' muslin.

She took a deep breath then, and nodded, her hazel eyes determined. ''Nora, come and unhook me!'' she ordered, reaching up to remove the hairpins that secured her elaborate coiffure. ''And while I am trying to do something to my hair, fetch the ecru evening gown and matching slippers.''

''But—but, Miss . . .'' her maid protested.

''At once!'' Merry ordered. ''We do not have much time.''

When she ran down the stairs a breathless quarter-hour later, Merry Lancaster looked a different woman. She was attired in the pale-colored ball gown, and with the Trumbull pearls at her throat, ears, and wrists, only the brilliant tint of her hair was a reminder of her earlier appearance. And even that seemed more subdued, arranged as it was in a simpler style.

Lady Gloriana looked surprised, but she had no time to question her future daughter-in-law, for Durfee was even then announcing the first arrivals. Merry's heart soared as Edward gave her a warm smile of approval and squeezed her hand tightly before he turned to greet the first guests.

Merry was sure she would never forget that evening. For from its unfortunate beginning, it had changed to become a magical, marvelous experience. All the guests congratulating them as they came through the receiving line, the first waltz with Edward that opened the ball, and the wonderful things he had murmured to her as they danced, the gay conversations and festive atmosphere, the delicious supper and sparkling champagne. It was as if all her senses were heightened, as if she knew she was storing up memories to be relived and sighed over when she was a very old lady. And she knew she would always smile when she thought of Jane's face as she danced with Jason Willoughby, and giggle when she remembered how difficult it had been to greet Mary Griffin with any degree of composure.

There had been only two times she had felt even the smallest pang. One was when Edward had asked her with a little frown if she were truly enjoying herself. He had said she was so quiet, so contained, he feared he had upset her more than he thought. Merry had shaken her head. She could not tell him that she was being even more careful than usual to present a modest, ladylike appearance, for with her brilliant hair, surely only that would carry the day. So, no matter how he had teased her or told her outrageous stories, she did not respond with anything more than a polite smile. She could tell he had been puzzled, but she could not explain. Perhaps she would be able to someday?

The other time had been when she had watched Edward dancing with his mother. How well they looked together, she had thought. Why, the lady was so dainty, Edward appeared very tall as her partner. Suddenly Merry had wished that she were not so tall herself.

And then there had been Edward's artless remark when he rejoined her, and she had complimented them both, that his mother had constantly told him he would always be her *premier cavalier*.

"She used to call me that when I was still a little boy, my dear," he had said with a reminiscent smile. "And she was the one who taught me to bow, and to dance, how to hold a lady's chair for her, and when to offer her my arm or kiss her hand. It was heady stuff for me, although I did not think so at the time. Then, you know, I considered such things namby-pamby and dull. No doubt I would have preferred to be riding my pony, or down by the river, fishing."

"But only see how it has answered, Edward," she had told him. "Surely there is not another gentleman in London to equal you."

His dark-blue eyes had softened as he leaned closer and whispered, "Nor any lady to equal you, my Merry. You are a treasure, and I adore you."

Ah, no! Miss Meryl Lancaster knew she would never forget that evening.

7

THE four inhabitants of the house on Mount Street met late the following morning for a delayed breakfast. None of them had been to bed till three, and in spite of the lavish super that had been served at midnight, Merry was starving. She had asked Nora to wake her early so she might wash her hair again. But although she told herself it was not as brilliant as it had been, she had been disappointed to see that almost all of the color still lingered. So much for Mr. Wilson's "special preparation"! No matter what Lady Gloriana said, she would never have the man touch her hair again.

As she took a full plate to the table and Edward rose to help her to her seat, she forgot the hairdresser in the warmth of his welcoming smile.

In her usual seat at the head, Lady Gloriana regarded her with her head tilted a little to one side. "Darling Merry," she said. "And now you must tell me why you did not wear the crimson gown last evening. It is so stunning. And I must tell you your choice did not go unremarked. Lady Feering was rather rude about your quiet little ecru. She said something to the effect that she was sure she had seen it before. Marianne is such a cat! But you may be sure I took care of her, my dears," she hastened to add. "Marianne Feering is no match for me! I told her she was quite right, but you were wearing it for sentimental reasons, since it was the gown you had on when Teddy declared himself. But I still don't understand why you changed your mind, nor did I understand your coiffure. Of course the color was most unfortunate, and so I shall tell Mr. Wilson when I see him next. But if he had anything to do with that simple milkmaid's do, I should be astounded to hear of it."

"I thought Merry looked lovely," Jane volunteered when it appeared Lady Gloriana had run down at last.

"And so did I," Edward agreed.

Lady Gloriana's expression did not change. "Well, of course she did. She is a very handsome young woman. But she would have looked a great deal more stunning if she had been dressed as we planned. Why weren't you, my dear?"

Merry put down her scone, but before she was obliged to invent a reason, Edward came to her rescue. "Because I asked her not to, *Maman*," he said, passing his fiancée the marmalade. "I went in to see her just before she came down, to give her the Trumbull pearls to wear, and we, er, we decided that they would not appear to advantage with the crimson."

"I see," the viscountess said slowly. "Yes, I remarked the Trumbull pearls."

"In fact, I must say I am astounded you chose that gown for her, *Maman*," Edward went on, pouring both himself and his sister another cup of coffee. Even in all her distress at the current topic, Merry noticed Jane's almost empty plate. She had taken nothing but a small piece of fish and some fruit.

She forgot her as Edward added, "As I am surprised that your hairdresser thought she would be improved by dyed red hair. Did you give that order, *Maman*? I cannot imagine him doing it without some instructions."

Merry glanced quickly at Lady Gloriana. For one second she thought her eyes glittered strangely at her son's criticism. But then she lowered them to her plate so quickly, Merry could not be sure.

"I did ask him to use a simple special preparation, to bring out the highlights in her chestnut hair, that is true. That he overstepped his directions, surely cannot be laid at my door," the viscountess said. "I am truly sorry that my poor efforts to help Merry did not suit you, Teddy," she added in a forlorn little voice. "I was only trying to help!"

"Well, it is of no importance now," he said, trying to cheer her up. "But I do hope Merry will be gowned in more appropriate style in the future. That crimson gown was nothing less than a disgrace."

Now Lady Gloriana laughed at him. "How impossible you are, my darling," she said. "Now, do pay attention, Merry, Tiny, for I am about to instruct you about men. Men! Once they fall in love, there is nothing they want more than to drape their future wives in sackcloth and cover them with ashes, lest someone else see the prize they have discovered and covet her."

"But I wouldn't like Merry in either of those things," her son protested. "Especially the ashes," he added with a rueful grin.

Jane began to giggle, and in a moment everyone was laughing and the awkward moment was over.

But as the others continued to discuss the ball, Merry ate her breakfast thoughtfully. She wondered why suddenly she had had the very nasty thought that perhaps Lady Gloriana was not doing all she could to help, in spite of her words. She had no concrete evidence for such an awful suspicion, it was more an intuitive feeling she had. But it was true that it was only after they had reached London that she and Edward had begun to quarrel and disagree, had had so many unfortunate experiences to shake their love and their trust in each other. Could that possibly be Lady Gloriana's doing?

And then she told herself she was the most ungrateful wretch that had ever lived. The viscountess had taken her into her heart and her home without reservations. She had been more than willing to share her son, even give him up to her, and she had welcomed her as a daughter. To think that here she was in return, imagining the most dire, Machiavellian things about the kindest lady she had ever known! It was too bad of her!

Merry finished her breakfast and poured herself another cup of coffee. By this time, Lady Gloriana and Jane were discussing the day's activities, and Edward was opening his post. Suddenly he swore under his breath, and all eyes went to his face.

"What is it, my dear?" his mother asked quickly, a hand to her heart. "Not bad news, I trust?"

"It is a letter from my bailiff at Trumbull, *Maman*," he told her. "There was a fire not two days ago, and one of the barns and a tenant farmer's cottage were destroyed. Gates asks me to come down, and I suppose I must, if only to see about rebuilding. But if it is the barn I'm thinking of, I have long felt it would be better located in another part of the home farm. However, there is nothing I can do by post."

He frowned and then he looked at Merry. "How I dislike leaving you, my dear," he said. "Be sure I shall return as soon as I possibly can."

"But, darling Teddy, you are not thinking," his mother interrupted. "There is no reason why you should be separated. Well, at least not for more than a few days. Now that the ball is over, London will begin to become tedious. And there are not many more weeks before the Season will be over anyway. Since we have been planning to go into Hampshire for your wedding, we can just move the departure date from town forward. Why, I expect we could join you there in a few days' time or so, if that is agreeable to everyone?"

Jane's face had brightened, and she was the first to commend the plan.

"Ah, Tiny, I despair of you!" Lady Gloriana told her. "You are such a lover of the country."

She turned to Merry then and said, "Tiny has to be dragged to London for the Season. She has never cared for town as I do."

"But of course," the viscount said. "That is a splendid notion, *Maman*! And how I shall enjoy showing Merry her future home, and the land, introducing her to my people."

"Well, that's settled, then," the viscountess said as she rose from the table. "I shall inform the servants. Between them, Durfee and Mrs. Wilkie will take care of

everything. But now you must excuse me, my dears.
Lord Saterly is arriving soon to take me for a drive
before I must rest.''

She waved as she went quickly to the door, skipping a
little as was her custom.

Behind her, she left the three younger people discussing the removal to Trumbull Hall, all last night's
festivities forgotten.

The viscount decided he would leave early the
following morning, rather than today. He said he did
not care to rack up for more than one night on the road.
Jane made a great point of pretending she would not say
what she thought of such a plan as she followed her
mother's example and quit the breakfast room.

Edward ignored her as he took Merry's hands in his.
''Unfortunately I have a great many things to do today,
darling,'' he said. ''How I wish we could spend every
minute of it together! However, do say I may take you
for a drive late this afternoon, at least.''

Merry agreed, and when he asked her plans, she told
him she intended to return the crimson gown to
Madame Céleste when she went for a fitting on her
wedding gown. She was not released to this welcome
chore, however, until she had been thoroughly kissed.

Viscount Trumbull left very early the next morning,
long before Merry was awake. And when she did open
her eyes and realized instinctively that he was gone, she
felt bereft. Was this what it was like when you loved
someone? she wondered as she rang her bell. As if when
they were not with you, an important part of you was
missing as well? She closed her eyes for a moment,
trying to picture Edward cantering along the country
roads, his phaeton containing his baggage following at a
more sedate pace.

He had taken a tender and lengthy leave of her the
evening before, telling her he would count the hours
until they could be together again. And he urged her to
hurry his sister and his mother along as quickly as she
could. Merry had promised to do so.

But in the days that followed, there always seemed to

be one important reason after another why they could not take coach. And Merry had to admit it was not always Lady Gloriana who was responsible for the delay. True, she had had a number of engagements in the near future she said she did not feel she could cancel, but Jane also had had to make several trips to the dentist, and Merry herself did not care to leave London until she could carry her wedding gown with her.

A week went by in this fashion, and then one evening at dinner the viscountess was full of a new scheme. Although, as she said with an arch look at Merry, Teddy was so eager for a quiet wedding, surely he would not object if she had a small house party at Trumbull Hall first? For there were any number of people she felt obligated to entertain, and besides, she very much feared they would all be moped to death without some amusements to leaven the long, dull days spent in that rural location. And she had had the most delicious idea for an afternoon of fun and frolic there. She intended to have a treasure hunt around the hall, and she was going to write the clues herself. Everyone would pair off, and the first couple to guess all the clues and find the sovereigns she would hide would win a prize. Didn't the girls think it a wonderful idea?

Merry smiled at her. She didn't care who Lady Gloriana invited, or what amusements she planned, as long as she herself could see Edward again. But she saw that Jane was frowning a little.

"Tiny?" her mother asked. "Don't you think it a marvelous conception, my pet?"

"Why, yes, it sounds like it will be fun," her daughter told her. "But who are you planning to invite, *Maman*, and for how long? After all, we have a wedding to see to before the end of the month."

"Of course. But if we only invite them for ten days or so, there will be plenty of June left for any number of weddings," Lady Gloriana said as she drew a piece of paper out of her gown and smoothed it open. "And as you see, my dears, I have already been at work. Now!

Of course we must have Lord Saterly and Nigel Brethers,'' she began.

"But not Reggie Horton, *Maman*,'' Jane interrupted. "Teddy would be so very angry if he were included.''

Lady Gloriana sat up even straighter in her chair. "Of course we will not have Reggie, Tiny,'' she said with dignity. "I hope I am old enough to know what is becoming? Reggie shall be denied. But I must ask Marianne Feering. You remember how lavishly she entertained us all just last Christmas in Kent? And then there is Kitty Hardin. I cannot neglect her for she is one of my oldest and dearest friends! And perhaps Mr. Hardin would honor us as well? But if he should cry off, we must find another gentleman, for I am determined that the numbers must be equal. There is nothing so tiresome as a party dominated by spinsters, widows, and unaccompanied wives. And you must not worry that I only intend to ask older people, dear girls. No, indeed! Of course we cannot include Sir Frederick White, or darling Teddy would surely be incensed, but Tony Best and Miss Griffin would be jolly company. And Lady Amelia Rogers and her two brothers? But I will take of it all, never fear!''

Merry hoped the coming house party would spur Lady Gloriana to a quick departure, but that was not to be the case. Somehow, all the details that must be taken care of, the special provisions and wines to be ordered, and a series of new gowns for country wear to be purchased, delayed them further. The invited guests had all professed their delight in the scheme and were only waiting for word to leave town. London was growing ever more sultry this June, and besides missing Edward as much as she did, Merry longed for the cooler breezes of the country.

Jason Willoughby had called to take his leave of the ladies that week, his business in town concluded. Merry had been out when he came to Mount Street, but she met him coming down the steps as she was returning from some last-minute shopping.

"I understand you are to follow me to Hampshire

soon, Miss Lancaster," he said after he had bowed and greeted her.

"Pray it may be soon!" Merry exclaimed without thinking.

Mr. Willoughby laughed harshly. "I know exactly what you mean," he said. "But even circumstances cannot hold you here much longer, you know. Besides, Edward told me of your quiet wedding at the end of the month. I shall be delighted to stand up with both of you."

Merry thanked him, smiling, and then she wondered why his answering smile changed to a dark, forbidding look. "Miss Lancaster—Merry . . ." he said slowly. "May I say something to you? I know we are not very well-acquainted as yet, but may I offer you some further advice?"

"Of course you may," Merry told him.

He paused for a minute, as if gathering his thoughts, and then he said, "Much as I dislike playing some sort of Delphic oracle, I must warn you to beware. There are many things that can go wrong before your wedding day, and you must be prepared for them. But perhaps forewarned will be forearmed. We must hope so."

Suddenly, Merry had a picture in her mind of the lovely Lady Gloriana, and she remembered her earlier suspicions of her. She longed to ask Mr. Willoughby if he suspected that Edward's mother might cause a problem, but she did not dare. If he were thinking of someone, or something, else, she would look quite foolish. And although she had the impression he was not fond of the lady, she had no idea why that should be so. And she still did not have a shred of proof that Lady Gloriana was anything other than she appeared: a gracious, loving, concerned person.

Jason Willoughby watched the emotions that chased one another across her expressive face, and he gave that harsh laugh again. "Yes, I can see you do not need my warning," he said. "Well, it is a relief to me to know that I was not wrong about you, Merry. You are an intelligent young woman and you will make my cousin a very happy man. Just be sure that that wonderful day finally arrives, do not let anything delay it further.''

Merry curtsied, and he left her without another word, almost as if he felt he had been too free and open with his opinions.

An hour later, Merry left her room to fetch her needlepoint. She had left it in the drawing room the evening before, and she did not like to be so casual with her belongings when she was still just a guest in the house. As she came down the stairs, she saw Jane standing in the hall, staring at a box she was holding.

Merry called a greeting and Jane looked up at her. Her face was cold and set, and Merry came to take her arm. "Is anything wrong, Jane? Can I help you?" she asked, concerned.

Jane hesitated for a moment, and then she said in a rush, "May I speak to you, Merry? In private?"

"But of course, my dear," Merry said. "Why don't you go on up to my room, and as soon as I have fetched my handwork, I will join you there. We will be quite private, for I have given Nora the afternoon off so she may purchase a few small things for her family before we leave town."

Without a word, Jane nodded and went to the stairs. As she climbed those same stairs a few minutes later, Merry wondered what Jane wished to tell her. She had thought her so much happier lately, but perhaps knowing that Jason Willoughby was leaving had dashed her spirits. But now, no doubt, she will be glad to help me get Lady Gloriana to set a date for our departure, Merry thought as she hurried down the hall to let herself into her room.

She found Jane standing in front of the pier glass, turning this way and that as she inspected her figure, and still frowning.

"I know that I have lost some weight, Merry, but it all seems to be taking a very long time," she complained as she took the seat Merry indicated.

Merry clapped her hands. "Oh, good, Jane," she

enthused. "Oh, I don't mean it's good that it is taking so long, but that you have begun to lose weight at last," she added. "But you must remember that it took a long time to put that weight on. It will not disappear overnight."

"That would be wonderful indeed! However, I know you are right," Jane said ruefully. "If only I were not so hungry all the time! And then, this just came for me."

She held out her package and Merry saw that it was a box of candied cherries. They did look enticing, each sweetmeat set in its own little nest of different colored tissue paper.

"Would you take it for me? I don't care if you give them away, hide them, or eat them," Jane said, sounding more than a little desperate. "You see, it is my favorite sweet, and if I just put it away somewhere myself, I know I will not have the willpower not to eat 'just one,' and then 'just one more,' until before you know it, the box will be empty. And I will be fatter."

Merry took the package she held out, nodding as she did so. "Of course, my dear," she said. "You will not have to see it again. But, Jane, who sent it to you?"

Miss Willoughby turned to look out the window, her brow knit. "Can't you guess, Merry?" she asked quietly. "It was *Maman*, of course. She knows how much I love them. She is always sending me little gifts of cakes or candies. Even as a child, I had a sweet tooth, and *Maman* and Teddy were always teasing me about it."

"Perhaps if you were to tell her you are dieting, she would stop," Merry suggested. "I mean, I know she wants you to lose weight, for she told me so herself."

"Does she? Really?" Jane asked, her mouth twisted. Then she shook her head. "I don't know, Merry, I really don't know. All I have are some vague suspicions, and then I hate myself for even thinking of them when I love *Maman* so much and know how much she loves me. Besides, she knows how unhappy I have been. Perhaps she sends them to me to make me feel better."

As she shook her head again, Merry said, trying to turn a painful subject, "Have you always been heavy, Jane?"

"No, indeed. Until I was seventeen or so, I was quite slim. Oh, not to compare with *Maman*, but then I am much taller and my shoulders are so broad. But no one could have called me fat."

She bit her lip before she went on, "It started the summer *Maman* noticed how interested I was becoming in my cousin Jason. I had just turned seventeen when she had a serious talk with me. She told me that I was much too young to be thinking of any one man, that until I had had a few Seasons in town I should not make any such momentous decision. And she pointed out that marriage lasts a very long time, and she could not bear it if I missed my come-out and all the fun a young girl has. She said it had always been her wish for me, for she knew, married at sixteen, how much she had missed herself.

"I suppose she was right, but you see, my Seasons in town never made me change my mind. But it was more than just that. *Maman* said that Jason was not worthy of me, that I should set my sights on someone in the nobility, not an ugly, bad-tempered country squire."

She looked straight at Merry as she said, "But that ugly, bad-tempered country squire is the only man I want, Merry, worthy of me or not as he may be. I know that now." She sighed. "*Maman* had other arguments, of course. I must travel, become more accomplished, and then there was her most telling argument of all: Jason Willoughby does not like her. I don't know why this should be, and neither does *Maman*, but if I were to marry him, she told me he would be sure to forbid me to ever see her again. I love my mother, Merry. I could not bear to think about such a decisive break. And how she wept herself when she contemplated it. She claimed she did not know how she was to live without her dearest Tiny. So, you see, I stopped riding with Jason and refused to see him the few times he came to call. I—I had to."

Merry took a deep breath. The story had fascinated her, and although several questions had occurred to her during its telling, she had not cared to interrupt such a painful recital.

"It was after that summer, when I resigned myself to giving up any hope of attaching Jason, that I began to put on weight," Jane confessed. "I suppose I thought it did not matter how I looked. *Maman* chided me occasionally, but I persisted. The boxes of sweetmeats and packages from Gunters she sent me did not help, however."

"What made you decide to diet now, Jane?" Merry asked, reaching out to squeeze her hand.

Jane squeezed it back, her eyes suspiciously wet. "I think it was seeing how happy you and Teddy are together. I—I know I was not very friendly when you first arrived. I do beg you to forgive me for that, but I was so envious of you. And, of course, when you began to go about with Mary Griffin and her crowd, I did not care to join you. I know Miss Griffin does not like me, and she even makes fun of me. I have never tried to make friends here in London, first, because in my misery I preferred to be alone with my thoughts of Jason, and then, because I thought that when *Maman* saw I was not enjoying my Seasons, she would relent. She has never done so, however.

"But when Jason came to town this spring, I decided to diet anyway. I began to wonder, you see, if perhaps it was not too late for us even now. He has never married, after all."

"Does he know of your love?" Merry asked shyly.

"I am sure he suspects. I let slip too many little hints when I was that seventeen-year-old girl," Jane told her. "And I am sure he was attracted to me then, too. I do not think it was all cousinly kindness, for one day when we chanced to meet out riding, he said a peculiar thing. He stared at me so intently, and then he said, 'How ironic it is that you look so much like your mother when you are nothing like her at all. If you were not her daughter, how different things might be!'

"So you see, it is not all one-sided, or only my imagination, don't you agree, Merry?" she asked, leaning forward in her eagerness.

Merry really thought his words a very thin thread to be spinning dreams with, but she could hardly say so. She only nodded instead.

"But now I am determined to become that girl he knew five years ago," Jane went on. "And then, somehow, I will make him fall in love with me, and we will get *Maman*'s permission. After all, I am almost twenty-three, and she must accept such constancy. And even if Jason does not care for *Maman*, surely he would not stop me from visiting her alone occasionally."

"But you do not need her permission now, Jane," Merry pointed out. "You are of age. And furthermore, Edward likes his cousin. If he gives his consent to the match, shows his approval as viscount, your mother must accept it too. And I must disagree with her. Mr. Willoughby would never be so harsh as to sever all your ties with her. If he does love you, he will not want you to be unhappy."

Jane's face had brightened as she spoke. Now, as the first dressing bell rang, she rose, saying, "How glad I am that we met, Merry! And how sorry I am that it has taken me so long to ask you to be my friend. I—I am ashamed of myself."

At her words, Merry came to hug her. "I will always stand your friend, dear Jane, as I hope you will stand mine," she said. "After all, we will be sisters, will we not? And you may be sure I will help you with your diet as much as I can," she added. "And when we do get to the country and you have a chance to ride and hunt, go for long walks, I think you will find your weight will be less of a problem. And then we shall see."

"And then we shall see indeed," Jane echoed, all smiles.

When Merry came down to the drawing room shortly before dinner, she saw that an enormous bouquet of roses had been delivered, and she went to admire them.

"How very lovely they are," she enthused, stooping to inhale their sweet scent. "They remind me of the country, especially now when not only cultivated roses are in bloom, but every hedgerow sports its own garlands of wild pinks and whites."

"Perhaps Mr. Horton wished to remind *Maman* that he is still available to go into Hampshire with us?" Jane suggested with a little smile.

Lady Gloriana tried to look stern. "Do not be pert, Tiny," he said. "Poor Reggie! He was so cut up when I told him he could not come. But he has become tiresome, trying to get me to change my mind. The roses are but another way of begging."

She sighed, looking petulant as she added, "He was here this morning after you both went out. Such a scene as he enacted me! I finally told him his histrionics might do very well on the stage, but I found them offensive. And would you believe I had to threaten to ring for Durfee and have him removed forcibly before he would leave me? Young men can be so very tiresome! And to think I am burdened with him simply because I did not like to wound him earlier. It is too bad!"

She made a *moue* of distaste. "And when he did leave, he claimed that I had ruined his life and that he would never recover from the blow. Oh, he was in a rare hubble-bubble, I can tell you! He makes me quite sorry I ever encouraged him out of kindness."

While dinner was being served, Merry discovered there was a new reason why their departure from town might be put off, and her heart sank.

"Just a very little, Durfee," Lady Gloriana told her butler as he presented a platter of veal with some braised vegetables. "I have not been feeling at all well today. I almost did not come down to dinner. Farewell would have had me stay in bed, but I insisted on joining you. However, I think I must leave you both to your own devices later, my dears."

"I hope you are not sickening, *Maman*," Jane said, waving the butler away when he would have given her a larger portion.

"So do I, Tiny," her mother agreed. "It would be a shame if we had to delay any longer because I was unable to travel. And there is the house party to consider, too. We must hope for the best."

Merry kept her eyes on her plate, feeling she needed a few moments to compose her expression so not a hint of her disappointment would show.

"Mercy me! Is that all you are going to eat, Tiny?" Lady Gloriana asked next as she caught sight of her daughter's plate. "Are you feeling quite the thing? Perhaps you are sickening too."

Jane's color was a little high as she said, "I—I find I am not very hungry this evening, *Maman*."

The viscountess shook her head as she took a sip of water. "And of course that has nothing to do with a certain package that came this afternoon, does it, my dear? Oh, Tiny, to eat them all at once! What am I going to do with you?"

Merry spoke up then. She could see that Jane was uncomfortable and she wanted to draw her mother's attention from her. "I had a letter from Edward this morning," she said. "He wonders what can be delaying us, and I do not know how to reply. Please tell me, dear ma'am."

"Ah, he is missing you, as I am sure you are missing him, isn't that so, darling Merry?" Lady Gloriana said. "But you may tell him we will be on our way as soon as I feel better. Teddy will understand. He knows what a bad traveler I am, and if I were to venture forth in less than perfect health, it could be a disaster for me. How unfortunate it is that I am not robust. Being small and frail can sometimes be a trial, although that is something neither of you lucky girls will ever have to deal with."

Merry tried to hide her disappointment again, but the viscountess seemed to understand, for she reached out to pat her hand. "Indeed, I will try to be better soon, pet," she said with her warmest smile. "I promise I will."

8

I T was early the following morning, and only Merry and Jane were at the breakfast table, when a distraught Lord Saterly made an unprecedented call. He tried to insist on seeing Lady Gloriana, but when he was informed she had not left her room, he demanded Miss Willoughby instead. Durfee could tell he was big with news, but it was his worried air and agitated expression that convinced the butler he should go and see if Miss Jane would receive him.

Jane was surprised, but she asked that he be brought to the breakfast room, and she was quick to dismiss the servants after one glimpse of his apprehensive face.

"Won't you join us, m'lord?" she asked, indicating a chair. "Perhaps some food or a cup of coffee would be welcome?"

"No, nothing, thank you," he said, looking from one to the other and wringing his hands. "I have some terrible news, just terrible!" he went on quickly. "I had thought to tell your dear mother myself, but perhaps this way will be better. You can prepare her for the shock, which I, as a mere man, could not. Oh, dear, it is the most calamitous catastrophe there ever was! Pray dear Lady Glory will not be quite overcome, that is my primary concern."

Merry tried to still a wildly beating heart. Did this have something to do with Edward? Was he ill? Had he been hurt somehow?

She did not feel she could speak, and she was glad when Jane said briskly, "But what is it? Tell us at once!"

"It is Reggie Horton, my dear," the marquess said. "He is, er, he is dead! He shot himself late last evening in his rooms on Jermyn Street. The news is all over town.''

"Good heavens," Jane said faintly while Merry drew a deep breath of pure relief that Edward was all right. Not, she told herself, that she was not very sorry for poor Mr. Horton, of course."

"Well, that is very bad, to be sure, m'lord, but I fail to see why you are so agitated. He was only an acquaintance, and it is not as if *Maman* had a *tendre* for him," Jane went on.

"No, of course she did not!" Lord Saterly snapped as he dropped into a chair and wiped his brow. "But there is more, and it is worse, much worse," he muttered. "You see, the young idiot, er, Reggie left a note."

As the two girls exchanged startled glances, he went on, "In the note, he said he was taking his life because Lady Gloriana had scorned him. He said that she had been cruel to him and mocked him, and that he adored her so, he could not live without her . . . Oh, it was the ranting of a madman."

"Or a highly strung, sensitive young man," Merry said thoughtfully.

The marquess stared at her. "Well, of course he was rather more than that! Normal people, no matter how sensitive they are, don't go around blowing their brains out. Oh, I do beg your pardon, ladies, I am so upset! But perhaps you have not digested the disastrous portent of this affair? Everyone knows now that Lady Gloriana was the reason for his death, however misguided his motives may have been. She has been associated with this debacle in the most telling, disgusting way. Her reputation has been sullied, for her name is on everyone's lips."

The door opened just then and the lady in question came in. Merry could not help but have the irrelevant thought that for someone who was sickening, she appeared to be in blooming health. She was dressed in a simple morning gown of aqua, her hair perfectly coiffed, and her eyes and skin clear. As usual, she looked beautiful and young and serene.

"Jeremy?" she asked in some disbelief. "Durfee told me you were here, although I found it hard to believe at this early hour. What on earth has prompted such an unusual call?"

Merry rose to put her arm around her and help her to her chair. "You had best sit down, dear ma'am," she said kindly. "Lord Saterly has some very bad news."

The story was soon told again, for the viscountess did not interrupt once. Both Merry and Jane watched her anxiously, but outside of a faint expression of distaste when told of the suicide she did not appear to be at all affected until she was informed that Reggie Horton had named her the sole reason for his demise.

"Oh, but what a horrid thing to do!" she exclaimed then. "I would never have suspected he could be so ungentlemanly, so selfish! Had he no thought for anyone but himself?"

Merry was horrified at this callous assessment of the death, delivered in such a petulant way, too. Didn't Lady Gloriana think of anyone but herself? Didn't she even consider what that poor young man's state of mind must have been like, or what his parents, all his loved ones, were going through now? Was she a monster? She put such thoughts aside to concentrate on the situation at hand. Across from her, she saw that Jane had relaxed now she saw there was no possibility that her mother might faint or become hysterical.

"My reputation will be ruined, ruined, and all by a heedless boy," the viscountess moaned. "I will never be able to hold my head up again."

"Now, now, dear lady," Lord Saterly said, patting the little hand so close to him. "I am sure it is not that bad. Why, no one can blame you for this. The young man was unbalanced, that is plain to see, but you are not responsible for that. And after all, no lady can help it if a man adores her. And anyone who knows the glorious Lady Glory would never doubt that he did, or why, without any encouragement on your part. Why, the whole thing is very similar to the way a young woman may go into a decline, if the gentleman she fancies does not return her love. But is that the gentleman's fault? Of course not! Take heart, my dear, you are innocent!''

The viscountess did not appear to have been attending to this fulsome and optimistic recital. "We must leave London at once," she said in a hard little voice. "I shall tell Durfee that we will require the carriages brought around no later than noon. Until that time, none of us will be at home to anyone who may call."

"But what if the authorities come, *Maman?*" Jane asked. "Someone must see them if they insist on it."

"Oh, if only my dearest Teddy were here," her mother moaned. "I cannot be expected to deal with this alone! But then, men are never about when you need them, never!"

"I shall be glad to stay and see any callers, dear lady, and render any assistance you may need," the maligned marquess interrupted to say. He was rewarded with a tremulous smile.

"You are so very kind, dear Jeremy. Indeed, I do not know what I would do without you, my faithful friend," Lady Gloriana told him before she turned her attention rather briskly to the two girls. "You had better go up and set your maids to packing," she said. "Tell Farewell what I have decided as well. And do not fuss if you cannot bring everything now. In fact, have your maids pack only what you will need for a couple of days. Since you will be traveling together, you will not need them with you, and it will free them to help Miss Farewell this morning. Tomorrow or the next day they can follow us with the rest of the staff, after they have completed the packing and seen to the closing of the house. Be quick now, off with you!"

Merry hurried to do her bidding, followed closely by Jane. Behind them, they left the marquess and Lady Gloriana deep in a whispered conversation, their heads close together.

But although Merry was delighted to be going to join Edward at last, she could not help but wish it might have been done in less unhappy circumstances. Poor

Mr. Horton, she thought as she ran up the stairs. Poor misguided young man!

The two carriages left Mount Street on the stroke of noon. Merry was absolutely astounded at what had been accomplished in only a few hours. When she remembered all the days they had been dithering about, unable to so much as set the date of their departure, she would never have believed such speed to be possible. But she learned that a groom had been sent ahead as well, to alert the inns that enjoyed Lady Gloriana's patronage and to warn Edward of their arrival. The servants that were to be left in London had been given their orders too.

On hearing the news, Nora had begun to pack a small trunk for Merry, although she had been called away to assist Miss Farewell before she was finished. Merry had assured her she could handle the task herself. And when she straightened up from the trunk at last, she smiled. There, right on top so it would not be crushed, was her wedding gown. A bandbox nearby held her matching bonnet. Lady Gloriana might tell her only to bring what she needed for a few days, but she had no intention of leaving without that one, most important ensemble.

Although the authorities never did call, several other people sounded the knocker that morning. They were dealt with by the competent Lord Saterly, be they gentlemen come to offer their condolences and support, or ladies eager to express their sympathy and see for themselves "how dear Gloriana was faring." One and all, they were told the lady was prostrate on her bed, suffering from severe shock.

In reality, the viscountess had been as busy as any of them. She had interviewed her butler and housekeeper, and given them innumerable instructions, and she had written a number of notes to be delivered after her departure, canceling appointments and social engagements. She had even found time to write to the guests invited to the coming house party.

When she stepped outside, just before noon, Merry Lancaster was surprised at the amount of equipment deemed necessary for one tiny lady's comfort on the journey. She knew, of course, that Edward's mother was a very bad traveler, but she had not known she always traveled in solitary state, with only her maid in attendance. The seat facing forward in the old-fashioned, roomy barouche she favored had been turned into a cozy nest of lace pillows and soft throws. There was a basket full of food and drink, such as might be required as a restorative, and a portmanteau of medicines, lotions, and smelling salts was packed inside as well. Miss Farewell sat in the space that was left, facing back. Merry watched as she helped Lady Gloriana from the house and settled her in her place. The viscountess was wearing a heavy mask that completely covered her face and throat. Merry thought it was because of the scandal, until Jane told her her *maman* always used it when traveling, to keep out the dust of the road, which was so injurious to the skin.

When the carriage doors had been closed behind Lady Gloriana, Merry saw that all the shades had been drawn as well. As she followed Jane to the smaller carriage pulled up behind, she was glad they were not all traveling together. How dreary to sit in a darkened vehicle, unable to look out and pass the time by inspecting the towns and countryside. She thought it would make anyone feel queasy.

The journey seemed to take forever to Merry Lancaster. She knew how impatient she was to be reunited with Edward again, and she tried to tell herself she must not be unreasonable. But surely a journey of three and a half days was excessive for the short trip to Hampshire? It seemed that the viscountess had decreed a snail's pace, with lengthy stops. They never left an inn before midmorning and they stopped long before dusk. The two girls saw Lady Gloriana only briefly during this time, for she went immediately to bed and took all her meals alone. Forewarned by Jane, Merry had brought some books and her needlepoint, and they whiled away the long hours as the teams plodded slowly on their way, reading or deep in conversation.

The second day, Merry could not help asking how ill Lady Gloriana really was.

Jane Willoughby laughed at her. "She is not ill at all. In fact, my dear little mother is as strong as a wire," she said cheerfully. "But traveling has always been hard for her, for it means she must give up her solitary afternoons in her room."

"Surely if she is in good health, she cannot need all that sleep," Merry remarked.

Jane shook her head. "No, but she is not sleeping. I'll tell you about it, if you promise you will never let on you know, Merry. Word of honor, now!"

Fascinated, Merry promised as Jane's dark-blue eyes twinkled with deviltry. "There is a strict routine she follows. Once, when Miss Farewell was in an especially good mood, I coaxed her to tell me all about it. You see, I was a very curious little girl and I knew no one else's mother sequestered themselves for hours every day. What happens is this. First *Maman* undresses, and then she does a great many exercises. Don't ask me what they are, for I have no idea. Then she meditates for half an hour."

"Prays, you mean?" Merry asked.

"No, it is not precisely praying," Jane said, frowning a little as she attempted to make this clear. "It is something *Maman* learned from a man who had spent some years in India. After that, Farewell gives her a complete massage to tone the body, and a facial for her skin. This all takes about two hours. Around four, she might eat a piece of fruit, or drink a cup of bouillon or a herbal tea that Farewell concocts. I tried some once. It tastes vile, but it is supposed to be very good for you. She takes nothing more, lest she gain an ounce." Here Jane sighed and rolled her eyes in admiration, and Merry chuckled.

"Next she rests for an hour or so, covered with special creams and a mask. Around six, she gets up to be dressed for the evening. Of course, if she is bathing or having her hair washed, the whole routine becomes more hectic, but *Maman* seldom immerses herself totally. She says water is injurious to the skin, for it is drying."

"She really does all that?" Merry asked, her hazel eyes wide. "Every single day?"

As Jane nodded, her eyes dancing, Merry said slowly, "But why? It seems such a waste of time. And just think what she is missing!"

"I assure you *Maman* does not consider it in that light," Jane said. "It is the reason she looks so young, and that is all important to her."

Merry sat back on her side of the carriage, deep in thought. She wondered what the lady would do when she finally did get old, when all those creams and masks and massages could no longer disguise a blurred jawline, the little wrinkles and creases and spots that all humanity was heir to, and she shivered. She supposed no woman liked aging, but she could see the slow, inexorable progress of time would be truly catastrophic for the lovely Lady Gloriana.

Merry was sitting on the very edge of her seat when the carriages made their way at last between two wrought-iron gates, past the gatehouse, and up a long, winding drive to Trumbull Hall. As she looked around, she saw it all as Edward's bride. This was to be her home. No, *their* home. She admired the large wood they were passing through, all those impressive oaks and elms and chestnuts. And when the carriage left the woods behind and came out on a small rise, she reveled in the sweep of velvet lawn, the ornamental water, the gardens, and the distant views of the River Test. Set down in the midst of this lovely location and dominating it completely was the hall itself. It was large, massive, and she could tell it was very old, for it was made of weathered gray granite and had tiny mullioned windows, softened somewhat by a series of handsome terraces and judicious plantings.

As the carriages swept up to the front of the house, she willed Edward to be there, opening the front door and hurrying out to greet her. But the viscount did not appear. The underbutler who welcomed them informed the viscountess that, not knowing the exact time of their arrival, he had gone to one of the outlying farms with his bailiff.

Merry was disappointed, but she told herself it was just as well, for now she would have a chance to freshen up and change her travel-creased gown. She was given a charming suite of rooms overlooking the gardens, and a special smile from the maid who showed her there.

She had washed and changed, and was busy unpacking her trunk some time later when she heard an impatient tattoo on the sitting-room door. At once, her eyes lit up and she ran to open it. In only a second, she was caught up in Edward's arms, being thoroughly kissed. She was vaguely aware that he had slammed the door behind him with his booted foot, but this time she did not consider the proprieties. How wonderful it was to be with him again, to feel that sensual mouth on hers, the strength of his arms, his caressing hands. How wonderful to breathe the glorious, familiar scent of his skin, touch his black curls.

At last he raised his head and drew back so he could look deep into her eyes. Merry did not know whether she most wanted to laugh or cry for joy as they exchanged a searching glance. Then Edward buried his face in her hair and murmured, "Oh, Merry, my love, how I have missed you! Every minute was an hour, an hour a week, a week a year." His arms tightened as he growled, "You will never leave me again. Never, do you hear?"

"I shall try not to," she said, her voice as unsteady as his had been. "For Edward, my darling, I missed you the same way. I thought we would never get here, and if it hadn't been for poor Mr. Horton, I am sure we would be in London still."

He kept an arm tight around her waist as he led her to the sofa. "Yes, I am anxious to hear all about that, for the groom who came with *Maman*'s message had no clear idea what had happened."

Merry did not think he was at all as anxious as he

claimed, for he began to kiss her again and murmur his love instead of giving her a chance to tell him. It was only when there was a discreet knock on the door that he released her and moved away. Merry was sure the maid and the footman who were wheeling in a sumptuous tea knew exactly what they had been doing. And when she saw they had brought two cups and enough food for both of them, she was sure of it, but she did not care.

In only a little while now, she and Edward would be married, and then they could be alone anytime they wanted. Her cheeks flushed as she contemplated how they would spend their time alone, and she made Edward take a seat across from her, lest she be tempted to start kissing him again.

The account of Mr. Horton's suicide was soon told. The viscount looked upset when she finished, and Merry did not wonder at it.

"But I warned *Maman* how it would be," he muttered, putting down his cup to run a restless hand through his hair. "Not, of course, that I ever expected such a terrible thing to happen. But I knew no good could come of Reggie's infatuation, and now there will be a scandal. And *Maman* will be at the center of it."

"I am sure her leaving town so quickly will diffuse some of the gossip, Edward," Merry said quietly. "For if she is not there to watch and titter over, it will take some of the shine from the story. But I do feel so badly for the young man's family."

Seeing he was still frowning, she thought to ask him about the estate and everything he had been doing. He smiled when she told him how beautiful she thought it, how impressive.

"Yes, Trumbull Hall is a landmark, and the grounds are especially fine," he said. "We often have visitors asking permission to stroll through the gardens, or on the woodland paths. And there is a charming little gazebo near the river I am anxious for you to see, my Merry. I plan to show it to you tomorrow."

The time they were together passed quickly, and

Edward did not leave her until they heard the first dressing bell. As he took her in his arms for one last kiss, he smiled at her. "It is not only good to see you again, love, but if I may say so, good to see you looking so much more like the girl I fell in love with."

He reached up to touch her hair then, and Merry smiled back at him. "Yes, that awful dye is almost gone," she said. "Of course, poor Nora is tired to death of washing my hair so often, but I was determined to get rid of it as soon as I could."

Merry wore one of her old Bath gowns to dinner. Somehow, in the country, the London gowns seemed much too elaborate, and she knew Edward would approve her choice, no matter what his mother thought of it.

That lady was in the drawing room when Merry came in. She was sitting close beside her son, holding his hand tightly. Merry wondered at her arch look as she took a seat across from them, beside Jane. Then she smiled to herself. Obviously, the viscountess had not heard of their clandestine tea party.

At dinner, only casual subjects were discussed until the servants had been dismissed.

"Merry has been telling me about Reggie Horton's unfortunate death, *Maman*," the viscount said then.

Lady Gloriana shook her head. "Yes, was there ever such a terrible thing, Teddy?" she asked. "I was so vexed I cannot tell you!"

"Well, at least it brought you all into Hampshire, for which I am exceeding grateful, but still, it was most unfortunate," Edward replied, his voice serious.

"Are you going to read me a lecture, darling Teddy?" his mother asked, leaning forward to peer down the long length of the table at him. "But it was not at all my fault, you know. Never would I have guessed he was so unstable. But Lord Saterly assures me no one can blame me for what happened."

Edward shrugged. "There will be those who will, however, as you are well aware, *Maman*. But at least now there can be no question of a house party here. I think it best if we all live very quietly, in seclusion, for several months."

Lady Gloriana put her wineglass down untasted. "Whatever can you mean, my dear?" she asked, sounding incredulous. "Of course we are going to have the party! Why, I sent a note to everyone invited before I left London, telling them we would expect them by the end of the week."

"You did *what*?" the viscount demanded, frowning mightily now.

"But, Teddy, love, you are not thinking," his mother said lightly. Merry thought her face a little set, however, as she went on, "If we were to cancel the party, everyone would think that I really *did* have something to do with Reggie's suicide, that I was feeling guilty about it. I could not abide that! You must see how we are compelled to go on as planned."

Since the matter had been taken out of his hands, the viscount was forced to acquiesce to her plans, no matter how much he disapproved of them. Merry began to wish the house party had never been thought of.

But the next morning at breakfast, Lady Gloriana had a number of letters, and when she had read them all, her face was very cold and disapproving. It seemed that although Mr. Brethers, Lord Saterly, and Lady Feering were most certainly coming, all the other guests had canceled, for the flimsiest of reasons.

Lady Amelia Rogers had not written herself, but her Mama had, a cold, formal note that excused her daughter and her sons without a word of explanation. Mrs. Hardin, however, had written a long, effusive letter. She was full of sympathy for her dearest friend and begged her to forgive her for failing, but she said Mr. Hardin was being positively gothic about attending any party at Trumbull Hall. She was quick to point out that the fact he was distantly related to Mr. Horton had probably colored his thinking.

Anthony Best also begged to be excused. He said he was leaving for the north of England on a commission for his father. And Miss Mary Griffin's mother had succumbed to a mysterious illness from which it was implied she would never recover if her daughter left her side at any time in the foreseeable future.

As Lady Gloriana reported this news, Edward nodded, looking grim. But when he suggested notifying the rest of the guests that the house party had been canceled, his mother would not hear of it.

"What? And give all those old quizzes something else to chew over?" she demanded, sounding quite fierce. "Why, Marianne Feering would positively relish my receiving such a homestall! No such thing, dearest Teddy! We shall do very well as a small, select group. And for the treasure hunt and *al fresco* dance I plan, I shall invite some of our neighbors to swell the ranks. Perhaps Jason Willoughby might be persuaded to come, and then there are the Wardens, and the Holbrooks. Oh, we shall have a merry old time of it, in spite of everything."

Edward still looked grim, but Merry noticed he gave in to his mother with good grace. Later, when the two of them went out to the horses he had ordered saddled for Merry's first tour of the estate, he told her privately that he was still uneasy about the wisdom of holding the party.

It was not very long before he was able to put it from his mind, however, as he showed his fiancée over his fields and orchards and introduced her to those of his farmers and their families that they chanced to meet. Merry could tell that the news of the viscount's approaching marriage had certainly spread beyond the hall, just by the keen glances she received and the warm smiles she was given in welcome. Much later, the two of them ate a picnic lunch Edward had ordered left for them in the gazebo near the river. Merry was more than generous with her compliments for everything she had seen.

"Then you think you will be happy here, my dear?" Edward asked.

"Who would not be in this beautiful place?" Merry asked in reply. "But of course I would be happy anywhere you were, Edward," she admitted.

His dark-blue eyes brightened in that way she had come to love, and she wondered if it were possible to die with happiness.

"There is someone else I want you to meet today, Merry," the viscount told her as they rode away from the gazebo. "Someone who is very dear to me. She is my old nanny, Mrs. Drew. She is retired now and lives in a cottage near the village, and she is anxious to make your acquaintance."

As they rode, he told her about his nurse and how close they were still. And when Merry walked up the flagged path to her cottage, admiring the gardens that surrounded it, and met the lady, she could see why Edward loved her.

Mrs. Drew was a round little butterball of a woman with white hair and a serene, smiling face. Her gray eyes were still keen, and she chatted easily as she set out a plate of cookies and a pitcher of cold cider.

And when they were all seated on some rustic benches in her garden, she smiled at Merry and said, "Yes, I can see why Edward loves you, my dear. You have a compassionate face and a loving manner. I am so glad! Of course, it is hard for a nurse to think any young woman is good enough for her boy, but in your case, I am sure you will make him happy."

Merry smiled at her. "I shall do my best, Mrs. Drew, I promise," she said.

The old lady asked next about their wedding plans. Edward insisted she must be present. He said he would send word as soon as the actual date was set, and was told rather briskly that it was never a good practice to put off to tomorrow what was better done today.

The viscount grinned at her as he said he wondered where he had heard *that* expression before. Mrs. Drew smiled and nodded.

"And have you opened the dower house, m'lord? Ordered its cleaning and refurbishing?" she asked next.

Edward put his glass down with a little frown. "The dower house? But why would I do that?" he asked.

"If you take my advice, you will see to it at once," his nurse told him, reaching out to pat his arm. "It never answers, you know, having a bride and her mother-in-law in the same establishment. And Miss Lancaster deserves to be treated from the start as the viscountess she will become when you put your ring on her finger. You would not have her deferring to your mother or taking second place to her, would you?"

"No, of course not!" Edward exclaimed. "But I never thought of *Maman* moving out of the hall, living in the dower house from now on." He spread out his hands, looking rueful. "To be truthful, I never thought of it at all," he admitted.

Merry would have spoken then, and reassured him, but the old nurse was too quick for her. "Then you must think of it, m'lord," she said, nodding wisely. "And not only think, but act as well. It is the way of the world. The old order changes as it must, so the new one can hold sway. And the time to do it is now. Your mother will be the dowager viscountess with all that implies. Best she accustom herself to it immediately. And you, my dear . . ." she added, turning to Merry. "Yes, I can see you have a kind heart and you would hesitate to insist on it. But believe me, it is better to begin as you mean to go on. And having Lady Gloriana make the move while you are on your wedding journey is the least painful way for everyone. For if you do not and later decide you would prefer living as a couple alone, it would be very difficult to dislodge her without bad feelings all around."

She snorted a little and added rather tartly, "And let me point out to you, m'lord, that Lady Gloriana herself was very quick to make sure that *her* future mama-in-law was removed from Trumbull Hall even *before* her wedding to your father. I know, for I was there."

Her eyes grew distant then, as if she were recalling those long-ago events, and she nodded. "I remember your grandmother didn't like it, but there was nothing she could do, and she soon grew accustomed to it. Now it is your mother's turn to be displaced. I do beg you not to waver in your resolve in such an important matter. Be firm with her, insist!''

9

THE viscount seemed preoccupied when they rode back to the hall a little later, and Merry knew he was pondering the advice he had been given. And although at first she had intended to tell him that she did not think it at all necessary to have his mother move from the hall, something stayed her tongue.

Perhaps it was the little wink and the nod Mrs. Drew had given her as they were leaving, or it might have been the tartness in her voice when she discussed Lady Gloriana. It seemed highly likely to Merry that there was no love lost between those two women, and she wondered why.

But even though Trumbull Hall was a vast place, with room for any number of women, she could see it would be easier for both of them if she and Edward could begin their married life there, alone. For how was she to learn to manage the household and give the necessary orders when Lady Gloriana had always done so and was still there to be consulted? And how would that lady like taking second place, deferring to a young daughter-in-law? It would be very hard for both of them.

At the edge of the woods, Edward halted his horse, and she followed suit. Staring ahead of him at the hall in the distance, he said, "Yes, I can see that Nanny Drew is right. *Maman* should move, and shortly, too. I shall mention it to her and suggest she inspect the dower house before her guests arrive. I suppose Jane will remove with her. But I remember from the times I visited my grandmother there that there is ample room for both of them."

Merry nodded, although a little frown still lingered between her brows. "I had planned to tell you it wouldn't be necessary, but in thinking it over, I can see its merits," she said slowly.

She told him then what she had been thinking, and he nodded. "Yes, there is the matter of preference, and besides, it is to be your home to rule as you see fit, my dear," he said.

He slapped his horse lightly with the reins, and as they moved forward again, at a walk this time, he added, "I wonder how she will take the news? It is so difficult to think of *Maman* as a dowager anything!"

To Merry's ears he sounded a little uneasy, and she prayed Lady Gloriana would not be too upset.

To her surprise, when Edward brought up the subject after dinner that evening, the viscountess only looked confused for a brief moment. Then she began to laugh.

"But how guilty you look, Teddy! And Merry, too! And how apprehensive," she mocked them. "Did you think I would fall into a fit of hysteria? But I seem to detect the fine hand of Nanny Drew here, for I cannot believe either one of you would be so abrupt, so decisive with me. Did you visit her today?"

She waited until her son nodded before she waved a dismissive hand. "As you will discover, Merry, nannies seldom care for their charges' mothers. They consider us too frivolous a class of women, too indulgent where our children are concerned. And I am sure they truly believe that if they were not there to have the major part in the children's upbringing, they would all end up discredits to their name.

"As for my removal to the dower house, I meant to mention it to you, myself. I fear it will need to be extensively renovated, however. Your grandmother filled it with fusty old antiques, dreary hangings, and dark, depressing pictures, and that will not do for me at all."

Edward agreed and begged her to change whatever she liked.

"I am only afraid that it will not be ready for some time," Lady Gloriana said next. "Since I cannot go to London and shop, because of that awful scandal, I cannot avail myself of your generous offer. But at least we can set some workmen to painting it, both in and out. It is best we have that done as soon as possible, so it can be completely aired. You know how the smell of fresh paint upsets me!''

"You must take all the time you need, dear *Maman*," her son told her, giving her a fond smile and a kiss in gratitude.

Merry echoed these sentiments, but she could not help but wonder how long such a program would take. And then she scolded herself for being so suspicious, so petty.

For the next few days, the viscount was busy. The new barn was being built, and he rode out often to check its progress. There was also some sickness in the village that he was concerned about, and a great many decisions to be made with his bailiff, since he would be away in July. He had decided to take Merry to Paris for a long stay after their wedding, and as well as refurbishing the dower house, he wanted to have his mother's rooms redone for his bride. He spent an entire day in Basingstoke, the nearest large town, selecting materials, wallpaper, and new carpets in shades of soft green, as a surprise for Merry. Of course, nothing could be done until Lady Gloriana actually left the hall, but he wanted to have things ready when she did. And perhaps it would be possible for the work to be accomplished while they were in France. He himself intended to move into his father's rooms, which adjoined hers, when they returned.

Since he was so busy, Merry was happy to have Jane's company. She had hoped Lady Gloriana might instruct her in the ways of the household that would soon be hers, but now that the rest of the staff had arrived from London, the viscountess turned everything over to her housekeeper and never suggested that Merry join her when she conducted her interviews. Merry hesitated to approach Mrs. Wilkie until she was Edward's wife in truth, lest she be thought an inching, *coming* female.

The two girls spent a lot of time on horseback, by

Jane's choice. She was as knowledgeable about the estate as her brother, and if he were not available, she was often consulted by his farmers and workmen. Merry thought Jane seemed much happier now she was home, and she was looking better as well. Her eyes sparkled, her back was straighter, and she was definitely losing weight.

One afternoon, instead of riding, the two went to pay a call on Jason Willoughby's mother. Merry was a little surprised at their destination, but as she drove them there in the gig, Jane explained that she herself had always been friendly with the woman she called Aunt Alma, even though the families were no longer close.

"I feel sorry for her, you see," she said. "She has not been well for years, and there are all those children to see to. I know Jason takes as much from her shoulders as he can, and she has an excellent staff."

She looked puzzled for a moment, and then she said, "It is strange. When I was very little, I remember how she smiled and laughed so much, how she was always ready to give me a hug and a kiss. And the stories she told! She could keep us all spellbound for the longest time. I admired her very much. But then something happened, and she grew sadder and grayer and sicker."

"Perhaps it was the result of her husband's death?" Merry suggested.

"No, I don't think it was that," Jane said. "She changed long before he caught that fatal chill while hunting. But you shall see for yourself."

It was five miles to the Willoughby estate, and when she saw it, Merry was impressed. Although nowhere near as grand as Trumbull Hall, it had the look of a prosperous, well-run place.

The butler bowed and ushered them to the drawing room, where he said Mrs. Willoughby would receive them. As he did so, Jane chatted easily with him, asking about his rheumatism and the other servants with all the insouciance of an old friend.

Merry studied their hostess carefully while she and Jane were exchanging a fond kiss. Alma Willoughby was a tall woman, thin to the point of gauntness. She had graying brown hair, and her pallid face was heavily lined. But when she smiled and greeted them, Merry could see that at one time she must have been a lovely woman. It was clear her illness had taken a heavy toll.

As the three talked and enjoyed some refreshments, Merry noticed that Mrs. Willoughby's hands had a distinct tremor and that sometimes her voice faltered and trembled as well. But when her son Jason came in and joined them, Merry saw how her expression brightened. She had to hide a smile when she noticed Jane's face was identically eager and welcoming.

Jason insisted on escorting them to the gig when they left a short time later, and he thanked them for coming. It seemed to Merry that he was much more easy and natural here in his own home than he had been in London.

Lady Gloriana's three house guests arrived at Trumbull Hall the next afternoon. The viscountess was not there to welcome them, of course, but Jane and Merry showed them to their rooms and said all that was proper for her. Since Edward had gone to the dower house to see about the work that had to be done there, they made his excuses as well.

Later, Mr. Nigel Brethers came out on one of the terraces where Merry was sitting admiring the gardens beyond.

"Pretty spot, Trumbull Hall. Congratulate you," he said in his abrupt way as he sat down beside her.

"Yes, it is very lovely," Merry agreed, wondering what on earth she was going to talk to the old bachelor about.

"Lady Gloriana in her room?" he asked next, staring up at the granite walls as if trying to find her. "Got a surprise for her," he added with a grim little smile.

Merry began to explain that the lady always rested in the afternoons, and he waved his hand. "Know it," he said, which effectively disposed of that topic of conversation.

Fortunately, Mr. Brethers suggested a stroll through

the gardens, and it was there that Merry discovered his avocation. He was an avid gardener, and he knew so much about the roses and perennials that she was fascinated. Once, he paused, rubbing his chin with his hand as he said, "Perfect spot for a herb knot. Near the kitchens. Out of sight of the main gardens. Suggest you see to it, Miss Lancaster. Happy to advise you."

They discussed how the knot should be laid out and what should be planted until Lady Feering came to join them. Merry had met this lady many times in London, and she thought her very proud and sharp-tongued. She was a woman in her late thirties who had lost her husband early in the Peninsular Wars, when he had served under Wellington. She was of medium height with soft brown hair and a fair complexion, and although she had never been a beauty, for her nose was too thin and her mouth too wide, she had great presence. Merry had once had the irreverent thought that it was as if she had taken a good look at herself one day and then decided to ignore what she saw in the glass forevermore. She carried herself, spoke, and behaved as if she were a great beauty, and surprisingly, she was accepted as one without question by the *ton*.

Everyone assembled in the drawing room a little while before dinner. Rested and refreshed, a gay Lady Gloriana was lovely in a gown of soft primrose. She welcomed her guests with a warm smile and was enthusiastic about the entertainments she had planned for their pleasure.

"Just to be here enough," Mr. Brethers told her, shaking his head.

"Indeed, dear Lady Glory, I could not agree more," Lord Saterly chimed in.

"That is all very pretty speaking, sirs, but I agree with Gloriana," Lady Feering said. "One must have amusements in the country, or die of boredom. That treasure hunt sounds intriguing, my dear. But what a shame so many of your guests did not come, and so must miss it."

Merry thought the lady's gaze at her hostess very piercing, and she was glad when the viscountess gave a silvery laugh and shrugged. "We shall do very well without them, Marianne," she said. "I have invited several of the neighborhood gentry to join us, and they have all accepted. If the weather continues fine, we shall have the treasure hunt tomorrow, followed by a festive dinner in honor of the winners. Oh, we shall have a fine time!"

Lady Feering took a sip of her sherry before she said, "It was a very good thing you left London as quickly as you did, Gloriana. There was such a whirlwind of gossip about young Horton's death, you would not have cared for it at all."

The viscountess seemed to stiffen, and Merry saw Jane move closer to her, as if to protect her. She wondered that Lady Feering should speak so openly about the scandal when supposedly she was a good friend of the viscountess. But perhaps it was because it was such a small party of old friends and family that she felt able to do so. However, Merry did not think she would like to have the woman for a bosom bow herself.

"Soon die down. Man was an idiot," Mr. Brethers growled.

"He was unbalanced, that is true," Lord Saterly said. "But he was not an idiot, Nigel. No man who had the sense to adore the glorious Lady Glory could be considered in that light."

Edward took a hand then and changed the subject smoothly, as Mr. Brethers ruffled up at being contradicted by his old rival.

But later, after dinner, he came to Lady Gloriana's side. "Got a surprise for you, my dear," he told her, reaching into his coat pocket to bring out a folded piece of paper. As he waved it, he said, "Horton's note. Got it from the authorities before its contents could be generally known. Take it! Yours!"

The viscountess did not seem enthralled by the gift, and she hesitated until he put the note in her hand and closed her fingers around it.

"Don't read it," he warned her. "Burn it! Got it for you."

"Why, why, how very thoughtful of you, Nigel," she said, staring down at the note, her face pale. "Darling Teddy, would you. . . ?"

Her son came swiftly to her side and took the note from her. All the guests watched as he went to the dark hearth, placed the paper inside, and lit it. In only a second, the one bright flame was gone and there was only a small pile of ashes left. Merry could not help shivering.

"I suggest we all forget this now," the viscount said. "Indeed, it was good of you to act so swiftly, sir, and *Maman* and I both appreciate it."

Mr. Brethers waved a deprecatory hand, but Merry could tell he was pleased. Peeking at Lord Saterly, she saw he seemed disappointed, as if he were well aware he had been upstaged.

"Indeed we do," Lady Gloriana said, a little color returning to her face now that horrid note was gone. "You have all been so good! Why, I do not know what I would have done without Jeremy the morning we left London. And Marianne, always so faithful, so staunch a friend!"

Merry was relieved when the suicide was not mentioned again that evening. Instead, everyone discussed drives to scenic spots in the neighborhood, the alfresco dance, and of course, the treasure hunt.

The next morning dawned fair and warm, and by one o'clock the party was assembled in the drawing room, dressed for riding as instructed. Jason Willoughby had refused the treat, although he had consented to join them for dinner later, but both the Holbrook and Warden families were there. The viscount was quick to introduce Merry to them, and Jane had to smile a little at the pride in his voice as he did so.

Mr. and Mrs. Holbrook, identically fat and jolly, were accompanied by their son and daughter. Mr. Timothy Holbrook was only recently down from university, and he was trying so hard to appear sophisticated in such smart company that he only betrayed his youth. Merry could not admire his taste in waistcoats. His sister, Amy, was another matter entirely. She was a very pretty, very petite blonde with guileless blue eyes, and her blushing smile for the viscount was warm and intimate. As Edward led Merry toward the Wardens, Miss Holbrook subjected her to a searching head-to-toe glance before she went to sit down beside Lady Gloriana and clasped her hands. They were soon deep in a whispered conversation.

Mr. Matthew Warden was a widower, and the complete country squire. He had brought his sister Rose, a spinster in her thirties who was dressed in a very youthful-looking habit. The lady seemed of a nervous disposition, for she talked breathlessly in a high, quick voice, waving her hands as she did so, until her brother told her to "Cut line there, Rose, do!" Merry hid a smile at how quickly he was obeyed. It was very similar to what happens when the cover is dropped over a parrot's cage.

When all the London visitors had been introduced to the Hampshire people, Lady Gloriana rose and clapped her hands for attention. She waited until the room was quiet before she began to speak.

"Now, my dears, I shall give you your instructions," she said. "On the stroke of two, you shall all disperse in pairs. There are six hiding places and, of course, six clues. They are numbered, and you must follow the sequence exactly, lest you all be looking in the same place at once. And remember, this is a competition, so don't help any of your opponents!

"The sovereigns are all hiden somewhere on the grounds of Trumbull, and you will need your horses. And that is the only hint I am going to give you! Now, you will have until five o'clock before we reassemble here, and the couple who return the earliest with the most sovereigns will win the prize. Durfee will make a note of the time you come back and the sovereigns you have. Remember, you only have three hours. If you cannot guess my clue in half an hour or so, go on to the

next one." She laughed a little. "I do not expect anyone
to find them all, for I have been very, very clever. But
you shall see!"

"Here, here! We'll be on our mettle, m'lady,"
Timothy Holbrook said with his grandest bow.

His hostess smiled at him before she went on, "And
when you do find a hiding place, take only one
sovereign and replace the rest for those who come after
you." She paused before she said, her blue eyes alight
with mischief, "And lest some of you gentlemen think
to spend the afternoon resting under a tree somewhere
and substituting your own coins, let me tell you they are
all wrapped in different kinds of paper to prevent such
cheating."

"But dear lady," the jolly Mr. Holbrook exclaimed.
"How can you even think such a thing of us? Assure
you, we'll stand buff and play fair."

Lady Gloriana nodded. "Of course you will, Roger.
Now."

As everyone laughed, Merry sensed Edward moving closer to her side as his mother held out a silver
bowl.

"Now, my honest gentlemen," she said, "come and
take a slip of paper. On it, you will find your partner's
name for the adventure. Hurry now! It is almost two!"

When all the slips had been taken and read amid
much laughter, Merry was disappointed to discover
Edward had not chosen her name as she had hoped he
would. He gave her a rueful little smile as he moved
toward Amy Holbrook. Merry could not like the warm
welcome that lady gave him, nor the way she took his
arm and clung to it as her blue eyes adored him. And
then she scolded herself for her jealous disappointment
and tried to welcome her own partner, the young Mr.
Holbrook, with equanimity. But at least he is better
than some of the others, she told herself, seeing Jane
beside the crusty, inarticulate Nigel Brethers while Lady
Feering nodded coldly to Squire Warden.

When Jeremy Overton greeted Mrs. Holbrook, she
chuckled and said, "Well, and I hope you are feeling

very well today, m'lord. I warn you I may need supporting if the going gets rough.''

Lord Saterly assured her he was capable of the task as her husband wished him luck.

"But the numbers are unequal, Lady Gloriana," Squire Warden announced. "You have no partner!"

"But of course I don't," the viscountess replied. "That would not be at all fair, for I know where everything is. But you must not worry about me, for I shall spend a delicious afternoon wondering how you are all doing and hoping I have been able to confuse you."

The Cartel clock on the mantel struck two then, and she handed each couple a little packet of papers. "Off you go, now," she said, making shooing motions. "Remember, the first pair back with the most sovereigns wins the prize!"

Merry was surprised when Timothy Holbrook took her arm and hurried her outside at once. "Can't discuss our clue here, Miss Lancaster," he said softly. "We don't want anyone to hear us."

She saw how his face had lit up, how he seemed prepared to enter into the game with all the enthusiasm of any young man his age, and she began to think she might have a better time of it than she had supposed.

He led her to the far end of the terrace before he opened the paper that was marked with the number 1. His blond head and her chestnut one bent over it together.

"But—but I'm at point-non-plus," he said, looking disappointed. "Surely Lady Gloriana is being very devious."

Merry read the clue aloud, a little frown between her brows. " 'Hunt this hiding place thusly,' " she read. " 'In the S———, in the third s———, where lives a mighty S———.' It appears we must guess what the three words are that start with S before it is clear," she said. "Hmmmm."

Mr. Holbrook stared at her, bewildered. "But what mighty thing would live in something that starts with S?" he asked.

Merry's eyes grew distant with thought. "I wonder why she wrote 'Hunt this hiding place'?" she asked. "Why not just say 'look for it,' or 'seek it'?"

"I've got it," Timothy Holbrook exclaimed. "Of course! The *Hunt*, Miss Lancaster. Horses! And horses live in stables!"

Merry chuckled at his delight. "I do believe you are right, sir. The sovereigns are in the third stall of the stables where . . ."

"Where lives a mighty stallion," he finished. "Come, let us go there at once and hope the stallion is out to pasture."

As they ran down the terrace steps, Merry spared a glance around. Edward and Miss Holbrook were preparing to mount their horses, and once again she felt a pang that she was not to be his partner for this golden afternoon of frolic. But then Timothy Holbrook was urging her to make haste, and she put Edward from her mind. As they walked quickly to the stables, she let the young man ramble on about how clever they had been, and well within the half-hour limit, too.

They both laughed in delight when the sovereigns, wrapped in gold paper and ribbon, were discovered under the hay in the manger of the third, fortunately empty, stall.

Mr. Holbrook tucked one of them away in his coat pocket as they went outside again to read their second clue. This one was not as easily solved until Merry remembered the statue of Pan placed on one side of a woodland bridle path some distance away. She only recalled it because the day she and Edward had ridden by, it had startled her. Life-size, the weathered stone of the half-man, half-beast, had appeared almost real in that setting, and its eyes had seemed to leer at her over the pipes it played.

They hurried to the front of the house where their horses were waiting, and Merry let the groom toss her into the saddle. In the distance, she could see Jane and Mr. Brethers standing by the lake deep in discussion, and behind her, from the direction of the gardens, she heard Rose Warden's breathless voice urging Mr. Roger Holbrook to look harder, harder! Of Edward and Amy Holbrook, or the other couples, there was no sign.

By the time the second sovereign had been found and tucked away with its fellow, almost an hour had passed. Mr. Holbrook, now fully involved in the hunt and already anticipating their winning it, urged speed before he read the third clue.

" 'So might you, standing on this pleasant lea, Have glimpses that would make you less forlorn, have sight of Proteus rising from the sea; or hear old Triton blow his wreathèd horn,' " he read, his brow creasing. As he lowered the note, he said, his voice a little pompous now, "From Wordsworth's 'The World Is Too Much with Us,' of course. But we're nowhere near the sea, and surely the viscountess said all the hiding places were on the grounds."

"That is true," Merry agreed. "But obviously this clue has something to do with water. We have only to discover which water."

"Lord!" Mr. Holbrook muttered, removing his hat to run a hand through his wavy blond hair. "Well, there's the lake, of course, and the River Test, but there's also several brooks, the trout stream, even the duck pond on the home farm. Whichever can it be? We have no time to investigate all of them."

"Could it be another statue?" Merry asked, reading the clue again. "Do you know of any near water, Mr. Holbrook? I am so sorry I am not of more help, but I am only new come to Trumbull."

The young man paced up and down, deep in thought. "None near brooks or the stream, and certainly not by the duck pond," he said. "I am not sure, perhaps beside the gazebo?"

"No, there is nothing there. I would remember it," Merry told him. "That leaves the lake. And Jane and Mr. Brethers were down there earlier, so perhaps that is the place."

"Let us ride that way," her escort said, mounting again and turning his horse. "Perhaps something will occur to us as we go."

But when they reached the calm stretch of ornamental water, there was no statue either of Proteus or old Triton to be found. Merry gazed at the lake itself. Set in the middle was a small island where Edward had told her swans nested. Nearby, drawn up on the bank as if awaiting them, were a couple of punts. She wondered if the statue were on the island, although she hoped it was not, for she knew swans were apt to be viscious when their nests were threatened.

And then she thought of something else, and her face brightened. "Mr. Holbrook," she said quickly. "Perhaps the clue has nothing to do with a statue or water at all. Perhaps the clue is only the last words, a horn!"

"A horn?" he said, bewildered. "I know of no horns at Trumbull, but stay! I do remember that only today as we entered the gates, I noticed the design of them for the first time. And there was a frieze of warriors across the base, some armed with spears, and one blowing a horn."

"Oh, dear, if you are right, we have wasted a lot of time coming back here," Merry said as they urged their horses to a canter.

As they entered the wooded part of the drive, they met the viscount and Amy Holbrook returning. But although both couples slowed their horses to exchange a few words, neither pair lingered. Merry thought Miss Holbrook's open admiration for her partner's acumen a bit overdone, and Edward's smile as he teased them with the number of clues he claimed they themselves had already uncovered, entirely too carefree.

The cache of sovereigns was soon discovered at the base of one of the stone pillars that supported the massive gates. There was only one missing, so it was obvious the others were having trouble with this clue. The gatekeeper's young children giggled at the sight of these lordly grown-ups on their knees as they felt through the grass, and called out in triumph when the prize came to light.

The fourth clue was all about roses, and it seemed so easy to guess that Merry was suspicious. And when she saw the number of rose bushes in Trumbull's gardens when they returned there, she knew they were in for trouble.

"What kind of rose do you suppose a Gallica Glory is?" Mr. Holbrook asked as he lifted her from the saddle and tied their horses to a post.

"Mr. Brethers could tell us in a wink," Merry said, staring at what seemed to be a sea of pink, yellow, crimson, and white blossoms. "We shall just have to separate and search."

"I'll take this side, and you the other," her escort announced. "Do be careful of the bees, though, Miss Lancaster."

They spent well over half an hour in the rose garden, but their luck appeared to have run out, for no sovereigns came to light. At last they were forced to abandon the search and open their next clue. This one was very short.

" 'The serpent beguiled me, and I did eat,' " Timothy Holbrook read, and then he crumpled the paper in disgust. "But that doesn't tell us anything. We are supposed to look for a snake?"

Merry laughed at him. She was growing warm on this hot afternoon, her habit had acquired some grass stains, and she could feel that her face was flushed from the sun, but caught up in the game now, she ignored her discomfort. It was her turn to be clever, since it was obvious that for all Mr. Holbrook's university education, his knowledge of Holy Scripture was nil.

"It is from Genesis, the first book of the Bible," she told him. "Surely you remember? The Lord told Adam and Eve there was one tree in the Garden of Eden whose fruit they must not eat. The serpent tempted Eve."

Mr. Horton's face lit up. "Yes, now I remember," he said. "How clever of you, Miss Lancaster! I would never have guessed it."

As they rode, Merry told him more, and he was
delighted when she was able to narrow the clue down to
apple trees. But when they reached that section of the
orchards, he sighed again.

"There are so many apple trees, almost as many as
there were rose bushes," he complained.

Merry saw that another couple was before them, for
two saddled horses were grazing nearby. She sat on her
own horse, deep in thought, for she had no desire to
wander through the viscount's extensive orchard.
Besides, it had to be one particular tree. But which one
could it be?

"I know," she said, sliding to the ground. "Well, at
least I think I do, and pray I am right. Adam and Eve
were the *first* man and woman, were they not? So
perhaps the prize is under the *first* tree."

Mr. Holbrook nodded as he dismounted, too. And
then, as they entered the orchard, they saw Squire
Warden coming toward them, carrying a weeping Lady
Feering. As one, they hurried to meet them, the treasure
hunt forgotten.

The two men lifted the weeping lady to her horse,
while Merry tried to soothe her. It appeared, from the
squire's slightly breathless account, that the lady had
stepped into a rabbit hole and sprained her right ankle.
Merry could see how it was swelling, and she was glad it
had not been the left ankle. Now, at least, thanks to the
sidesaddle, she could ride her horse back to the hall for
some much-needed attention.

Lady Feering was most upset and angry. She and the
squire had only found one sovereign all afternoon, and
she was sure it was all his fault, for a more chuckle-
headed bumpkin she had never met. And now to injure
herself in the bargain . . . well! She wondered that dear
Gloriana could ever have thought such an afternoon at
all enjoyable. She was tired and hot and now her whole
stay here would be ruined. It was too bad!

Neither Merry nor Timothy Holbrook was at all sorry
to see the back of the unhappy pair as they hurried back
to the orchard again. "But 'ware rabbit holes, Miss

Lancaster," he said with a warm smile. "We still have one more clue to go!"

The cache was soon discovered at the base of the first tree. Mr. Holbrook complimented his partner on her religious knowledge before he checked his watch again. He frowned when he discovered they only had fifteen minutes left, but when he opened it, they discovered that the last clue was no problem at all.

" 'Tomorrow, and tomorrow, and tomorrow, Creeps in this petty pace from day to day. . . . Yet time and tide wait for no man,' " he read quickly. "Shakespeare, Miss Lancaster," he instructed her, that little pompous note creeping into his voice again.

"Time, time . . ." Merry mused. "A clock?"

"It cannot be a clock, for it must be outdoors," he told her.

Then they both beamed at each other as they said in unison, "A sundial!"

"In the perennial gardens," Merry went on. "Oh, do hurry! We may just have time to reach it before five."

But when they galloped up to the hall, it was to find Durfee standing on the steps, ringing a large bell to announce the end of the treasure hunt, and they were forced to give up that one, last prize.

"If only we had not taken so much time in the rose garden," Timothy Holbrook mourned as he helped Merry up the steps.

"But we have all but two sovereigns," she consoled him. "Surely we must be the winners."

When they entered the drawing room, it was to find everyone before them. And although some of the guests were chatting and laughing over their adventures, others looked decidedly glum. Lady Feering was there, her bandaged foot propped up on a large, soft footstool, and Rose Warden sat beside her, her thin shoulders drooping. She held a cloth to her mouth, and when she lowered it to dip it into a bowl of water set nearby, Merry saw that she had been badly stung. One whole side of her upper lip was swollen and distorted. Miss Amy Holbrook's curls hung in limp clusters, and she had torn her habit. Merry soon learned that her mother had had to retire and change. Jeremy Overton, himself dressed in different clothes now, told her why. It seemed they had taken one of the punts out to search the island and had been chased away by angry swans. Mrs. Holbrook had become so agitated by their hissing attack that she had upset the punt, tossing both of them into the water and necessitating a gasping, floundering retreat to the nearest shore.

"Fortunately," as Lord Saterly said tartly, "the lake is very shallow, or I fear the lady might have drowned me, she clung to me so!"

Merry tried to look properly concerned at the very small nobleman's report, but her eyes twinkled remembering Mrs. Holbrook's girth. And when Edward's eyes caught hers for a pregnant moment, she had to look away from him before she disgraced herself. But, oh, how she wished she might have seen it all!

Telling herself she was very bad, she looked around again. Jane appeared very hot and disheveled, she thought, before she looked down at her own dusty habit with the grass stains at the knee. Catching a glimpse of her gleaming, sunburned face in the mirror over the mantel, she realized she herself was no pattern card of propriety, either. In fact, the only woman in the room who looked her usual self was Viscountess Trumbull, the Lady Gloriana Regina Willoughby.

Merry wondered why the sight of the beautiful, perfectly groomed and elegant little lady did not please her more. But when she considered the afternoon m'lady had spent resting and being pampered with facials and massages, she was not surprised at the sharp stab of dislike she could not suppress. For one mad moment, she wondered if the viscountess had somehow anticipated the misfortunes of her feminine guests, had even hoped they would happen.

And then Merry told herself that, besides being very bad, she was nothing but a horrid cat.

10

WHEN Merry returned to the drawing room later, she found the guests reassembling there, rested and dressed for the evening. She herself felt much better after a refreshing bath and the cool lotion Nora had put on her sunburned face. She was even looking forward to the fun that was to come. Earlier, the viscountess had told them she would not announce the winners until dinnertime, and she had begged everyone not to divulge how many sovereigns they had found until then.

Timothy Holbrook had winked at Merry before he went to the room assigned to him for the evening, and she had smiled back at him. He was so sure they were going to win! Edward had questioned her then, but she had only returned evasive answers to all his queries.

"You shall hear all about it later, Edward," she had said. "But what of you? When we saw you on the drive, you were all smiles. But I do not think Miss Holbrook looked best pleased just now. And how did she tear her habit? Are you still stepping on ladies' gowns, my dear? You really must do something about that awful trait of yours."

The viscount had laughed as he took her hand in his and squeezed it. "I'll have none of your sass, my girl," he told her in a mock growl. Then he smiled and added, "But you must wait until later to find out, too. Sauce for the goose, my dear." He lowered his voice then to whisper how much he had missed her as a partner this afternoon, and Merry had laughed.

"But if we had been, sir, I doubt we would have solved any clues at all," she told him pertly, and he grinned and nodded.

Now, looking around the drawing room, she saw that Lady Feering and Miss Warden still held center stage, as the wounded members of the party. It was a situation Lady Feering seemed to expect, and one that Miss Warden appeared gratified by. Jason Willoughby had arrived, and Merry sent him a warm smile. And then she wondered why he looked so grim this evening.

There was much hilarity both in the drawing room and at table later, as everyone recounted the adventures of the afternoon. Only the viscount and Miss Holbrook, and Merry and her brother, had found the hiding place at the front gate. Squire Warden was quick to take Lady Gloriana to task for her misleading clue.

"For you must admit, m'lady, it had very little to do with the actual location of the sovereigns," he said in his hearty, positive voice. "All that nonsense about the sea, and Triton! There is nothing like that at the gate."

Lady Gloriana waved a dismissive hand. "No, you are quite right, Squire," she said. "But I have always admired that sonnet by Wordsworth, and I wanted to use it. Besides, surely I was allowed one tiny little red herring to make the search more difficult? And after all, you must not forget I did mention the horn!"

She was roundly scolded by everyone, although Mrs. Holbrook declared she had quite forgiven her, in spite of her ducking. Turning to the viscount, she said, "I do advise you to get rid of those swans, though, m'lord. Such nasty-tempered things they are! And when you consider how beautiful they look floating so effortlessly in the calm water . . .Well, it is most misleading! Swans are really horrid and vicious. I do not think I will ever forget trying to escape them, and if it hadn't been for Lord Saterly, they might well have been the end of me."

She smiled warmly at her late partner, and he bowed. Merry noticed he kept his distance, however.

Everyone had found the sovereigns in the stables, with the exception of Lady Feering and the squire.

"But, my dear Marianne, that was one of the easiest

clues," Lady Gloriana teased her. "How was it possible for you not to guess it?"

"The squire was sure you were referring to pigs. In fact, he was positive," the lady replied, her voice barely disguising her disgust.

"Pigs?" her hostess asked, looking puzzled.

"Yes. We must have inspected every sty in the vicinity, searching for swine," Lady Feering told her, much to everyone's delight as they tried to picture the elegant London sophisticate in such malodorous, messy locations. Merry noticed that even Jason Willoughby was smiling now.

But if the stables had been easy for most of the teams, only Jane and Nigel Brethers had found the Gallica Glory rose. Everyone else had wasted far too much time searching the rose garden. Miss Warden waved her hands and begged everyone to please stop reminding her about *that*! The swelling on her lip had gone down a bit, but it would be some time before it was back to its normal shape again.

Nigel Brethers had been quietly preening himself. "No Gallica Glories there," he said loudly, to silence the voluble Miss Warden, who, in spite of her supposed distaste for the subject, seemed prepared to tell the story of her sting once again. "Saw that at once. The only Glory roses are planted down by the gazebo."

The viscountess called the party to order then. "I do hope you all had a good time, in spite of a few, small mishaps," she said with her lovely smile.

Miss Warden sniffed sadly, and Lady Feering shifted her bandaged foot, looking affronted that her accident should be dismissed as a "small mishap!"

"And now it is time to award the prizes," Lady Gloriana went on. "We have two couples tied for first place, and for a moment when I learned that, I was quite sunk. But then I thought it would be only fair to give the lady's prize to darling Amy, and the gentleman's prize to her brother. You see, Teddy, being viscount here, had a definite edge on the rest of you.

And of course I know dearest Merry must agree that as
the future viscountess, she should forfeit the prize to a
guest of Trumbull. Isn't that so, my dear?'' she asked,
spinning around to smile at Merry.

Merry nodded, and Lady Gloriana gave two gaily
wrapped packages to the Holbrooks. Everyone crowded
around as they opened them. For Amy, there was a
delicate painted fan with diamond chips on the handle,
and for Timothy, a handsome onyx stickpin set in gold.

As the others exclaimed, the viscount asked Merry if
she minded his *Maman*'s decision, and she shook her
head. ''Of course not, my dear,'' she said. ''But I am
disappointed Mr. Holbrook and I wasted so much time
searching the rose garden. We knew the last clue was the
sundial, but we didn't have time to reach it before the
hunt was over. If we had, we would have beaten you fair
and square.''

He laughed at her, and she went on, ''But how did
Miss Holbrook tear her habit, Edward? You cannot
imagine how eager I am to hear about that.''

''Oh, that happened in the orchard,'' he said carelessly. ''Would you believe we saw a snake there? It was
almost too much like the Garden of Eden, or so Amy
told me later. But when she saw it, she screamed, and in
her haste to put as much ground between herself and the
reptile, she stepped on her train. I had nothing to do
with it, darling. Word of a Willoughby!''

Merry nodded, but still a little bothered by the
relationship between him and his lovely neighbor, she
said, ''I must admit I was quite perturbed when you
drew her name, Edward. I have seen how the lady looks
at you, the warmth and admiration in her eyes. I suspect
Miss Holbrook is in love with you.''

Edward smiled. ''Oh, surely not anymore. When we
were very young—just growing up, in fact—we did talk
about marrying each other someday,'' he admitted.
''But that was long before I met a tall and lovely lady
with chestnut hair who has quite bewitched me. Amy
understands. Indeed, she was so very sweet this
afternoon when she wished me happy. But I must warn

you that she did say she expects us to give a great many smart balls and house parties at Trumbull so she can meet a number of London gentlemen. She claimed that was the least I could do for her after jilting her."

He chuckled, but Merry watched his eyes soften as he looked toward the little blonde. Amy Holbrook was showing her fan to Lady Feering now, and dressed in a gown of periwinkle blue, with her curls in order again, she was a very attractive picture.

The evening was one of Lady Gloriana's triumphs. Dinner was excellent, the wines superb, and the company relaxed and full of good spirits. The only person who did not appear to be having a very good time was Jason Willoughby, but perhaps that was because he had not participated in the treasure hunt and so therefore could not join in the fun of discussing it, Merry thought. She saw Jane watching him a little anxiously, and she noticed how quickly she went to his side when the gentlemen rejoined the ladies in the drawing room after their port.

Sometime later, she chanced to overhear Jason as he spoke to Lady Gloriana. At that moment, they had their backs to her, and there was no one else nearby. She heard the viscountess quite clearly as she inquired for Jason's mother.

"I am afraid she is not at all well today, Aunt," he said, his deep voice even harsher than usual. "Mother is sunk into the depression she suffers so often, and has taken to her bed again."

"But how sad!" Lady Gloriana exclaimed. "Do remember me to her, Jason, and tell her I hope she will feel more the thing soon."

"Somehow I doubt your good wishes will do anything to speed her recovery!" he snapped. Before his hostess could reply, he changed the subject. "But what of you, Aunt? Of course I can see you are as young and lovely-looking as ever, and I must say I am relieved."

"Relieved?" Lady Gloriana asked faintly.

"Why, yes. I was sure you must be prostrated your-self, from contemplating your future, ma'am," he told her. "After all, in a short time, you will be the dowager viscountess, will you not? It is hard to picture you in the role, or living in the dower house, indeed it is! And when I try to imagine you as a grandmother, with all those little ones toddling at your feet . . . Well, it quite boggles the mind, does it not?"

"A grandmother?" Lady Gloriana echoed.

Merry knew she should not eavesdrop on a private conversation, but she could not move away. Had she imagined that faint note of disbelief, even horror, in Edward's mother's voice?

"Oh—oh, yes, of course," that lady was saying now. "But it is early days yet, Jason. Why, my darling Teddy is not even married as yet!"

"But he will be, no matter what, er, *obstacles* are put in his path, for it is plain to see it's all April and May with him. And time has a way of flying, Aunt," he told her. "Someday, sooner than you might like perhaps, Edward and Merry will have children. There might well be a little granddaughter for you to dote on, Aunt. She is sure to be lovely, too, don't you agree? And so *very* young and fresh."

Merry saw Lady Gloriana rise and watched Jason follow suit in his leisurely fashion, and she drew back a little.

"Please excuse me now, Jason," she heard the viscountess say with great dignity. "I must not neglect my other guests."

As she moved away, Merry heard Jason chuckle, and she was not surprised at the shiver than ran over her skin. He had sounded almost vindictive! And why was he twitting Lady Gloriana about her age? It was not at all kind. She wondered if she would ever discover the motive for the antipathy he had for Edward's mother. He had to have a reason, a very good reason, but no one seemed to know what it was, including, Merry thought, Lady Gloriana herself. Yet, if at one time something had happened to cause his dislike—no, almost hatred— surely she would be aware of it? And yet she seemed as much in the dark as Merry was herself. It was a puzzle.

Merry looked about the room and caught sight of Jane. She was looking very well this evening in a simple gown of pink muslin. It was obvious she had lost quite a bit of weight, and as her features thinned down, she looked more and more like her mother. Merry shivered again. She did not think Jane's chances of ever capturing Jason's heart were at all good, for what man would want a wife who reminded him constantly of a woman he loathed? She prayed she was wrong, for Jane's sake, and then she made herself join a group chatting nearby and put the whole thing from her mind.

The next morning, Merry was surprised to receive a note from Lady Gloriana, asking her to come to her rooms as soon as she had had her breakfast. Edward's mother had never honored her this way before, and somehow Merry felt uneasy. She could think of nothing she had done lately that deserved a scold or more advice about her behavior, so why was the lady requesting a private interview?

When she knocked on her door, Miss Farewell admitted her and curtsied. Merry looked around as Lady Gloriana dismissed her maid, saying she would ring when she needed her. The viscountess's boudoir was decorated in soft shades of rose. At the large windows that overlooked the front of the house, formal draperies of deep-rose brocade were softened by sheer undercurtains. Near them was a chaise and two satinwood chairs, separated by a small dainty table in the French style. Lady Gloriana had been reclining on the chaise, but now she rose to come and kiss Merry and draw her toward the seating arrangement. She was still wearing one of her charming robes.

"What a lovely room, ma'am," Merry said, her voice admiring. "It looks just like you."

The viscountess smiled. "Yes, it is pretty, isn't it?" she asked as she took her seat and gestured to Merry to sit across from her. "I am very fond of rose, as you know. But no doubt Teddy will have it completely redone for you, my dear. I believe he mentioned it to me only a few days ago."

Merry tried to relax, but there was something in the atmosphere that made her uneasy. She watched the viscountess look down as she clasped her little hands in her lap and bit her lip, and she steeled herself for whatever was coming.

"Merry, my dear, I have called you in here so we could be private," the viscountess began. "In just a short while now you will be married, and there are things you should know. And since your own mother is gone, it is clearly my duty to speak to you. I know it is not done as a general rule, that most girls go to their marriage beds with no more idea of what will happen to them there than a lamb does that is being taken to the butcher. But I have always felt that was so wrong! For example, my own mother just told me to be brave, and that was not much help at all. Far from it!"

She shook her head, and then she raised it to look straight at Merry, her expression full of loving concern. Merry wished she were not blushing, but she could tell from the heat rising in her face that she was.

"You must not be embarrassed, dearest girl," Lady Gloriana said quietly. "It is a fact of life all women must face. But I would like to prepare you for it as best I can. You see, Merry, whatever you have imagined about it, when a man makes love to you, it hurts. Especially at first. It was such a shock to me, who had only been kissed a few times, that first intimacy. And men are such selfish creatures at heart. They think only of their own satisfaction, and your feelings are quite unimportant to them once they become lost in desire and sensation. I suppose they feel that having given you their name and title, promised to support you and the children you may have, you will have to accept whatever indignities they subject you to. And they are indignities, Merry. There is no other way to describe them. They are disgusting, loathesome, and yes, you certainly must be brave to endure them. My mother was right about that!"

"But—but surely if you love someone, you will not feel like that. You will welcome their lovemaking,"

Merry interrupted. She did not want to hear this advice —she hated it!—but she did not know how to refuse. She could hardly excuse herself and flee.

"Yes, that is what all young girls think," Lady Gloriana told her. "They have read so many romances, heard so many love songs, dreamed so many dreams. And then they fall in love, and the man they choose becomes some sort of magical being, able to transport them to joy with his touch, his lips." She shook her head a little, and then she asked, "Do you think I didn't love my husband? Of course I did, darling girl! As fervently as you love Teddy, you may be sure."

She rose then and walked a little distance away. With her back turned, she said, "But the act of sex is not like love or romance. When men finally get you in their beds, they are rough and harsh. Oceans of tears do not move them. You are their wife, you see. You must let them do what they want."

She turned back then and sighed. "And that is not the worst of it, my dear. When you finally become *enceinte*, although they do tend to leave you alone then—concerned for their heir, mind you, not you, yourself—you must suffer nine months of sickness and discomfort. And when your labor comes, the birth . . . Ah, you feel as if you are being ripped apart. And it goes on and on and on, sometimes for days, until you wish you could die, even pray for death to release you."

"Why are you really telling me all this, ma'am?" Merry asked, trying to keep her voice steady.

"Because I want you to know what you are getting into. I want you to approach your marriage with your eyes open," Lady Gloriana said, taking a seat on the edge of the chaise and reaching out to take Merry's hands in hers. "It will be easier for you, and you will not have to suffer the heartbreak I did, innocent that I was."

But it won't be like that, Merry cried silently. Not with Edward! He is not cruel or rough, and he does love me. Comforted by this thought, she said, "Perhaps it was only that you are so very small, m'lady? But as you can see, I am not. Why, I am sure, er, everything will be easier for me."

Lady Gloriana shook her head sadly. "It will make no difference, darling girl. I thought much the same and asked other, larger women, and they had identical experiences."

Merry wondered then why all brides looked so happy, why young wives seemed so overjoyed to bear their husband's child, and she began to suspect that this might be just a ploy of Edward's mother. Perhaps, in spite of all the times she had said how much she wanted their marriage, she had been lying.

"It is a burden all women share," that lady was saying now, and Merry pushed her suspicions aside to consider later, when she was alone.

"But why are women so anxious to marry then, ma'am?" she asked. "And why do so many mothers encourage their daughters to do so, if they know what horrible experiences they will be facing?"

"It is the way of the world," the viscountess told her. "an unwed woman is no one. She has no respect, no status in society, and she is ridiculed by everyone. What mother would want such a life for a beloved daughter? No, she promotes a match, even knowing the price of respect and status is very expensive indeed."

Merry withdrew her hands from the lady's grasp and took a deep breath. "I could almost think you do not want me to marry Edward at all, ma'am, you paint such a gloomy picture," she said. She was more than a little angry now, and that anger made her brave.

The viscountess's eyes opened wide. "Oh, no, no, dear Merry, you are wrong! How many times have I told you how I long for your marriage? But I do admit that is why I have tried to get you both to delay it a little. I did so want you to enjoy a happy time! You see, my dear, it is not only the episodes of lovemaking that you must face. There are other things as well—things that in their own way hurt just as much, even though they affect your spirit, not your body."

She paused for a moment, and Merry found herself

holding her breath. What, now? What could possibly be coming next?

"After marriage, men change," Lady Gloriana began. "Oh, they still want you in their beds, of course, but they tend to return to their own pursuits after only a few months, and leave you very much on your own. It can be so terribly lonesome! And whatever a man was before he married, he will become again."

She shook her head and took out a handkerchief to wipe away a tear. Her voice shook as she said, "I wish I did not have to tell you what I am about to say now, dear. It is very difficult for me. You know how I adore Teddy, but you must also know I am not blind to his faults. Neither should you be. You see, he is more than just a handsome beau. In reality, he is a rake, a voluptuary. I cannot begin to tell you of the number of mistresses he has had, all those opera dancers and demimondes, even married women of the *ton*. He is discreet, of course, so his reputation has not suffered unduly, but you must be prepared to look the other way when he takes a mistress, perhaps right after your wedding."

"No. That is not Edward," Merry whispered, her face white now.

Lady Gloriana looked even sadder. "Yes, Merry, it is your Edward," she said quietly. "The Teddy *I* know that *you* have yet to discover. I am sure yesterday you saw how Amy Holbrook adores him. She has for years. It is only by her mother's vigilance that she is still pure, not from any forebearance on my son's part. When he sees any woman—girl—he wants, he takes her. I have scolded him time and time again, but now he is a man, I have little control over him, as you can imagine. But there have been others as well, even here on his own estate. Dairy maids, farmer's daughters, once even a pretty upstairs maid until I dismissed her. I can tell you I have had my hands full!"

"I do not believe you. I won't!" Merry tried, rising swiftly, her fists clenched. "Edward is not like that, he is *not*!"

Forgetting to curtsy, she ran to the door. As she wrenched it open, she heard Lady Gloriana say, "I quite understand your anger at me, my dear. I expected it. It is the price I must pay for honesty. But someday, we will have another talk, and then you will thank me, even though we weep in each other's arms."

Merry did not wait to hear another word. She closed the door behind her and ran blindly to her room. She could barely see for the tears that were streaming down her face. Fortunately, Nora was nowhere in sight when she gained that sanctuary. But before she could throw herself down on her bed and weep as she wanted to, she was forced to hurry to the dressing room for a basin to be sick in. Retching and miserable, she tried to forget what she had just heard. It was not true! It couldn't be! She would never believe it. For surely she would have sensed such things about Edward if they were true, wouldn't she? And how could she had fallen in love with a man no better than the satyr his own mother claimed he was? But no, no, she knew it was not true. Edward had never treated her to anything but honor and respect, even though he must have known she loved him so, she would not have objected to it if he had wanted to consummate their love.

Merry washed her face at last and went to lie down. She still felt sick, and she was exhausted. Perhaps if she slept awhile. . . ?

But she could not sleep. Instead, she lay on her back and stared up at the hangings above her head. The tears had vanished as quickly as they had come, and all she felt now was a helpless hopeless despair.

She stayed in her room all that day, dozing and waking to her terrible thoughts again, and refusing to see anyone. Even when Jane came, concerned for her, she refused to have her admitted. Nora shook her head, but since she suspected this sudden illness might be the result of yesterday's party and the hot sun, she was not alarmed. But she did wonder when Miss Lancaster asked her to remove the bouquet of flowers the viscount sent up to her, even though her mistress claimed that the scent of them was so strong it was making her dizzy again.

By the following morning, Merry had herself well in hand. She was awake very early, and as she sat up in bed and watched the sky lighten as a little breeze stirred her curtains, she came to a sudden conclusion. It was as if everything that had happened to her since Edward had first brought her to London had become crystal-clear, and there was not a doubt in her mind.

She would never believe Lady Gloriana ever again. It was all so plain to her now, as if something had swept aside layers of veiling that had been hiding the truth. Lady Gloriana did not want her to marry Edward, any more than she had wanted Jane to marry Jason. She did not want them to marry anyone, for then she would not be the most important person in their lives. And Lady Gloriana Regina Willoughby must always be that. If her son married, she would not only have to adopt the hateful title of dowager viscountess, but her *premier cavalier* would be forever gone. And if Jane married, she would lose an adoring handmaiden.

That was why she had discouraged Jane and Jason, why she had tried to delay her son's wedding, not so Jane could have her Seasons, or Merry enjoy being an engaged girl, as she had claimed. It was why she had insisted Merry buy all those elaborate clothes that did not become her, told the hairdresser to cut and dye her hair, promoted other men's attentions, made her late to appointments when she knew how Edward hated tardiness—all under the guise of helping her. Merry was sure of it. And no matter what the viscountess had said about Edward—his innumerable mistresses, his philandering—she would not believe that either. It had been nothing more than a ploy to get her to cry off, break the engagement. But she believed in Edward and their love. Nothing Lady Gloriana could say would shake her trust in him.

But how was she ever to tell Edward such horror stories about his own mother? She shook her head, for she knew she could never do that. It would hurt him, and she could not bear to bring him pain. Besides, he loved his mother, and he did not suspect she was anything but what she appeared to be. And even if she did manage to convince him, it could only cause estrangement between mother and son, something she did not care to contemplate. No, somehow she must find a way to live with Lady Gloriana, even with all her new knowledge of the lady's true nature. For now she understood what those cryptic hints of Jason Willoughby's had been all about, why he had urged her not to delay or let anything stand in the way. And his conversation with the viscountess last evening was so very clear, now. Somehow, he knew what she was like, but he was the only one besides herself who saw through the lady's loving, caressing facade, to the selfish, shallow witch beneath it.

As she rang for her maid and swung her legs over the side of the bed to put on her robe, she told herself that she must make sure nothing interfered with her future— hers and Edward's—ever again. And no matter how distasteful Lady Gloriana's private interview had been, she realized the lady had done her a singular service. For now, of course, that she knew what the viscountess was really like, she would be very much on her guard.

And this very day, she would see Edward, and they would choose their wedding day.

And nothing—nothing!—would stop it, for she would see to that!

11

THE viscount was delighted when Merry sought him out in the library later that morning and told him she thought they should set the date of their wedding without further ado. Since the last calling of the banns was this coming Sunday, and the London guests would be leaving next week, they chose the following Saturday.

Merry felt great relief as soon as this had been decided, and Edward's possessive arms, caressing hands, and passionate kiss did much to restore her spirits. Later, they sat close together while they discussed that happy day.

When he learned she was to wear a gown of ivory silk for the ceremony, he promised her the most lavish bouquet of creamy roses to carry that his gardeners could pick, and a festive wedding breakfast to follow, complete with his finest champagne.

"And what happens then?" Merry asked, a little shyly.

"Oh, then we will leave for London, and for Paris," he told her, his dark-blue eyes alight as he caught her close again.

A lot of time elapsed before Merry was able to ask him the question that was burning in her mind. "Will your mother move into the dower house while we are gone?" she asked.

"I do hope she can," he told her, smoothing back the chestnut hair at her brow. "But you know she has not been able to choose new furniture, indeed look for any of the things she will need."

"I was in her rooms yesterday," Merry told him, trying to control the breathlessness she was feeling.

"They are so very lovely, so like her. Why don't you have all her pretty things moved to the dower house? I am sure that would please her and make her feel more at home there. As for the other furnishings, surely she can live with them until she goes to London in the fall, don't you think?"

"But what an excellent idea!" he exclaimed. "It is so kind of you, my darling Merry, to try to make this as painless as possible for her. But then, there is no one as good and thoughtful as you are. How lucky I am that I found you and you fell in love with me."

Merry put her head on his chest and closed her eyes, feeling like the worst hypocrite on earth. This was going to be a lot harder than she had imagined, knowing what she did and yet pretending that everything was just as it always had been. She hardly knew how she was to face Lady Gloriana when the time came, or how she was to act the part of future, adoring daughter-in-law without giving herself away. But she was glad Edward had agreed to strip the viscountess's rooms, for she knew she couldn't have borne to live there, decorated as they were now, a constant reminder.

When Merry and Lady Gloriana did meet later, there were others present, and she managed to brush through the encounter without incident, for the viscountess was her usual, charming self. Indeed, she acted as if they had never had that distasteful conversation, or that Merry had run from her room exclaiming her disbelief, her defiance, at all. And when Edward announced their wedding day, she checked for only a moment, her eyes slightly narrowed, before she clapped her hands and declared she was so pleased! Only once, when her son turned away to answer a question of Lady Feering's, did she look directly at Merry. Her eyes were sad and resigned, and she shook her head a little, as if in sincere regret that her good advice had been ignored.

Merry did not flinch as she met that gaze. It had suddenly occurred to her that she was not the only hypocrite in Trumbull Hall.

She was not present when Edward informed his

mother of the scheme to move all her furniture, hangings, and carpets to the dower house, but when she asked Jane about it later, she learned the viscountess had professed to be delighted and had agreed at once.

"Teddy has set me the task of seeing to it, as soon as you both have left," Jane told her. "And I am to oversee the refurnishing of the rooms for you, Merry. I shall be so pleased! But if my humble attempts do not please you, I hope you will make any changes you want when you return."

Merry thanked her quietly, and Jane came and took her hands. "Is everything all right, Merry?" she asked, a little frown between her brows. "You seem so different lately, as if there was something bothering you. Can I help in any way?"

Merry made herself smile as she reassured her sister-in-law-to-be that everything was just fine. Then she was quick to change the subject to the amount of weight Jane had lost, and made a jest about how busy her maid must be, taking in all her clothes. She was relieved the ruse worked so well, and Jane rose to show her how loose her gowns were becoming.

But although Merry entered into all the amusements Lady Gloriana had planned for her London guests, was pleasant when spoken to and quick to join in any conversation, the viscount noticed as well as his sister had that the lovely, lilting laugh he had admired so long was conspicuously absent. He wondered at it. Merry seemed so quiet, so remote of late. He had no idea if all girls about to wed behaved in like manner, but he finally convinced himself that that must be the reason. No doubt his darling Merry was feeling shy, perhaps overcome with the seriousness of the step she was taking. Well, he would show her, with all the love and tenderness he could bring to their marriage, how much he adored her, that there was nothing whatsoever to worry about.

The *al fresco* dance had to be postponed because of a heavy rainstorm on the original date set. The evening it finally took place would have pleased even someone who hated the country. It was warm and balmy, with only a little breeze, and the gardens and terrace looked festive in the lantern lights Lady Gloriana had had installed. Part of the terrace had been swept and polished for dancing, and the orchestra installed at one end. Farther away, small tables and chairs were set out, and inside one of the salons, long tables had been arranged for food and drink. There were flowers everywhere, in urns and vases, and in fragrant garlands hung in swaths between the lanterns. But Lady Gloriana's most original touch was the champagne punch that flowed in the fountain in the center of the garden.

To the applause of the guests, Edward opened the dance with Merry. A great many people from the neighborhood were present, all interested in meeting the future viscountess. So many, in fact, that Merry had thought they would never have done with the receiving line.

Once again, she wore her ecru ball gown and the Trumbull pearls, and she was greatly admired, or so Edward told her as he bent closer to whisper to her as they danced. Merry smiled up at him, trying to keep her face serene. She knew from the way several young ladies had stared at her, their intent faces not quite hiding their disappointment, that her capturing such a handsome peer did not sit well with the neighborhood belles. One young lady, with a wealth of black curls and a pert little nose, had even gone so far as to tell her that everyone's heart had been broken at her stealing the viscount away. Edward had laughed at this remark and called the lady a dear exaggerator, but Merry had not felt reassured when she saw the girl's seductive pout for him, or the way he slid his arm around her for a moment, to hug her close. Sometimes, it seemed to Merry that Edward was a great deal too free with his favors. But then she would chastise herself for such ignoble thoughts, telling herself that if the viscountess had not put such poison in her ears about Edward and his philandering ways, she would not have thought a thing of it. He had grown up with these girls; they were all old friends. Naturally, he felt affection for them.

At one point during the evening, Merry found herself beside the viscountess, and she was quick to congratulate her on the success of the evening.

"Yes, everyone is having such a good time, are they not?" the little lady asked with a smile. "Why, even Tiny is dancing and laughing and happy tonight! And by the way, dear Merry, I must thank you for everything you have done for Tiny. I can see the weight she has lost, and I am sure that is all your doing." She laughed then and added, "And to think she would take your advice, but not mine! But you must not be concerned, dearest girl. I am not the least angry or disappointed, for I learned long ago that the expression 'Mother knows best' is never heeded by grown-up children. My, no, quite the contrary. Naturally Tiny would prefer to listen to someone her own age."

"Jane," Merry reminded her, before she thought.

Lady Gloriana stared at her for a fleeting moment before she smiled again. "Of course. *Dearest* Jane! I do try to remember, you know, Merry. Truly I do!"

Mr. Brethers bowed to them then, come to take the lady away, and Merry was delighted to see him. There were only seven days to go before her wedding day, and she knew she must take every precaution to act as if everything was as it had been before, lest Edward learn what she had discovered of his mother's Janus face. She found it quite the hardest thing she had ever had to do in her life. And it was made all the more difficult by Lady Gloriana's acting as if there had been no change in their relationship at all.

When Jason Willoughby asked her to dance, she was glad to put all thoughts of the lady aside and take his hand.

"Edward tells me you have chosen a date at last, Merry," he said as he bowed to her.

"Finally," she replied, curtsying in return. As he drew her up, she added, "I must thank you for all your good advice, Jason. It has been invaluable to me."

She looked up into his harsh face to see him staring at where Lady Gloriana was standing, teasing her two elderly beaux. His mouth grew grim as he looked back at his partner and said, "So, you yourself have discovered the lady's true nature, have you, Merry?"

She nodded. "I could not believe you or your warnings at first, but now my eyes are open. Lady Gloriana does not want me to marry her son; she does not want him to marry anyone, at least for years. And she doesn't want to lose Jane to any man. Yet neither of them is aware of this. But as soon as I discovered it, I went to Edward and we named our wedding day. For she must accept a new viscountess once we are married, don't you think? There can't be anything else she can do, can there?"

He saw the little worry in her hazel eyes, and he said, "No, my dear. Once you exchange your vows, there will be nothing she can do at all."

Merry's sudden smile was dazzling, and his harsh face brightened in response. "But don't break any bones or catch an infectious fever, my soon-to-be cousin," he warned her.

Merry assured him she would be on her guard. For a fleeting moment, she wished she might ask him to tell her about Edward's past, but there was no way she could think of to initiate such a conversation. Besides, it would be disloyal to Edward. She knew what she should do was ask her fiancé herself, but every feeling was offended at the thought. How would he take her distrust of him and being accused of raking and immorality? And how could she ask him such a thing without revealing the source of her information? No, no, for his sake, and the love he had for his mother, however misguided that love was, she must hold her tongue.

Although Jane danced with a great many others as well, Merry noticed that Jason Willoughby asked for her hand three times. The girl was aglow with happiness, and Merry could see he was attracted to her. In some trepidation, she looked around for Lady

Gloriana, wondering how the little viscountess would take his sudden renewed attentions. But Lady Gloriana appeared to be ignoring the sight of her daughter with the tall dark man she had warned her away from once before.

It was very late and some of the guests were beginning to take their leave when Merry looked around for Edward. She had not seen him since their last waltz. But he was not dancing now, nor sitting out at one of the little tables, and curious, she wandered through the salons, stopping every now and then to speak to people she had met that evening.

Eventually, she made her way to the gardens. Surely it was most unusual for the host to absent himself during the party? Wherever could he be?

She was about to give up her search when she saw him a little distance away. He was standing close to Amy Holbrook, holding both her hands and looking down into her uplifted face. They seemed to be having a serious conversation, for she saw Miss Holbrook's inquiring face and moving lips, as well as the way Edward shook his head before he began to speak to her at some length. Merry wished she had never come upon them, but although she also wished she might turn and walk away, something held her there, watching them carefully.

At last the viscount stepped back and let the little blonde's hands go. As he offered his arm, she grasped it in both hands and began to speak to him again, and in a moment, her arms crept up to his shoulders. Merry held her breath as Edward's arms went around Miss Holbrook's waist, and he bent his head further to kiss her. Merry drew a ragged breath and whirled and ran away.

She was so upset at what she had witnessed that she went into the hall and up to her room to compose herself. Perhaps Lady Gloriana had been right, after all? And if she had been right about Edward's amorous activities, might not Merry have misunderstood all her intent during their conversation?

No, I didn't, she told herself as she smoothed her
curls before the dressing-table mirror and tried to pinch
some color into her pale cheeks. I know I am not
mistaken in her, for look how Jason agreed with me this
very evening.

There had to be some simple explanation for the kiss
she had witnessed. Edward and Amy Holbrook had
known each other from childhood, and at that time had
talked about marrying someday. Surely, such closeness
did not disappear simply because the viscount was about
to wed another. What she had seen must have been a
final farewell to childhood fantasies. She must not
elaborate on it, nor give it any special significance.

Still, Merry was up early the following morning. She
had not been sleeping well for some time now, and she
knew from past experience that there was no sense in
lingering in bed, hoping to doze off again. The uneasy
thoughts whirling about in her brain would not permit
it. Without summoning Nora, she dressed in one of her
old habits and made her way through the sleeping hall to
the stables. Perhaps a good ride would shake the
cobwebs from her brain, sweep away all her depressing
thoughts.

A startled stable boy saddled a mare for her, but
when he would have summoned a groom, she refused
any escort. Alone, she rode farther than she had ever
gone before, trying to enjoy the freshness of the
morning, the mist rising from the fields, and the dewy
grass and wildflowers.

At last, she turned her mare for home and slowed her
to a trot. As she approached a small lonely farm she had
passed earlier, she saw the inhabitants were now up and
about. The sturdy farmer, a blond with a freckled face,
removed his cap as she rode nearer, and bowed. A
young woman, as blond as he was himself, stood in the
doorway of the cottage. She was holding a fair-headed
baby in her arms, and close beside her was a little boy,
his dark-blue eyes round at the sight of the strange lady
on horseback.

Merry smiled and would have spoken to them, even as

her eyes went back to the little boy. She wondered why she felt so uneasy until she noticed his hair. It was as black and curly as Edward's and her gaze returned to the two blond parents. Surely such coloring was unusual, with two such fair parents? She stared at the young mother again. She was a pretty thing, with a voluptuous figure and tiny waist that any man would admire. As Merry watched, the farmer's wife bobbed a curtsy. She must have seen the questions in Merry's eyes then, for she flushed scarlet as she lifted her chin in defiance and reached out to pull the little boy closer to her skirts.

Merry kicked her mare then and cantered away. The bright fresh morning was forgotten now, for her eyes were bleak and she was having trouble restraining her tears. That was Edward's son. She was sure of it. And he must be sure of it, too, for why else had he avoided this part of the estate whenever he had taken her riding? The omission was a sure sign of his guilt, as was the young mother's reaction when brought face to face with her master's future bride.

As Merry jumped the mare over a fence, she wondered how Edward had persuaded the farmer to marry the girl and take care of his bastard. Perhaps he had given him the farm as payment? Or perhaps he had promised money for the boy's upbringing? How dreadful this was, now she had real proof of his vice!

She had almost reached the hall again when she halted her mount. The mare dropped her head and began to crop the new grass as Merry considered her predicament. Even now, as distraught as she was, she knew she still loved Edward Willoughby. She would always love him. And no one is perfect, she told herself stoutly. Surely when they were married, his philandering would be a thing of the past. Every young man had his flings, his affairs—she was not so naïve she did not know that. How could she help but be aware of it when it was so common in 1816? She must not place too much significance on the accepted practice. But as she shortened the reins and clucked to the mare, she wished she had never gone the way she had this morning, nor even that she had searched for Edward at the dance. It was very true that what you did know could hurt you.

She was especially quiet for the rest of the day, and when Edward tried to tease her into going for a drive or a ride that afternoon, he could not persuade her to leave the hall. As she excused herself and left him, she did not see his frown, the bewilderment in his eyes.

It was very late that evening when the viscount tapped softly on his mother's door. He had been uneasy all day, for not only had Merry refused to go out alone with him, he had had the feeling she was trying to avoid him. Yet how could this be? Their wedding was only a matter of a few days away, and he could think of nothing that might have happened to upset her, make her shy of him. But although he had been happier since their engagement had been announced and had thought Merry happier as well, surely she was acting very strangely now. He went over their time here in Hampshire, turning his mind this way and that, desperately searching for some reason, some happenstance, some little thing that he might have missed. Nothing came to mind. Every moment they had been together had been wonderful—perfect, at least for him. And he knew he could never have felt that way if Merry did not think so too. Moreover, it had been Merry herself who had come and begged him to set the date of their wedding at last. Would she have done that if she were having doubts, or was upset about something?

It occurred to the viscount that women were complicated creatures, much more complicated than he had ever given them credit for being. And since this was the case, perhaps seeking another woman's council might be helpful? For even if his mother did not know what the trouble was either, as another woman at least she could advise him, reassure him, about the capriciousness of her sex.

Miss Farewell admitted him to her boudoir, and curtsied before she left them alone.

"My dear one! But what a lovely surprise!" Lady Gloriana exclaimed.

He bent and kissed the soft, scented cheek she offered before he led her to the chaise.

As they sat down, his mother searched his face, her eyes intent. "What is it, Teddy?" she asked, serious now as she pressed his hand between both of hers. "I can tell there is something very wrong."

The viscount ran a hand through his black curls. "There is something very wrong indeed, *Maman*. I have come to see if perhaps you can help me."

"But, of course, dear. I will do anything I can, you know that," Lady Gloriana assured him. Then she moved closer and said quietly, "It is Merry, isn't it, my son?"

He nodded, looking bleak. "So, you have noticed the change in her too, have you, *Maman*? I thought perhaps only I was conscious of it."

"No, no," his mother said. "I agree that she has changed, but I have no idea why," she added, throwing out her little hands in bewilderment. "Are you aware that I spoke to her a day or so ago, here in my rooms?"

She paused until he nodded, and said, "Yes, she did say you had asked to see her privately, but she did not tell me the subject of your conversation."

The viscountess sat up a little straighter. "I called her in here to see if I could discover why she has seemed so unhappy lately. Surely it is very unusual for a young girl in love, and one about to wed as well! In reality, she should be ecstatic. But in spite of my most gentle questions, she would not tell me anything, and, well, I hesitated to press her. I am not her mother, my darling, and no matter how I have tried, I do not seem to be able to get her to regard me in that light, even as a substitute. And lately, it is as if she suddenly does not trust me. You do see how difficult it would be for me to do anything further, no matter how much I wish to help the both of you?"

The viscount smiled down at her concerned face and hugged her close for a moment. "Ah, *Maman*, was there ever anyone to equal you?'' he asked, his dark-blue eyes full of admiration. ''You are so kind, so understanding!''

Lady Gloriana waved away his compliments. ''Has she said nothing to you, Teddy? Nothing at all? And have you asked her, straight out, what is bothering her?''

He rose to pace the boudoir. The viscountess never took her eyes from his handsome, worried face. ''No, not as yet,'' he admitted. ''I thought to see you first, hoping you might be able to shed some light on this dilemma. You see, *Maman*, Merry used to be so gay and happy, so quick to laugh! It was one of the things about her that made me love her. But now she never laughs, and she is not happy. I don't think she has been since we arrived in London.''

''Perhaps she is having second thoughts about the wisdom of her marriage to you?'' Lady Gloriana asked a little shyly. As the viscount looked astounded, she added, ''You must know, dearest, that some young women tend to, er, leap before they look. And then, after they are better acquainted with their fiancé, they realize that the great love they thought they felt is no such thing, after all.''

The viscount was frowning now, and she went on quickly, ''You must remember what a whirlwind affair your courtship was, dear. A mere three weeks' acquaintance! Even so, I cannot understand why Merry would change, stop loving you. Why, you are the nicest man I know! But a mother's affections are nothing like those of a strange young miss. No doubt I am prejudiced—''

''It cannot be that,'' Edward interrupted, ignoring her compliments. ''Merry loves me, I know she does!''

''Does she? Then why is she acting this way?'' Lady Gloriana persisted. ''And with her wedding less than a week away?''

She saw his frown deepen until his black brows were a solid bar across his forehead, and she said, ''It was one of the reasons I tried to get you to delay the wedding.

Marriage lasts a very long time, my son, and I could not bear it if you married someone who would make you unhappy as the years passed. But, oh, how I hoped that your love for each other would deepen, grow stronger throughout your engagement! Yet from what you have just told me, it is obvious that the opposite has occurred. Perhaps . . . Oh, dear, no, I cannot bear to say it!''

She put her hands to her face and bowed her head. The viscount strode back to the chaise to sit beside her and take hold of her shoulders so she was forced to look at him.

"Can't bear to say what, *Maman*?" he demanded.

She swallowed a little and whispered, "Perhaps it would be better for you to cry off, darling? Or let Merry do so? But, oh, how disappointed I am! I was so happy for you both, and I have learned to love Merry so much that I hate to even *think* of such a move!"

His sudden strong grip caused her to cry out, and he was quick to release her. "No, never," he said, his jaw tilted at an arrogant angle. "I will not cry off, and neither will Merry. Instead, I will find out what is bothering her and take care of it."

"Teddy, perhaps it would be best if you were not so, er, direct?" Lady Gloriana suggested a little diffidently. "Her concern might be about any number of things. Why, just consider, darling. Perhaps she is worried about the physical side of marriage, and she would be embarrassed to discuss it with you. Let me talk to her again, my son, and see if I can't find out the root of the problem. If it is a fear of intimacy, I can reassure her, comfort her."

The viscount kissed her cheek in gratitude. "Do everything you can, *Maman*," he said. "I love Merry. Any life spent without her by my side would be too miserable an existence for me to contemplate."

"I shall do my best, dear one," the viscountess said, stroking his cheek. "But please, do not speak to Merry until I have had a chance to, I beg you! This may only be feminine shyness and reluctance. We must pray so."

The viscount's eyes grew distant with thought. He found it hard to believe that Merry had suddenly retreated into maidenly modesty, for she had always been so passionate when he embraced her. But what else could it be? And although he wished he himself might go to her and hold her in his arms while he told her how marvelous their love was going to be, he could see that speaking to another woman might be less upsetting.

"It shall be as you say, *Maman*," he told the viscountess. "But do try to speak to her soon, for otherwise I know I will not be able to contain myself."

His mother wrinkled her nose at him as she rose and gave him a little push. "Men," she said, her voice amused. "How impatient, impetuous, and impertinent you all are! Away with you at once, and leave all to me. I shall see to it, and you will be happy very soon again, I am sure."

The viscount's hug was fervent as he kissed her good night and thanked her. As he went along the corridor to his own rooms, he was sure there wasn't another man on earth who had such a wonderful mother. He certainly was a lucky man.

The next day was dark and stormy, and Lady Feering began to pack, even though she had intended to remain till the end of that week. But as she told the company at dinner, when she announced an early-morning departure on the morrow, the country in foul weather was an abominable place. Furthermore, since she was still incapacitated by a sprained ankle and therefore unable to join in any festivities yet to come, there was no point in her remaining. She said she intended to see her London physician as soon as she reached town again.

Lady Gloriana did not try to persuade her to remain. In fact, rather surprisingly, she suggested that Lord Saterly and Mr. Brethers might like to decamp as well. "I quite agree this weather is dreary beyond belief, dear sirs," she told them. "I shall not insist on your attendance. Besides, there is darling Merry's and my Teddy's wedding to see to, you know. Yes, I do think it might be best for you to follow Marianne's example."

Although neither gentleman would have left a second before the other ordinarily, now they were perfectly agreeable to the plan. Lord Saterly only tried to discover when his Lady Glory planned to return to town herself, and Mr. Brethers insisted she must journey to his estate in Kent in the near future, so he could show her his gardens.

The London guests left very early the following morning, in a little cavalcade of carriages. Merry stood beside Edward on the steps of the hall, with Jane and the viscountess waving their good-byes as well. She had not thought she would be sorry to see them all leave, but now, somehow, their departure made her uneasy, for it meant she would be alone with Lady Gloriana again. She had caught the viscountess staring at her, deep in thought, several times yesterday, although she had made no move to see her alone. Merry wondered what she was planning now. The wedding was only four days away. Surely Lady Gloriana had some further scheme in mind to delay it if she could. She could not know that Edward was disturbed that his mother had not sought his fiancée out. And when he taxed her with it, she had told him she had been so busy with her guests on the last day of their stay that she had not had the opportunity.

When the post was delivered, the four regular inmates of the hall were together, back in the breakfast room to discuss the house party while they enjoyed another cup of coffee. Jane remarked how nice it was to have the hall to themselves at last, for now she and *Maman* could concentrate on the wedding. Merry made herself meet Edward's questioning eyes, and when she saw the puzzled look there, she made herself smile a little.

As he smiled back and sent her a silent message of love, she heard a stifled gasp. Quickly, she looked up to see Lady Gloriana clutching a letter she had just received, her face white with shock. For once, Merry thought she looked every year of her age.

"*Maman*, what is it?" Jane asked, rising quickly to go and kneel beside her.

"I cannot believe it," the viscountess moaned as she put her handkerchief to her eyes. "How dreadful! How very, very dreadful!"

"What is dreadful, *Maman*?" Edward asked, getting to his feet now, too.

"It is my dear sister Jane," his mother wailed. "She is gone, gone! This letter is from your Uncle Henry telling of a sudden illness that resulted in her death. Why, Jane has been buried for three days, and I never even knew it!"

A younger Jane got up to take her weeping mother in her arms and pat her back. "There, there, dear *Maman*," she said, her voice soothing. "Let me take you up to your rooms. Perhaps if you lie down and rest . . . But Miss Farewell will know what to do. We can discuss all this later."

"Yes, I am so distraught, so terribly upset," Lady Gloriana managed to get out between her sobs. "Thank you, dearest Tiny. Whatever would I do without you? Or my Teddy, either?"

Her daughter led her to the door, supporting her with an arm around her waist. She paused there long enough to say over her shoulder, "Do not be concerned, Teddy, Merry. I shall see to *Maman*."

Left alone together, Merry only stared into her coffeecup. Edward took his seat again, reaching out to squeeze her shoulder as he passed her. He held his uncle's letter in his hands.

As he read it aloud to her, Merry was more than a little surprised. Mr. Henry Grandford had written a cold, factual account, from which even a vestige of family affection had been removed. It might well have been a notice sent to mere acquaintances, she thought. But perhaps he had been overcome with grief and dared not give in to it? Yes, of course, that must be it!

She reached out to take Edward's hand in hers, to comfort him. But when she questioned him about his aunt and uncle, he divulged the fact that they rarely saw each other. He said it was something he had wondered about before. Of course, as he pointed out, the Grandfords lived near Harrogate and seldom came to town. But he seemed a little surprised nevertheless when he recalled how few times they had been together as a family, how little he knew of his cousins or their life.

Trumball Hall was very quiet all day. There was a fine rain falling, and everyone was kept inside. But Merry saw Edward only briefly, for he had been busy writing letters of condolence and asking what, if anything, he could do for his uncle. Jane, too, had been closeted with her mother most of the time, so Merry had spent a dreary day of introspection, alone with her thoughts. And although she had never had a sister, she remembered how she had felt when her father died, and her heart went out to Lady Gloriana.

All her charity fled in a moment at dinner that evening, however. She had been surprised that the viscountess had felt strong enough to join them at the table, accompanied by Jane. Both of them were dressed all in black, and Lady Gloriana's face was pale and subdued, her mood somber. It was not long before they learned that she was most displeased that neither the viscount nor Merry had thought to don mourning, too.

"Of course, I do not think Merry is required to," she said sadly as she took her seat at the head of the table. "I am not quite sure of the etiquette for engaged ladies."

Before Merry could comment, she turned to her son and said, "But, Teddy, for shame! You must see to your mourning clothes at once, dear boy. It is necessary that you show your respect for such a close member of the family, no matter how disappointing it is for you personally."

Merry had a sudden premonition and she looked quickly at Edward. He was facing his mother at the other end of the table, an arrested expression on his face.

"Why should it be disappointing personally, *Maman*?" he asked quietly. "What do you mean?"

Lady Gloriana looked at him sadly as she took the napkin the butler handed her, and put it in her lap. "My dearest Teddy, you are not thinking. Of course we must all go into mourning for my sister, your dear aunt! And for a full year, too. I cannot tell you how sorry I am for you and Merry, that your marriage must be delayed for such a time."

She sighed and then she added in a fading voice, "It is too bad."

12

MERRY stifled a gasp, but the viscount was not so restrained. "No," he said in a flat, authoritative voice.

Merry stole a glance at Lady Gloriana and saw that she was observing her son with sad eyes. Try as she might, she could read nothing in the lady's expression but somber regret.

"What do you mean, 'no,' Teddy?" she asked. "You have no choice in the matter. You must."

The viscount turned to the butler. "Clear the room, Durfee," he said. He waited until the butler and two footmen had left and closed the door behind them, before he spoke again. "I mean that Merry and I *cannot, will* not delay our marriage for an entire year, *Maman*." He paused, but when the viscountess did not speak, he went on, "It is too much to expect of us. And since the ceremony is to be private, and we are going abroad immediately, I do not see why it is at all necessary. As for mourning, we will wear it when we return, for the prerequisite amount of time, if you insist on it. But know that Merry and I will be married on Saturday, as we planned."

Merry had listened to him with a great deal of relief, but now she looked almost apprehensively at Lady Gloriana. She was very pale and her eyes were filled with tears.

"How can you be so unfeeling, my son?" she asked, her voice breaking. "My only sister, your dear aunt! And when society hears of it, you will be an outcast. Is that what you want for your bride? Are you truly *that* selfish?"

Merry took a deep breath. "I don't see how it can be

as bad as that, ma'am," she said, trying to keep her voice steady so her rising anger would not show. As Lady Gloriana turned to her, her face expressionless, she went on quickly, "We will not be here for some time. And if we do not go to London in the autumn, entertain or attend parties, who can fault us?"

Unexpectedly, Jane took a hand. "I know how upsetting this is for you, *Maman*, but I think Teddy and Merry are right. You and I are in the proper mourning, and if we remain in the country, live quietly at the dower house, no one will be able to say a word."

The viscountess straightened in her chair, her back ramrod-straight. "I never thought to hear such things from either one of you, Tiny, Teddy," she said, her voice constricted. "I never realized I had brought you up to be so inconsiderate, so cruel. Is it nothing to you how this reflects on me? Nothing at all that I must live with this scandal for the rest of my life? Nothing, that your dear *Maman* can never hold up her head again?"

Merry bit her lip, lest she vent her anger. How dare the viscountess speak to Edward of her shame, accuse him of cruelty, after the scandal she herself had been involved in when Reggie Horton committed suicide because of her. And what had she done then? Retreated from the world? Been concerned about the shame her children felt? No, she had had a house party!

She glanced at Edward's face and saw how it had paled, and still she dared not speak. She was not family yet. She clenched her hands together in her lap, praying Edward would find a way to circumvent what she knew was only another delaying tactic on his mother's part. True, the viscountess had not known her sister would die, but look how quick she had been to use it to her advantage! And since Edward had told her only this morning that the families had never been close and rarely saw each other, how much real affection could Lady Gloriana have had for her sister?

Merry suddenly felt a wave of weariness sweep over her. She was so very tired of all this—this pretending! She wished suddenly that she could stand up and scream at them all. Scream at Lady Gloriana for her deceit and selfishness, reveal her for the witch she was; scream at Edward for his raking, and tell him how much she hated the way his mother ran his life, and hated him, too, for letting her do it!

She lowered her eyes to her lap, her head spinning. No, I didn't mean that, she cried silently, her fingernails biting into the skin of her palms. I don't hate you, Edward. I could never hate you.

But a sudden vision of the little boy with curly black hair she had seen this morning, swam behind her eyelids, and when she forced that picture away, it was replaced by Amy Holbrook's arms stealing around Edward's neck, and his immediate response. She swallowed.

"You are distraught, *Maman*," Edward was saying now. "I believe the news of Aunt Jane's death has overset you more than you imagined. Why don't you go back to your room, try to sleep?"

His mother did not move, nor take her eyes from his face. She seemed about to speak, and then she gave a choking little cry. Horrified, Merry watched her put both hands to her heart and gasp. "Aah, the pain, the pain!" she cried, and as her eyes turned up in the sockets, she slid from the chair into a little heap beneath the table.

All three younger people were on their feet at once. Jane was the first to reach her mother, and as she felt for her pulse, she said, "Tell Durfee to send someone for the doctor, Teddy, and call Miss Farewell. Hurry!"

As he hastened to do so, running across the dining room and flinging open the door, Jane continued, "Merry! Wet a napkin in some water. We must see if we can't revive her."

She stretched her mother out on the floor, supporting her head in her lap. Merry handed her the napkin and knelt on the lady's other side. She was relieved to see the slight movement at the neck of her gown that showed the viscountess was breathing, for for one horrible moment, she was sure she had died, right before their eyes. As she picked up a cold little hand to chafe it, she

remembered how, for a split second, she had wished
that it were so. Now, she hated herself for such an
unchristian thought, and she made herself pray for forgiveness, and Lady Gloriana's recovery.

When she felt Miss Farewell's hand on her shoulder,
she rose and moved away, to give the maid room to see
to her mistress. A short time later, Edward had his still-
unconscious mother in his arms, for he would let no one
else carry her upstairs.

Merry sank down on a dining-room chair as she
watched him leave the room, followed by Jane and the
maid. How tiny the viscountess had looked, how frail
and helpless, she thought. And how concerned and
upset Edward had been.

Merry was left alone with her thoughts for a long
time. She leaned her elbows on the table and put her
head in her hands. Where was all this going to end? she
wondered in despair. And even if Lady Gloriana made a
complete recovery from what appeared to have been a
heart attack, how could they marry on Saturday now,
leave her for weeks while they traveled? She shook her
head. It was almost as if the fates were against her
marriage to Edward Willoughby, as if something,
someone, even beyond Lady Gloriana was trying to stop
it.

She sat up straight and lifted her head as she clasped
her hands in her lap. Perhaps those fates are right, she
thought. Perhaps everything I have learned here has
been for my own good. And perhaps, no matter how I
think I love Edward now, I will be sorry if I do not heed
their warnings.

The butler came in some time later, to ask if she
thought he should hold dinner. She shook her head. "I
do not know when the viscount or Miss Willoughby will
return, Durfee," she told him. "I do not think they will
care to eat now, nor do I."

The elderly butler's lined face showed his concern.
"The doctor has just come, Miss Lancaster," he told
her as he straightened Lady Gloriana's chair and bent to

pick up the napkin and jug of water that Merry had used. "He is with Lady Gloriana now."

"Where is the viscount?" Merry asked, rising and smoothing her skirts.

"He is waiting for word in the library. Miss Jane remains with her mother," Durfee told her.

"I must go to him," Merry said. "He should not be alone now."

As she walked to the door of the dining room, Durfee said, his voice sad, "We, the staff, are all so sorry, Miss Lancaster. We were looking forward to seeing you installed as viscountess here, in the near future."

Merry's eyes filled with tears, remembering how Durfee had always been such a staunch conspirator of theirs. She made herself thank him before she went to Edward, to wait for word of his mother's condition and comfort him as best she could.

The doctor did not join them for half an hour—half an hour that Edward spent pacing the floor, and Merry tried to think of things to talk about, to distract him. Since there didn't seem to be a single suitable topic of conversation that would not be considered frivolous under the circumstances, she soon fell silent.

But when she saw him bow his head for a moment and clench his fists at his side, she went to him and put her arms around him. "Edward, my dear," she whispered. "I know what you are going through . . . Ah, I feel for you so! We must pray Lady Gloriana is all right, pray that she will make a complete recovery."

His arms came around her hard, and he buried his face in her hair. "Thank God you are here, Merry," he said. "I could not have borne this without you."

"Has your mother ever had a spell like this before, my dear?" she asked, smoothing his dark hair and feeling a stab as the dark curls twisted around her fingers the way they always did.

"No, and that is what is so very worrying," he said. There was a slight pause before he added, "Merry, do you think it was caused because I insisted on our

marriage taking place as planned? For if I was the one
to blame for it, I shall never forgive myself!''

His voice sounded despairing, and Merry's arms
tightened. ''You must not think that, Edward,'' she told
him. ''No, no, such things cannot be! I am sure it was
just a sudden indisposition, for her breathing was
normal even in her faint. You must remember she has
had a severe shock today. If anything caused this, it had
to have been that cold, factual letter from her brother-
in-law. I wondered, when you read it to me, that he
could be so dry, so unaffectionate. But perhaps that is
his nature?''

Edward drew away and frowned in thought. ''I seem
to remember Uncle Henry as a quiet man of few
words,'' he said slowly. ''But you are right. The letter
was cold, wasn't it?''

Before Merry could reply, the doctor knocked and
entered the room. Edward spun around.

''How is my mother?'' he asked, forgetting to offer
the man a chair in his haste to learn the news.

''She is fine, m'lord,'' Dr. Redding said. He was an
older man with only a fringe of white hair left. Merry
saw that his ruddy countryman's face was easy, and she
drew a deep breath of pure relief.

''There is no sign of any heart disease, or permanent
damage, so you may be calm. I have left her some
sedatives, and she is sleeping now. She agreed to my
suggestion of bed rest for a few days.''

''She came to herself, then? You spoke to her?''
Edward asked eagerly.

The doctor twinkled at him as he rocked on his heels.
''Indeed she did, sir! So much herself that she begged
me to tell you that she was sorry.''

''Sorry?'' both Merry and Edward echoed.

''Why, yes. She said it was very important that you
know at once that she thinks she was wrong about your
marriage. Oh, allow me to wish you happy, Miss
Lancaster, m'lord,'' he added, bowing.

''But we can hardly marry on Saturday now, with
Maman confined to her bed,'' Edward muttered.

"Well, the lady said nothing about Saturday, sir," Dr. Redding told him. "But she made me promise to tell you that she has no objection to a Christmas wedding, for that is half a year of mourning, and although it is not quite correct, she says she is sure you can all of you together brazen it through. I cannot remember all her words, but she said something about how stunning crimson velvet would be. Lady's talk, m'lord."

When she saw Edward nod in agreement as the doctor chuckled, Merry's heart sank. Then her eyes went up to the lofty ceiling above her. So, you have won after all, haven't you, Lady Gloriana? she thought. And so much can happen in six months, can't it?

When the doctor had taken his leave, after a glass of Edward's best madeira and a good many more reassuring words about the viscountess's condition, Merry excused herself almost at once. She said she had no appetite for the supper Edward said he would ask the servants to bring them, and she knew she could not sit and talk about the delay of their wedding, not until she had time to think, alone.

For a moment she thought Edward might protest, and she was glad when Jane came in, smiling and nodding, and he let her go.

When Merry came down to breakfast the following morning, she found Edward and Jane before her. Her fiancé welcomed her with such a broad smile and fervent kiss that it was almost unnecessary for her to inquire how the viscountess had passed the night.

"Well, I have always said *Maman* was as strong as a wire," Jane remarked as she stirred her coffee. "The main problem now will be to convince her that she must stay in bed."

As the viscount reached for the marmalade, Merry noticed for the first time, the broad black band high on his right sleeve. She was not at all surprised to see it.

"I agree," he was saying now. "However, I shall insist on it. We want no repeat of last night, and until

Doctor Redding is completely sure there will be no danger of it, *Maman* must follow orders.''

Merry made herself eat a spoonful or two of eggs, a bite of toast, although she was not a bit hungry and didn't feel she would ever be hungry again. As Jane and Edward discussed estate matters, she reviewed the decision she had reached late last night. It was almost as if she were trying to find a flaw in it, something that would keep her from announcing it. But nothing came to mind. And nothing will, she told herself. You know it is the only thing you can do.

At the first lull in the conversation, she said, "I have been thinking, Edward. About the situation here, your mother's illness, and the long mourning period. I believe it would be best if I went back to Bath now."

The viscount spun around to stare at her. "What?" he asked, his voice incredulous. "Go back to Bath? Whatever for?"

She made herself smile a little. "You know I cannot stay here for that length of time," she said. "It would not be right. A short visit is acceptable, but six months? No, no! And Great-aunt Elizabeth will be delighted to see me again, I am sure."

"I am sure she would," Edward told her. "But I would not be delighted to see you go."

Merry looked away from his grim face, to add sugar to her coffee. "But I myself would prefer it, Edward," she told him. "And I know when Great-aunt learns of the delay of our wedding, she will insist on it anyway. My remaining here is not seemly."

Before the viscount could reply, Jane rose from the table. "I must ask to be excused," she said. "Surely it would be better for you to discuss this alone. But Merry, you know I am always there, if you want to talk to me."

Merry murmured her thanks, and Jane nodded. She looked confused and a little uneasy, and as she shut the door behind her and left them alone, she wondered what Merry's real reason was for this sudden, startling decision.

Her brother was having similar thoughts. "And now

perhaps you would be so good as to tell me why you really plan to go to Bath, Merry?'' he asked. ''I was not at all taken in by that Banbury tale you just told me.''

Merry made herself look back at him steadily. ''It is as I said, Edward. I cannot remain here for such a space of time.''

''Did you make this decision because *Maman* thinks to make us wait till Christmas?'' he persisted. ''For if that is the reason, let me tell you I am very sure that we shall be married long before that. As soon as *Maman* is well again, I intend to set a new date.''

''But then there will be something else, some other pressing reason why we must delay,'' Merry said before she thought. Quickly, before he could catch her up on it, she went on, ''My mind is made up. I have already set Nora to packing. I intend to leave early tomorrow. Perhaps you would be so good as to arrange the hire of a carriage for me? I am not sure where I should go to find one, in Trumbull Village.''

''If you go anywhere, you travel in my carriage, of course. And a groom will go ahead to apprise your great-aunt of your arrival,'' the viscount replied. Then he rose and came to draw her to her feet. ''What is it, Merry? What is it really?'' As he spoke, he put his hands on her shoulders and shook her a little. ''This is your Edward, remember? You can tell me!''

His handsome face was so close to hers that she could smell the lotion he used, even see where his valet had nicked his chin a little that morning, shaving him. For one mad moment, she thought of telling him the truth, but cold common sense stopped her just in time. What good would it do to destroy his love for his mother, especially since she herself was having second thoughts about taking a rake to husband, no matter how much she loved him?

''I find I need some time to think, Edward,'' she made herself say instead. ''I am troubled, confused, and I do not want to marry you feeling this way. Let me go back to Bath for a while, and then we will see.''

He moved closer, as if to kiss her, and she stepped

back. For a second, she thought she would cry at the
bleak disbelief and disappointment on his face. She had
never refused his embrace before.

"Please let me go now," she whispered, her throat
dry. "I must help Nora with the packing."

Edward nodded, but he didn't say a word as she
curtsied and turned to leave. Even after she shut the
door to the breakfast room behind her, Merry could feel
his piercing eyes on her back, and she had to lean
against that door for a moment to calm her rapidly
beating heart. How very difficult that had been! How
painful!

The viscount took his seat again, but he made no
move to finish his breakfast. When Durfee came in,
bearing the post, he waved him away. He was still sitting
there when Jane came back some time later, and at the
expression on his face, his sister could hardly restrain a
gasp.

"What is it, Teddy?" she asked, sitting down beside
him in Merry's empty chair and taking his hand in hers.
"What was Merry's explanation?"

"She would not tell me her real reason for wanting to
leave," he said. "She only repeated that she had to, that
it was not seemly for her to remain." He made an
impatient gesture. "*Seemly*, Jane!"

He rose then and went to the window. Jane stared at
his cold, set profile silhouetted so clearly in the warm
sunlight, and her heart went out to him.

"Perhaps if I speak to her?" she asked a little shyly.
"Merry is my good friend now. She might tell me.
Besides, I think I know what the trouble is." As her
brother turned to stare at her, she added, "Oh, it is
nothing I can talk about, just some vague suspicions I
have, have had for some time. But if she is still determined to return to Bath, Teddy, you will have to let her
go."

"I know," he said quietly. Then his face brightened.
"Jane, if she does not relent, would you go with her? I
would feel so much better knowing you were there,
watching over her." He paused and frowned then. "Of

course, I do not know if *Maman* will like having you away on a visit just now.''

As Jane rose, he saw she was smiling. ''But *Maman* has the faithful Farewell, Teddy. I am just in her way in the sickroom. I think you have had a splendid idea, and it will be such an adventure for me! You know I have never gone anywhere except with you or *Maman*.''

Her brother had to smile at her excitement. ''Bath is hardly a place frought with excitement or intrigue, my dear. And I doubt you will have many adventures there, swathed as you are in black.''

Jane tossed her head. ''We shall see,'' she said. ''Now I must leave you, Teddy. I must tell *Maman* our plan, after, that is, I ask Merry if she would care for my company. And then there is the packing to see to and a special letter I want to write.''

As she spoke, she colored up a little, but the viscount did not notice, for he was thinking hard. ''Jane, whatever you do, do not tell Merry that this was all my idea. Let her think that you, and you alone, thought of it.''

''Of course, Teddy,'' Jane agreed as she hurried to the door.

The viscount followed her in short order, to repair to the library and his neglected post. He felt a little better, knowing the two girls would be traveling together. And trust Jane to keep the memory of him green and eventually find out why Merry was behaving this way, he thought.

Merry was confused and not best pleased when Jane told her of the scheme.

Seeing the little frown between her brows, Jane said, ''Oh, do say that I may come, Merry! I have longed to see Bath ever since you told me about it. But stay! Perhaps your great-aunt would not like me to visit? Perhaps she does not have enough room for me?''

Merry shook her head. ''Great-aunt will be delighted to welcome you, I am sure, and she has room for any number of guests,'' she said.

Jane waited quietly, and then she added, ''Very well, Jane, if you think you would care for it.''

That Merry's reply was less than gracious bothered Jane not a whit, and she kissed her before she went to tell her mother.

Lady Gloriana seemed neither surprised nor disappointed to learn that Merry was leaving Trumbull Hall, but she did pout a little when apprised of Jane's plan to go with her. "So, you would leave me now, when I am ill, Tiny?" she asked. "I wonder how I am to take that."

"Now, *Maman*, you know I am only in the way here. And neither Teddy nor I like to have Merry traveling alone. Besides, I have never seen Bath. I quite look forward to it."

With her eyes lowered, Lady Gloriana pleated the satin coverlet on her bed. Jane held her breath until she said, "Very well. Come to think on it, it might be a very good idea for you to leave Hampshire for a while. And while you are gone, Tiny, I want you to ponder long and hard about what you have been doing, the course you have set for yourself. I believe you know what I mean."

Jane nodded, and she did not look away from her mother's serious face, although she did not trust herself to speak.

Merry was able to avoid Edward all day, by remaining in her room, supposedly packing. But of course they met at dinner, and although Jane was there as well, she was quick to excuse herself and leave her brother and his fiancée alone soon afterward.

The viscount took Merry in his arms even before the door of the drawing room closed behind her. His kiss was gentle and tender, and Merry could not resist returning it, her arms going around him in turn. But when his kiss deepened and grew more insistent and passionate, she put her hands on his chest and pushed him away.

"Please, Edward," she pleaded. "All this is hard enough, believe me."

"You still insist on leaving, Merry?" he asked. "You will not tell me what is troubling you?"

"I cannot. You must not ask," Merry whispered.

His face grew cold. "I remember a time when we told each other everything, a time when there were no walls between us, not an unsuitable subject in the world that we could not discuss freely and openly. How sad that that time is no more!"

He paused and waited, but when she only shook her head, her eyes lowered, he went on, "Will you at least write to me? I will be writing to you almost constantly, trying to get you to change your mind, come back to me."

"Yes, I will write," Merry promised. "But now I must ask to be excused. As you know, we are leaving very early in the morning. I must get some sleep."

The viscount nodded reluctantly, but as she curtsied, he said, "You do intend to see *Maman* before you go, don't you, Merry? She has been asking for you, and I know she is wondering why you have not visited her today, to see how she did."

"I shall go in tomorrow just before I leave, to say good-bye," Merry told him over her shoulder. She was glad she had her back turned, so he would not see the revulsion she was sure showed on her face for such a disagreeable chore.

True to her word, Merry went to the viscountess's rooms the next morning. She was glad to meet Jane on the same errand in the hall, so she would not be alone with Edward's mother again in her rose-colored retreat. Together, they went in and found the lady in bed, reclining on a number of lace-edged pillows. Merry thought that, outside of a faint pallor, she looked as well as she ever had.

"I have come to bid you good-bye, ma'am," she said as she curtsied. "And to thank you for your hospitality, and all your—your kindness."

"Pooh!" the viscountess said, waving an airy hand. "It was nothing, and I enjoyed doing it, darling Merry. I am so sorry you must leave us, that circumstances were such . . ." Her voice died away as she peered into Merry's composed, expressionless face. Then she held out an imploring hand. "However, I quite understand your reason, and I am sure it is all for the best. You may rest easy knowing I will keep Teddy safe for you, until your Christmas wedding, dear girl.''

Merry was glad when Jane spoke up then, from the other side of the bed. "As to that, we must wait and see, *Maman*. I am sure Teddy has no intention of waiting such a length of time, and it is his decision, his and Merry's, of course.''

What Lady Gloriana might have said in reply was not heard, for Miss Farewell came in then to tell them the carriage was waiting and all the baggage strapped on.

Merry was quick to curtsy, but she was not to escape so easily. "Do come and kiss me good-bye, dearest Merry,'' the viscountess begged, holding her arms wide.

Merry could not restrain a little step backward. "I do not think I had better, ma'am,'' she forced herself to say. "I—I feel a cold coming on, and in your condition—''

"Heavens, no!'' Lady Gloriana exclaimed, shrinking back against her pillows. "I shall let you go at once. Ah, darling Tiny, how I shall miss you! Do not stay away too long, if you please.''

Merry left the two embracing. When she reached the hall, she leaned against the wall there to wait for Jane. She knew Edward was waiting for her below, and she wanted no repeat of last night's scene. Much better to say good-bye with Jane beside her.

She was surprised when she saw Miss Farewell come out of the adjoining dressing room and pause to stare at her. Then the maid said in a deep, gruff voice, "If you go, you'll lose him, miss. She'll win.''

It was not the unusual sound of her voice but her words that made Merry start a little. She put up her chin. "If I do, Viscount Trumbull is not the man I thought he was, nor the man I want,'' she said, her quiet voice steady.

Miss Farewell seemed about to say something more, but then she nodded and shrugged. A moment later, Jane came out, and she turned away.

"Quickly, Merry, quickly!'' Jane whispered, taking

her arm and hurrying her toward the stairs. "I am so afraid *Maman* will think of something to keep me here, and I could not bear it."

Edward was waiting to escort them both to the carriage. Merry thought him pale this morning, and stern, for he did not smile and his eyes never left her face as she said good-bye to Durfee and Mrs. Wilkie.

The two maids were already seated in the carriage, and after a fervent kiss and a hug, Jane climbed in to join them, and allow her brother a moment alone with Merry.

Completely ignoring the interested house servants, the coachman, and the grooms, the viscount took her in his arms as if they were all alone. "I shall never understand this, Merry," he told her. "But perhaps you will tell me about it someday. Oh, not that social gibble-gabble you have been mouthing, but the real reason. Remember I love you, that I will always love you. And remember that I will be waiting for word that I may come to you. You have only to send a message, you know."

Merry nodded, her eyes searching his face. Perhaps she would never see Edward Willoughby again, and she wanted to impress the memory of those handsome features on her mind. She saw a little muscle moving in his cheek as he returned her gaze before he bent his head and kissed her, long and hard. Merry closed her eyes and prayed she would not weaken. But of course she could not do that. Everything was over and done, the baggage loaded and her farewells said. By her own choice, she was for Bath.

When she was settled in the carriage, she turned for one last look at him where he stood on the steps. Then her eyes went up the granite walls of Trumbull. Somehow, she was not at all surprised to see Lady Gloriana holding back the sheer curtains at one of the windows of her bedroom. The tiny, elegant lady smiled down at her and blew her a kiss before she waved a fervent good-bye. Sick at heart, Merry turned away.

13

ABOUT a week after Merry left for Bath, the viscount spent an evening alone in his library. His mother had come down to dine with him earlier, for the first time since her heart attack, and he had set himself the task of being charming and talkative, although seldom had he felt less like doing so. But after dinner, he excused himself, claiming a press of estate business. Lady Gloriana frowned a little and shook her head at him, but she did not try to stop him or say anything to him, for which he was grateful. He could not discuss Merry with anyone just yet, not even his mother.

It seemed an age to him since he had kissed Merry good-bye on the steps of Trumbull Hall. He knew she and Jane were in Bath, for the carriage had returned three days ago with a short message from his sister, telling him of their safe arrival. But although he had written to Merry twice since then, there had been no word from her.

He had intended to write to her again this evening, but now he only stared at the blank sheet of hot-pressed paper that lay on the desk before him. What could he say that he had not already said so many times before? And he knew his words would not change her mind. For whatever reason she had decided on the course she had chosen, it was clear she was determined to pursue it.

Perhaps he should not have let her go. Perhaps he should have insisted that she remain with him. But how could he have done that? He could hardly have kept her here by force, and that was not how he wanted her. No, he wanted her here because she could not live anywhere else, without him.

If he only understood why she had gone! What had happened, what had changed, to make her so distant, so unlike the Merry he had come to know and love? And why couldn't she tell him her reasons?

He sat very still for a moment, deep in thought. Then he picked up his pen and pulled the paper closer. He would not write to her tonight. Instead, he would review these past weeks, try to discover some clue to her present, unfathomable behavior.

He cast his mind back to their meeting in Bath, their whirlwind courtship, and he smiled a little at his memories. No, the trouble did not lie in Bath. They had been happy there, so happy he had felt blessed. And he knew Merry had been happy, too, for look how quickly she had agreed to marry him and come to London with him.

London. Frowning again now, he wrote the name at the top of the sheet. It was there in town that all the trouble had started. He drew a line down two-thirds of the way across the paper and began to take notes. It was well over an hour later that he sat back and rubbed his eyes before he read over his impressions. As he did so, his frowned deepened. Surely it could only be a coincidence that one name appeared in the right-hand column next to every misfortune they had ever had?

The delay of their engagement, Merry's new haircut, the dye the hairdresser had used; the unsuitable, flashy clothes; the attentions of other men; other parties, other friends; Merry's sudden tardiness to appointments, the way she had grown so quiet and subdued, her reluctance to see him alone anymore . . .

His eyes ran down the right-hand column. No, there was no mistake. It had been his mother who had been responsible for each and every problem he and Merry had had from their arrival in London right through her stay here in Trumbull Hall.

The viscount rose so quickly that he almost upset his chair. He did not want to believe that *Maman* had been devious, he couldn't ! Yet still his mind remembered other instances of her interference, all done under the guise of being helpful, loving, concerned. He remembered how quick she had been to stop him from announcing his engagement as he had wished, her delay in coming to Hampshire, how she had tried to put off the wedding once she was here, even how she had suggested he cry off only a week ago.

But *Maman* had not known her sister was going to die, he told himself as he read over the last sheet. No, that was truly a coincidence. But then, when he had refused to observe a full year of mourning, there had been that heart attack.

Edward stared into space. Had she really suffered such an attack, or had it all been just an act? He shook his head, completely baffled. He would see the doctor tomorrow, question him in more detail.

There was someone else he could question, too. He was well aware that Nanny Drew did not like Lady Gloriana, although he had never thought to question why that should be so. Instead, he had taken his mother's word that nannies seldom care for the mothers of their charges.

The viscount went and poured himself a brandy, and he was not at all surprised to see that his hand was shaking a little. This was terrible, horrible! As he twirled the golden liqueur in the large glass, he tried to think of some way to disprove his theory. Surely, he must be losing his mind, to have such awful suspicions about his own dear mother!

But when he sat down beside the small fire Durfee had lit to take the chill off the evening, he remembered how Merry had kept to her room for an entire day after her interview with the viscountess. Could it be that she had not been ill as she had claimed? Had *Maman* said something to her that had distressed her to the point she could not bear to see him? He recalled Nora coming down the stairs with the roses he had sent to Merry, and how, when he questioned her, the maid had said the scent was too strong for her mistress. But Merry had never refused his flowers before, and why would one bouquet bother her when she had made no demur at the dozens he had had placed in her room in London the day they had announced their engagement at last?

He sipped his brandy, to steady himself. There was another thing, too. The morning Merry had revealed her plan to return to Bath, and he had told her they would not have to wait an entire year to marry, she had blurted something out and then, quickly, gone on to speak of other things. He had taken no special note of it at the time, for he had been upset, but he remembered it now. What were her exact words? Ah, yes! "But then there will be something else, some other pressing reason we must delay."

Of course she must have meant *Maman*. He wondered how long she had known the lady's true colors? He shook his head. It was all so very clear now. And because it was his mother, and she knew how he revered her, she could not tell him what was troubling her. It was the *only* thing he could think of that she would *not* be able to discuss with him openly, and it was this realization that convinced him of his mother's guilt at last.

And all this time, Merry must have been waiting for him to see his mother's true nature for himself. How frustrating for her, how agonizing it must have been. And he had been so obtuse, so blind!

He ran a hand through his black curls, in that familiar gesture. Surely it was inexcusable that he had not seen through the lady long before this. And yet . . . and yet, she *was* his mother. He had loved her all his life. For her gaiety, her kindness, her constant admiration of him, her loving, wonderful caring. How would he have been able to suspect such a lovely paragon of treachery? Yet, coldly, his brain reminded him that his mother had known how much he loved Merry, how important she was to his future. And she had done this terrible thing anyway. *Why*?

Suddenly he remembered Jason Willoughby. He would write to him, ask him to call. He had often wondered why Jason did not like his mother. Now he would force him to reveal why this should be so.

The following morning, he sent a groom with a message to his cousin before he went out for an early-morning ride. As he cantered down the drive, he wished he were setting out for Bath right now, but he knew he must see the viscountess first and hear her side of the story before he did so.

He rode home by way of the village, but Nanny Drew's cottage was empty. A neighbor told him she had gone to Basingstoke for a few days, to shop, and his frown deepened as he made his way to Dr. Redding's dispensary.

The doctor had little more he could tell him about his mother's condition. He said he could see no sign of damage, and so he had given the lady permission to resume her normal life, since she seemed so well. Indeed, he claimed he had been completely dumbfounded that a woman in such excellent health for her age could have suffered such an attack.

There was no way the viscount could think of to ask the doctor if this particular attack might have been just a pretense. But as he rode home later, he knew it was entirely possible. Why, who would be able to tell?

On arriving at the hall, he discovered that Jason was in Basingstoke too, and he was not expected to return until tomorrow. He had seldom felt more frustrated.

Later, he realized that all this probing was not at all fair to his mother. He should not go behind her back, no matter what she had done. What he should do—would do—was confront her himself. He was repulsed just thinking of such a meeting, but he knew there was no escape from it. He must have the truth.

Accordingly, he asked Lady Gloriana to join him in the library after dinner, and he told his butler that they were not to be disturbed. This evening she was wearing a high-necked black silk gown, and even in her mourning, she looked as beautiful as ever, and impossibly young. The viscount watched her as she came in and took her seat. How was it possible for such a lovely woman to be so evil? he wondered.

"Darling Teddy, don't stare at me so!" she scolded as

she arranged her skirts. "You are looking at me as if you had never seen me before in your life."

Before he could reply that perhaps he had not, she went on, "However, I am glad to have this opportunity to speak to you, my dear. I was about to request a private interview myself. You have been such a terrible grouch lately, Teddy, and it is not at all becoming. You really must strive for a little more conduct. Yes, yes, I know that you are missing Merry, and that this is a sad time for you. But you have my word that you will recover, my darling. And although my heart goes out to you in your disappointment and distress, how much better it is that you discovered her true nature before you married her. It is clear now that she never loved you as she should."

"Didn't she, *Maman*?" he asked. "How do you know that?"

Lady Gloriana opened her blue eyes very wide. "Why, it is as plain as the nose on your face, Teddy! Once she knew she must wait such a time, she lost all interest in marriage and went away. Then too, remember how she changed. It is just as I told you, my dear. Some girls are too hasty, and then they begin to regret their impulsiveness. You have had a lucky escape. And someday, when you find the woman you will truly love, one who loves you in return as you deserve, you will look back on this experience and be grateful for your escape."

"And when will that be, *Maman*?" he asked, never taking his eyes from her face. "In a year? Ten, perhaps? When do you think you will decide it is time for me to marry, and finally agree to it?"

Lady Gloriana looked confused. "But I do not understand you, Teddy. Why, it is nothing at all to do with *me*!"

"No, it is not," he agreed. "Yet somehow, I find you have had everything to do with it, for it was you who caused Merry to go away."

His mother put a little hand to her heart, and he said, "No, there is no need for that. Dr. Redding tells me there is nothing wrong with your heart, and both of us know he is right. And if you think to faint, I want you to understand that I will simply wait for you to come to yourself before I continue."

"Teddy!" she gasped. "Can this be possible? Can I really be hearing these terrible words from my beloved son?"

The viscount rose to pace the room. Over his shoulder, he said, "I wish I had said them weeks ago, ma'am. Merry Lancaster and I were happy and in love, until we came to London. But once we were there, you took as many steps as necessary to estrange us, all under the guise of being helpful."

Now Lady Gloriana rose as well, her hands clenched at her side. "Merry told you all these lies about me, didn't she, Teddy?" she asked in a fierce little voice. "How hateful of her, how devious! I assure you I have never been more mistaken in a young woman! And to think how I began to love her, and all the things I did to help her—"

Her son held up his hand. "Merry did not tell me anything, *Maman*. She has never spoken a single word to your discredit."

"Then it had to be Jason," his mother said quickly. "He has never liked me, never!"

"No, it was not Jason, nor Nanny Drew, either. I was able to figure it out all by myself, and there can be no doubts. For some reason, known only to yourself, you have tried to prevent my marriage to Merry Lancaster. I wish you would tell me why you did such a terrible thing. It is the only thing I do not understand."

He paused and waited, unmoved by the tears he saw in her eyes.

"Very well, darling, I do admit it," she said in a soft little voice. "Oh, not that I was trying to prevent it so much as I was testing you both. I wanted to be sure, you see, that this sudden violent love you both felt was real. And now you see how right I was to do so, for Merry has left you. And if she really loved you, she would not have gone away, no matter what I did, now, would she?''

The viscount ignored her pleading look, her outstretched hands. ''You have interfered in my life quite long enough, madam, but understand that you will do so no longer,'' he said, his voice cold.

His mother sank back into a chair. ''Whatever can you mean, Teddy?'' she asked.

''I am going to Bath tomorrow,'' he said. ''I shall tell Merry what I have told you, and beg her to forgive me for being so blind. Then I will bring her back to Trumbull, and we will be married at once. I order you to beg her pardon most humbly, too, and confess all your faults. And while I am gone, I expect you to remove to the dower house immediately.''

''But I cannot do that! You know it is not ready,'' she argued.

''I said 'immediately,' and that is what I meant, *Maman*,'' he told her, his voice implacable. ''There will be no more occasions for you to make mischief in the hall. This is Merry's home from now on, not yours.''

''And, of course, mourning your dear aunt does not matter to you at all,'' his mother said bitterly. ''Are you so lost to decency that you would forget what you owe her?''

''I have explained before what I intend to do,'' he said. ''Perhaps if I had ever known my aunt, I might feel more regret at her death. But I did not know her. I think I only saw her a few times in my life, many years ago. And why was that, *Maman*? If she was your dear sister, why did you never meet?''

Lady Gloriana sniffed. ''That was all her husband's fault,'' she said crossly. ''For some reason, Henry doesn't like me, and he poisoned her mind against me . . .''

''There seem to be a great number of people who do not like you, isn't that so?'' the viscount remarked. ''I wonder I never noticed it before.''

Lady Gloriana rose then and tilted her chin at him. ''I

have no intention of sitting here and listening to your insults, Teddy," she said. "It is obvious to me that you have gone mad! But because of my great love for you, I will try to forgive you for the awful things you have said, accused me of. But you will regret the move you are about to make, just see if you don't!"

She sobbed as she turned and went swiftly to the door, skipping a little as she was wont to do when she was in a hurry.

Edward watched her, his eyes bleak. As she put her hand on the doorknob, he said, "I shall never regret marrying Merry, ma'am. I only regret that I am bringing her into a family that is so divided, so unhappy. And I do not ask your forgiveness; I see no need for it when I was simply telling you the truth. Instead, I will try to forgive you. Perhaps in time, I will be able to do so. For now, I think it best if we do not see each other for quite some time. Good-bye, madam."

Lady Gloriana's only response was to slam the library doors behind her.

Viscount Trumbull was on the road to Bath early the next morning. Right after his mother had left him, he had given his butler and housekeeper orders for Lady Gloriana's removal to the dower house, saying he expected her to be in residence there when he returned in a few days' time. Then he had ordered his tilbury and fastest team for eight in the morning, and had his valet pack him a few essentials in a portmanteau.

As he tooled the team through the stark and lovely Salisbury Plain, his heavy heart began to lighten. It was as if in leaving his mother behind, he was truly separating himself from her and her influence on him. Besides, every mile brought him closer to his Merry. It was no wonder he felt so much easier as the hours went by, he thought.

He had almost reached Trowbridge late in the afternoon when he heard hooves thundering behind him. A moment later, he glanced left to see his cousin Jason keeping pace with him astride a huge black gelding. At his signal, Edward pulled his team to a halt.

Jason nodded to him. "I came as soon as I could, halfling," he said. "I am sorry I did not get Jane's letter until my return from Basingstoke, or I would have been with you sooner."

"Jane wrote to you?" the viscount asked a little bemused.

"Yes, to tell me of her trip to Bath with Merry. It was then I realized that I must speak to you. I have not done so all these years, because, well . . ."

He paused and the viscount said, "There is no need to pull any punches with me, cousin. Finally, I have discovered my mother's perfidy for myself."

Jason looked around the lonely plain. "Well, we could discuss it here, but let us make for some more comfortable location. Where did you intend to put up tonight?"

"Nowhere. I meant to go straight on to Bath, no matter how late I arrived," the viscount told him.

"Well, you can't call on Merry at midnight," Jason said curtly. "Break your journey in Trowbridge, cousin! We will be able to talk there, and then when you do see Merry, you will understand everything, and it will be easier for both of you."

The viscount nodded. "Very well, lead on," he said.

The two cousins stopped at The Fox and Grapes on the outskirts of Trowbridge. Two bedchambers and a private parlor were bespoke, and dinner ordered. It was only after this repast had been consumed and another bottle of wine broached that Jason Willoughby began his tale.

"But first, I must have your promise that you will hear me out, Edward," he warned. "Furthermore, no matter what I say, nor how you think your mother is being maligned, know that I don't intend to arrive in Bath sporting a broken nose, a black eye, or a mouthful of loose teeth. You may be shorter than I am, halfling, but you are much quicker, and I have seen your prowess at Gentleman Jackson's often enough not to risk it. Are we agreed?''

His cousin promised he would have a care for Jason's rugged face as he poured them both another glass of port.

"Well, I discovered the kind of woman your mother is from my father," Jason began. "Not directly, mind you. Oh, no, my father would not tell his son anything of that nature! But he kept a journal, and I found it when I was going through his papers after his death. In it I discovered why my mother is so often ill, why she suffers from fits of depression. You see, my father thought he was in love with your mother. From what I read, I gather she gave him good reason to believe that she returned his regard."

Edward Willoughby started up and would have risen, except his cousin held him in his seat with a large hand while he reminded him of his promise.

"But she did not care for him at all," Jason went on as the viscount settled back in his chair. "She was only toying with him, trying to make him an admirer of hers, one of her flirts. My mother found out about the whole thing, late in one of her pregnancies, and quite by accident. She has never been well since. You see, she loved my father, and she had been sure he loved her the same way. When she discovered he did not, she grew more and more despondent, suffered ever more recurring spells of bad health, for she felt her life was ruined. The fact that my father continued to bed her, and produce even more children, only made it worse. And when three of those babies died in infancy, it was too much for one in such fragile mental health." Jason paused for a moment before he added, "You must know she only told me all this when I taxed her with it later, thinking it might help if she shared it with me."

The viscount waited, a deep frown on his face as his cousin sipped his port.

"I have hated the lovely Lady Gloriana ever since that time," Jason remarked conversationally. "Perhaps I would not have, if she had been in love with him, too.

These things do happen, as we both know. But she was not in love at all. She did not want a lover . . . any lover. Your mother just wanted to be placed on a pedestal and worshiped from afar. And to gain her ends, she ruined a decent marriage without a single regret."

Jason shook his head and grimaced, and then he stared straight across the table at his cousin. "There are women like that, Edward," he said. "They are like queen bees. Everything, everyone in their sphere of influence—their 'hive' if you like—must revolve around them, for they are completely selfish. They expect adoration and instant obedience. And woe betide anyone who tries to cross them, for they have absolutely no hesitation in stinging!

"But know I do not excuse my father, Edward. He was a weak man and as such, greatly to blame himself. And when I think of what he did to my mother, that gay and lovely woman, I . . . I . . ."

He paused and rose to turn his back for a moment, his shoulders squared and his hands forming large fists at his side. The viscount waited patiently.

At last Jason took his seat again and went on, "My father was not the only man your mother went after. Even her own sister's husband was not safe. In my father's journal there was an account of quite a party at Trumbull Hall, and how your Aunt Jane and her husband left at dawn the next day, vowing never to return. And as you are well aware, there have been others over the years, any number of them, culminating in the young and foolish—and late—Reggie Horton. I am sure he will not be the last."

"But even so, why would *Maman* try to stop me from marrying Merry?" the viscount asked, sounding perplexed and pained. "I am her *son*, not one of her beaux."

"Think, Edward, think!" Jason told him. "By falling in love with another woman, you replaced your mother as the most important woman in your life. The Queen Bee would not like that, no, not at all. Furthermore, she could not like becoming a dowager viscountess, living in the dower house, deferring to another woman, and a younger one too! You know what store she sets on her youthful looks! They are an obsession with her. And as long as you and Jane are unmarried, she can pretend you are still children, for it makes her seem younger.''

He finished his port and poured another glass. "Talking is thirsty work," he remarked as he did so.

"This is all so difficult to take in," Edward said, moving his own glass in an aimless little circle on the table. "It is like discovering I have loved a phantom all these years, someone who did not even exist."

Jason squeezed his shoulder roughly. "You will soon forget her in your Merry's arms, my friend," he said.

A moment later, he rose to go and lean against the mantel and say, "I don't think you ever realized it, but about five years ago, your sister and I were in a fair way of falling in love ourselves. Your mother took care of that, however, and in short order, too."

"How do you know this?" Edward asked. "Did Jane tell you?"

"No, she didn't have to. Suddenly, Jane would not see me, and we never met by chance anymore, nor was I ever invited to the hall. And then Lady Gloriana took her off to London. Haven't you ever wondered why Jane put on all that flesh? Why she has not seemed as happy as she used to be when she was a little girl?"

The viscount shook his head. "How very unseeing I have been," he said. "Did *Maman* do that because she could not bear to lose her faithful, admiring daughter?"

Jason nodded. "Yes, and I imagine, to prevent the dire possibility of becoming a grandmother. How that would destroy her image! And she had only to look at me, and all my brothers and sisters, to realize that the male branch of our side of the Willoughby family was, er, shall we say, not only virile but prolific as well?"

"Do try not to brag about your unfulfilled accomplishments, Jason," Edward said wryly.

Jason's eyes lit up at the jest, and he chuckled a little in relief. "Shall we have a contest, Edward?" he asked.

"I am even prepared to accept the challenge, although you will have a head start."

The viscount's faint smile faded. "Only if I can convince Merry that all will be well now," he said.

"I am sure you will have no trouble at all," his cousin told him. "Merry Lancaster loves you, my boy. You are a lucky man. At the *al fresco* dance, she thanked me for all my hints—by the way, you should know I had been trying to put her on her guard, for she was in danger of becoming another adoring handmaiden of your dear *Maman*'s—and she asked me if marrying you would solve the problem. I assured her that it would, for there would be nothing further that Lady Gloriana could do."

He frowned then. "But I do not understand why she decided to give you up and go back to Bath. It could not have been just the mourning period that Jane mentioned. I know Merry would wait for you no matter how long it took."

"I do not understand that, either," the viscount admitted. "But I agree with you. There had to be something neither one of us has discovered. But perhaps Jane has been able to find out."

"No matter," Jason said carelessly. "You can ask Merry her reasons tomorrow."

The viscount rose and stretched. "You remind me that I must get some sleep. I plan to leave early."

His cousin would have made a jesting remark then, but Edward forestalled it by holding out his hand to him and saying earnestly, "Thank you for coming after me and telling me what you did, Jason. I know the story of my mother's true nature is safe with you. I also know how difficult it must have been for you to keep it a secret all these years, especially since in effect she ruined your own mother's life. I—I appreciate it."

Jason threw a casual arm around his shoulder as they walked to the door. "Think nothing of it, halfling," he said. "But know that I do believe I will be asking quite a favor of you in return, and very shortly, too. Indeed, you may count on it."

* * *

Back at Trumbull Hall, Lady Gloriana Willoughby was lying on her stomach nude, on a bed in one of the guest rooms. Her own suite of furniture had been removed to the dower house earlier, but she was determined not to quit the hall until everything was in order to receive her, and so she had told Durfee when he had relayed the viscount's orders. However, even with all the upset, she had no intention of forgetting her usual routine. She had done her exercises and tried to meditate, although this afternoon, that had hardly been a success.

The faithful Miss Farewell had arrived a few minutes ago, but the viscountess was still so distraught, she could not relax, even now that her maid was giving her the usual soothing massage.

"I would never have believed that Teddy could be so cruel to me, Farewell," she was saying now. "If you could have heard half the things he said to me . . . Well, you would have been sure your ears were deceiving you. My darling, loving Teddy! That awful girl has bewitched him!"

"Indeed, madam," Farewell replied in her gruff voice. Then she added rather tartly, "Do try to relax, m'lady. Your muscles are so tense I cannot help you."

Her mistress sighed and tried to comply as she added, "And then to insist on my removing to the dower house, and announcing his immediate marriage to that—that creature!

"Oh, Farewell, Farewell," she wailed, suddenly pounding her pillow in frustration. "I *won't* be a dowager viscountess, I *won't*."

"I see no reason why you should be, m'lady," Miss Farewell said as she rubbed a little more fragrant oil between her palms.

Lady Gloriana twisted and sat up, clutching a towel around her. "Whatever do you mean?" she demanded. "If Teddy marries—and I hardly think there is another thing I can do to prevent it—then it is as good as a *fait accompli*. You make no sense at all, you stupid thing!"

"But you are a dowager viscountess only as long as you remain unwed yourself, m'lady," her maid reminded her. As the viscountess's eyes began to glow, she added dryly, "It is only a matter of deciding whether you would rather be Mrs. Brethers, or the Marchioness of Saterly."

"Oh, but a marchioness, of course!" Lady Gloriana crowed, bouncing a little on the bed in her excitement. "And I will outrank a lowly viscountess that way, too, won't I? That nasty Merry will have to curtsy to *me*, give *me* preference in affairs of state. How very splendid! And I shall give her the cut direct if she ever dares to approach me, you may be sure of that!"

She thought for a moment before she stretched out again on her stomach. "Of course, it is a shame that Nigel Brethers is not the peer. He is so very wealthy, you know, and his estate is outstanding. Then, too, he is tall. I do so dislike standing beside the marquess, for I think we look like dwarfs together, and people are laughing at us."

"They would never dare to laugh at you, m'lady," Farewell told her. And knowing you, I don't believe you will make a habit of standing beside him very often, she thought to herself as she began to rub the oil into that satiny back. As she did so, she noticed how puckered Lady Gloriana's elbows were becoming, and she smiled grimly to herself.

"I wonder if I should write to Jeremy, or just arrive in town unannounced," Lady Gloriana mused.

"Oh, much better to surprise him, ma'am," Miss Farewell advised. "Then, too, you would hardly wish to be here when the happy bridal pair arrives, now, would you?"

Lady Gloriana shook her head. "Most assuredly I would not," she said. "Why, Teddy even insisted I apologize to that *inching* girl, and I absolutely refuse to do so! How fortunate we are all packed for the move. Now we can just order the carriage and be off tomorrow. And I can discard these dreary blacks as well. I will leave a cold letter for Teddy . . . But stay!

No, no, I won't! I will make my letter as loving and tearful as I can, and then he will be sorry he has driven me to this step by being so horrid to me.''

"But what about Miss Jane, ma'am?" her maid asked next as she covered the lady with a soft throw and began to put her creams and oils away.

"Oh, Tiny can stay here with Teddy," Lady Gloriana said carelessly. "She deserted me for that Merry, after all, and even though I was only pretending to be ill, she hurt me badly. And Tiny is defying my express wishes by trying to attach Jason Willoughby again as well. I wash my hands of her, she is so willful, so selfish! I do not see why I should give her another thought, do you?"

"Indeed no, m'lady," Farewell said obediently. She saw that her mistress's eyes were closed at last and that the lady was smiling a little.

She herself grimaced. She did not like Lady Gloriana, she never had. But though she had taken her measure even before she had taken the position ten years earlier, she had not refused it, for the salary was excellent. Now, however, she rather thought she would move on, and she would do so without a single regret. She had gained quite a reputation as a lady's maid who could hold back time, but if she were not mistaken, Lady Gloriana's days of glory were numbered. There was that little sag to her breasts. And the wrinkles forming around her eyes were growing more noticeable. Massage and exercise could only do so much, after all.

Miss Farewell decided she would see about another position as soon as they reached town. The Duchess of Glebes had tried to bribe her away before, and then there was the rich Lady Constance Waverly, who was such a leading beauty. And both of them were years younger than Lady Gloriana Regina Willoughby, who was soon to become the next little Marchioness of Saterly.

Yes, it was definitely time to move on.

14

AFTER she and Jane were in residence at her great-aunt's house in Bath, Merry Lancaster tried to be content as she resumed her former life. Miss Elizabeth Lancaster was not a bit hesitant to inform her her efforts were not at all successful, for the elderly spinster had never believed in mincing her words.

She did not do so, however, until Merry had been in Bath for a week. During that time, the two younger women had explored the town, from the Royal Crescent to the Roman Baths and the Pump Room. Jane had been delighted with everything she saw, and even the steepness of the hills on which Bath was situated could not dampen her good humor. She rode and walked and drove, and begged Merry's advice when she went shopping for new clothes. As she did so, she explained she would not be in mourning forever, and she had always admired Merry's taste. She was kind and cheerful and good, the sister that Merry had always longed she would be. But now, of course, it was too late for that.

During those days, Merry found herself waiting for Jane to ask her the real reason she had left Edward as she had. She was determined to say nothing further about it, for she knew she could not tell Edward's sister the truth either. To her surprise, Jane did not ask for any explanation. Merry was astounded that she was not more curious, that she seemed so happy and content. It was almost as if she knew some delicious secret.

As it turned out, she did confess the truth to Jane in the end, on the evening at dinner when her great-aunt taxed her with her lack of spirits. The butler had poured his mistress her usual glass of port and left the decanter handy before he bowed himself away.

As soon as he left the room, Miss Lancaster began to berate her great-niece and call her a perfect bubblehead. Jane sat quietly and listened. She had liked the old lady on sight, and had come to admire her curt, forthright speech. Miss Lancaster was only of medium height, but her snow-white hair and regal bearing made her seem taller, more commanding. And whenever she spoke, Jane had noticed that everyone listened with the same awed respect they would have accorded royalty.

"And I am sure it is all just a great to-do about nothing," the old lady was grumbling now, fixing Merry with a steely eye. "Yes, yes, I understand all about the viscount's aunt and the mourning period, all the rest of that faradiddle you told me, too. But it is as plain as plain can be that you and Edward Willoughby have agreed to disagree. It is not only that you are so glum, I know he would never have allowed you to return here otherwise. Why did you do so, Meryl? What has happened?"

Merry looked helplessly from her aunt to Jane, trying to keep her face expressionless. She found herself quite unable to speak a word.

"Very well, then, don't tell me," Miss Lancaster said, her voice tart. "But know that if you ever do want to confide in me, my dear Meryl, you have only to say so. And in spite of my single state, you may be assured that I understand the male sex and all their ways very well. Indeed, knowing them as well as I do was the major reason I never married one of 'em."

Jane had been sipping some water during this speech, but at that remark she swallowed the wrong way and choked a little with laughter.

"You find that amusing, Miss Willoughby?" Miss Lancaster asked, the twinkle in her eyes belying her stern words. "But there is no mystery about men, you know. At heart, they are simple creatures, and easily read. And if ever I saw a man in love, one so eager for his wedding, it was your brother. I am astounded he and Meryl were not married weeks ago!''

"I am afraid the delay was all my mother's doing, ma'am," Jane admitted. Startled, Merry stared at her, but Jane's eyes were fixed on her hostess's face. "*Maman* did not want my brother to marry Merry. In truth, I do not think she wanted him to marry anyone, ever. Neither did she want me to marry," she added with a wry smile.

"She is self-centered? Conceited? Selfish?" Miss Lancaster inquired briskly.

"All of those things," Jane admitted. "It took me a very long time to figure the situation out, but now I wonder that I could have been so dull-witted. However, I loved my mother, as my brother did, and it was hard for me to believe that she would do things that would make us both unhappy. You must know she always pretended to have a kind, loving nature."

She turned to Merry then and said, "You knew what she was really like, didn't you, Merry? I suspect you found her out quite a while ago."

Merry nodded, looking concerned. "Yes, I did know, but I could not tell you, or—or Edward either," she said. "I did not think either one of you would be able to believe me, and it was the outside of enough for me to be criticizing the viscountess. How very horrid I would have appeared, if I had done so!"

"Well, I think you should write to the viscount and tell him now," Miss Lancaster said in her positive way as she poured herself another glass of port. "What you have done by keeping your knowledge secret and running away is hardly fair to him."

Since Merry was shaking her head, Jane said, "Perhaps it would be better if I were to do so, ma'am? After all, Merry is in a delicate position here, and any revelation of hers might be taken as backbiting. But as Teddy's sister, I have every right to tell him the truth."

As her great-aunt nodded at this wisdom, Merry said slowly, "I thank you, Jane, but still, I wish you would

not. You see, until he discovers it for himself, and acts
on it one way or the other, I can never be sure . . .''

"Do you love him or don't you?" Miss Lancaster
asked, looking quite fierce.

"Yes, I love him, but I do not want a husband who is
ruled by his mother and who cannot see the kind of
woman she really is," Merry told her.

"Of course you don't!" her great-aunt snorted.
"Who would? But until the viscount knows everything
you have told me tonight, he can hardly act on it. And
men do not always grasp the facts of life as quickly as
women do, poor things. And so often they need help,
for they have no intuition and only a little
imagination."

She rose then, and the two younger women were
quick to follow suit. Jane handed her her cane, and
Merry came to support her other arm. At their feet, one
of the two pugs who had been sleeping under the table
began to yap, while the other made little darts at Jane's
ankles. Jane ignored them both. For some reason,
Caesar and Brutus had decided she had dire designs on
their mistress, and they never ceased trying to disconcert
her. Now, Miss Lancaster ordered them to behave, and
when her words had no effect, she rapped them lightly
with her cane. They subsided then and went ahead to
their cushions in the drawing room with the air of a
loyal escort congratulating themselves on a job well
done.

When Edward and Jason Willoughby arrived in Bath
the next morning, Merry and Jane were taking the pugs
for their walk. Jason went on to York House to reserve
rooms, while the viscount drove immediately to Great
Poultney Street. His eyes lit up when he saw Merry
tugging a stubborn pug a short distance away. His
sister, Jane, was similarly engaged with the other dog,
but the viscount never took his eyes from Merry's face.
Jane's radiant smile when she caught sight of him
forgave him his discourtesy.

"Merry!" he called as he beckoned to a boy to hold

the team for him, and prepared to step down from the tilbury.

Merry stood very still for a moment, one hand going to her mouth. And then, as Edward started toward her, she saw that he looked different, that he seemed older and sterner somehow, as if he had recently suffered pain or disillusionment. Her concern for him made her forget everything she knew to his discredit, and she dropped the leash she was holding and ran to meet him.

The viscount caught Merry up in his arms and bent his head and kissed her, long and hard, before she even had time to breathe his name. It was scandalous behavior for Bath, and two old ladies on the opposite side of the street averted their eyes as they hurried past. The boy holding the viscount's team whistled under his breath, and the two pugs, both now in Jane's care, began to bark in earnest. Neither Merry nor Edward was aware of the commotion they were causing.

When the viscount raised his head at last, Merry's face was flushed. She tried to pull away from him, as if suddenly aware of the proprieties, but he was having none of that. Keeping one arm tight around her waist, he waited for his sister to reach them.

"Teddy, how lovely to see you!" she exclaimed, nudging Brutus away from her ankles. "Did Jason speak to you as I asked him to?"

"Indeed he did, but it was unnecessary by then," her brother told her. "I had figured the whole thing out before he returned from Basingstoke, and I had already confronted *Maman* with what I knew."

"I long to hear all about it, but we cannot talk here," Jane said. "Do come back to the house with us, so I can take the pugs inside. I can't hear a word over the din they make, the nasty little things!"

Her brother shook his head, still looking stern. "I shall be delighted to tell you everything, Jane, but you will have to wait," he said in a firm voice. "Right now, I am taking Merry for a drive. We have a great deal to discuss, and I have a lot of explaining to do."

Jane waved them good-bye with a smile. "Off with

you, then," she said. "Just leave everything to me, Merry. I will tell your aunt where you are, and we will not expect you until later. Much later," she added with an even wider smile.

Edward helped a silent Miss Lancaster into the tilbury. As he climbed to his own seat, he tossed the boy a coin that had him scurrying away before the fine gent could discover the amount of largesse he had bestowed for such a simple chore.

The viscount had intended to drive out to the Mendip Hills, where he had first proposed to Merry, but the dear sight of her so close beside him on the perch, her rosy cheeks and chestnut curls, the sweet scent of her skin, had him pulling up only a few short miles from town.

They had not spoken a word to each other all this time. From a few quick glances, Edward could see that his Merry was deep in thought. The fleeting expressions that crossed her face would have discouraged a lesser man, but still, even though he knew now what the problem between them had been, he realized he had his work cut out for him.

He jumped down from the tilbury and tied the team to a branch before he came and held out his arms to her. "Will you walk with me, Merry?" he asked.

She nodded and bit her lip. As he swung her to the ground, his hands tightened at her waist, and she spoke for the first time. "No, please don't, Edward," she said with a dismissive gesture. He bowed, and took her arm instead.

"I do apologize for running to you in town like that," she said next. "I was not thinking."

"Then I must hope you seldom think in the future if I want a kiss, mustn't I?" he asked.

She ignored his pleasantry as she said, "But nothing has changed between us in spite of that. Nothing at all."

"I intend to convince you differently, my dear," he told her. "Because, you see, everything has changed. I know now why you went away, why you could not be honest with me. I have been so stupid, so blind! But when I had time to sit down alone and think it all through, I was quick to see that it was my mother who caused our estrangement. It was she who discouraged us, poisoned your mind against me, and she who separated us. She will never do so again. I have had it out with her and ordered her to the dower house, after, that is, she apologizes most humbly to you. She will never bother you again. I only wish it had been possible to banish her from Trumbull forever, but—but I could not do that. She is, after all, and no matter what she has done, my mother."

He looked so anguished that Merry could not resist squeezing his arm in sympathy. Her spirits had risen throughout his speech, but now she was reminded of her other reason for leaving him, and they plummeted again.

As they reached the banks of the Avon, the viscount indicated a stretch of grass. "Let us sit down, Merry," he said. "I can see you are still troubled, and I must know why. You do see that you must tell me, don't you?"

Merry nodded reluctantly as she sank to the soft turf. The sun was warm on her skin, and she could smell the fresh scent of the wild flowers, hear the soft song of the birds. It was a beautiful day, but to her, it might just as well have been as dark and forbidding as her spirits.

"What did my mother tell you the day you went to her room, Merry?" the viscount began. He took a seat beside her, being careful not to touch her.

As she swung around to stare at him, her eyes widening, he went on, "That day when you claimed you were ill and never left your room afterward? The same day you refused to accept my flowers?"

As she hesitated, he reached out and took her chin in his hand and forced her to look at him. "I see I must remind you again that this is your Edward," he said. "Remember you can tell me anything. You know you can."

Merry took a deep breath and he let her go. "Yes, I know I must tell you," she said. "It isn't easy, though."

She paused and he waited quietly. "At first, Lady Gloriana spoke to me of marriage," she began. "She claimed it was her duty to prepare me for it, since my own mother was dead. She said—she said your love-making would be painful, that it would not only hurt me but disgust me as well."

The viscount wore a black frown now. "But you didn't believe her, did you, Merry?" he asked. "It will not be like that, I promise!"

"No, I couldn't believe her," she answered, and his frown disappeared. "I had begun to take her measure some time before, and I knew it was only another ploy of hers to get me to cry off."

"But if that didn't upset you, what did?" he persisted. "Come now, I will have the answer, you know!"

Merry looked away from him, her eyes lowered. He waited as she picked a daisy and began to strip away the petals. "Your mother told me you were a great rake, a satyr," she said at last. She could feel him stiffening beside her as she continued, "She claimed that you would take mistresses again, almost at once. And she told me what a terrible time she had always had keeping you away from innocent girls—older women— even those on your own estate. She said no girl was safe from you, that you had even tried for Amy Holbrook."

"My mother is even baser than I had thought possible," the viscount said grimly. "But surely you did not believe that either, did you?" he asked.

He waited, but this time she was not quick to reassure him. "Not at first, I didn't," she said slowly. "If you remember, I went to you the next morning and asked you to set the date of our wedding. But then, that same evening at the *al fresco* dance, I happened to see you talking to Amy Holbrook in the garden. I saw you embrace her, kiss her, and then I didn't know what to think."

She stole a glance at his face and was astounded to see that instead of looking guilty or conscious, he was wearing a glowing smile.

"Of course I kissed her," he said. "Amy is a dear old

friend. She had asked me to go apart with her, for she needed my advice about her brother. That Bartholomew-baby had gotten himself rather badly in debt while he was up at Oxford, and Amy had just learned of it. Her parents did not know, nor did she wish them to find out, and she did not know where to turn. I was able to reassure her that Timothy was not becoming an inveterate gambler as she had feared, that he had only been making a fool of himself, as a lot of young men do at his age. You see, he had spoken to me earlier about it, and I had had it out with him and loaned him the money to repay his debts. When she heard that, Amy kissed me to thank me for my help. That was all there was to our, er, tryst."

"I did not know. I am sorry that I was mistaken in you," Merry managed to say.

"Instead, it was easier to think me a loose screw, was it, love?" He chuckled. "I will *try* to forgive you!"

But when he saw her still-troubled face, his own grew sober again. "There is more, isn't there, Merry?" he asked. "Something worse. What is it?"

She nodded. "Yes, there is more," she told him. "The next morning, I took my mare out for an early ride. I went a long way, to a part of the estate where you had never taken me. And as I was returning, I saw the family who live on that lonely farm."

"And?" he prompted, looking confused.

"The farmer and his pretty young wife and baby were blond, but the little boy there was not. He had black curly hair, exactly like yours," she said, wondering why he needed the explanation at all. Surely he wasn't going to try to bluff this through!

The viscount appeared stunned, and even though she felt great disappointment, she told herself it was only what she had expected. She prayed he would not lie to her about this, for she did not think she could bear that. And then she was amazed when he began to laugh, great shouts of complete amusement. She was so angry at his reaction that she reached out and tried to shake him.

"It is not a laughing matter, Edward," she scolded

him. "How can you think it funny? You should be
ashamed of yourself for fathering a bastard, not
amused by it!"

The viscount grabbed her arms and shook her in
return. He was completely sober now. "Now, just you
listen to me, my girl," he told her, his dark-blue eyes
glittering. "I have been very patient with you, but my
patience is not inexhaustible. You're right, though. The
boy is indeed a bastard. The pretty Molly Breen was at-
tacked by a black Irish tinker just before her marriage to
Sam Hill. She is a good girl, and she told him about it.
He came and asked my advice. I told him he must decide
if he loved her enough to forget the rape, take in
another man's by-blow, and he said he did. I arranged
for them to farm that lonely place, because Molly could
not face the scorn of the villagers. For even though the
rape was not her fault, some of the *good* wives never let
her forget it. But to think that you, my own dear love,
could actually believe that *I* was the father! Merry,
Merry, for shame!"

He dropped her arms then and rose, to walk away
from her and stand stiffly with his back to her. Merry's
hand crept to her throat. What had she done? Could he
ever forgive her? Had she destroyed his love forever?

He turned at last and came to kneel beside her again.
When he saw the tears running down her cheeks, he
took out his handkerchief and wiped them away as he
said, "But of course I do not blame you for thinking
such a thing, my darling, not after the lies my own
mother told me about you. She has even more to answer
for than I thought.

"But although you never asked before, I will be
honest with you now. I have indeed had mistresses. I
am, after all, a man. But I have not had the never-
ending stream of them my dear mother suggested, nor
do I have any bastards that I know of. And no woman
in my care was in that care unwillingly, and I always left
them ample funds for their future. But since I met you,
there hasn't been any other woman, nor will there be
again. How could there be? You see, I have never been

in love before. There! That is a full confession for you, my heart. Do you believe me?''

"Oh, Edward," she cried, swaying toward him, "of course I do! But how unhappy I have been, and even more miserable now that I could think ill of you."

He caught her in his arms then and she melted against him. Just before his mouth came down on hers, and she closed her eyes to savor it fully, she saw the love he felt for her blazing in his own. It was so fervent, so strong, that she was humbled by it.

Viscount Trumbull and Miss Merry Lancaster did not return to Bath until late in the afternoon. They had talked for hours beside the slow-moving river, revealing everything that had happened that they had not been able to discuss before, and vowing never to be separated again. Eventually hunger had driven them to seek an inn, and even there they had lingered over their simple repast of wine and bread and cheese.

Edward kept his arm around Merry as he helped her up the steps of her great-aunt's house. He could tell she was a little worried about how that elderly lady would take her long absence, and he meant to go in with her to make sure she did not have to suffer a massive scold.

To their surprise, they found Miss Lancaster all smiles. She was presiding over a tea tray, and Jane and Jason were with her. Edward saw how happy his sister was, how often her eyes went to the rugged face of his cousin, and he was glad for both of them.

"So, you decided to join us at last, did you, sir?" Miss Lancaster demanded as she readied two more cups. "As for you, Miss Meryl, you should be ashamed of yourself! But there was never anything to be done about a pair of lovers, as I learned more years ago than I care to remember. Sit down, the both of you, and tell us when the wedding will take place."

Edward hugged Merry close before he said, "As soon as we can return to Trumbull, ma'am. We are off tomorrow."

"I take it that the Lady Gloriana has been vanquished?'' Miss Lancaster asked, bending closer to peer at him. "I do not want my niece to be unhappy, you know.''

"My mother will never trouble her again,'' the viscount told her, his voice grim. "She has removed from the hall.''

"And gone to live in the dower house, ma'am,'' Jason added. The dark planes of his face broke into creases of amusement. "However, knowing her, I doubt she will remain there for long where she will be reminded so constantly of her dowager status.''

"How very much trouble *Maman* has brought to all of us,'' the viscount mused. "I am still stunned that I was taken in by her so, and for so many years as well.''

"I am not,'' his sister said with a chuckle. "Why, dear Miss Lancaster was telling us just last night how very slow men are to grasp even the simplest deception.''

"Jane!'' both gentlemen exclaimed together, and she dissolved in laughter. It was not long before everyone joined in.

The viscount hired a carriage for Merry and his sister, and their maids, and it was at the door early the following morning. He and his cousin were to follow in the tilbury, trailing Jason's black gelding.

Although Edward would have liked to return to Trumbull as quickly as possible, he did not want Merry to arrive there exhausted. Accordingly, the little cavalcade stopped in a village a few miles west of Andover, to spend the night. Edward knew it was better this way, for they could reach the hall easily the following morning, and be married that very day. He sent one of the grooms ahead to alert his butler and the vicar of their arrival, and to carry a special message to Nanny Drew.

As he explained to his sister as the four of them ate their supper that evening, he did not care to have her alone at Trumbull, and he could not like her living with her mother in the dower house. He said he had asked Nanny Drew to move back to the hall until he and Merry returned from their wedding journey.

Jane opened her mouth to protest such an arrangement, but then she caught Jason's eye and saw the amused twist to his mouth, and she subsided, her color high.

The carriages came to Trumbull Hall the following morning as planned. The viscount himself insisted on helping Merry alight from the lead carriage. He kissed her soundly, as if even this short time apart had been an age.

"Off you go, my love," he whispered as they walked together up the steps and into the hall. "You must make yourself fine for our wedding. I shall be waiting for you here in an hour."

"An hour and a half, if you please, Edward," she corrected him. "I have no intention of being married when I am looking every which way."

He nodded reluctantly. "But not a minute longer," he said.

Before he followed her upstairs to bathe and change, he asked Durfee for news of the viscountess, and learned she had left for London the day after he himself had gone to Bath. The butler bowed as he presented him with the letter the lady had left for him.

Edward would have preferred to read it later, or even not at all, but he made himself take it into the library. He was careful to close the door behind him before he broke the seal and spread the sheets out on his desk.

Darling *Premier Cavalier*,

Yes, my dear Teddy, as you can see, I have forgiven you for your harsh words, your cruelty. I know you only spoke to me that way because you have been bewitched, but someday you will come to your senses and realize what your *Maman*'s love truly means.

Besides, I thought it only right to tell you my plans, plans I never thought I would be making. Your love was always enough for me; alas, you did not feel the same about mine!

If you remember, it was not too many weeks ago when I received a letter from you, announcing your engagement. I was happy for you then, but now that I have been driven from my home, I cannot stay here and watch that horrid, devious girl ruin your life. Remember, my dear Teddy, if you please, that I told you she was not worthy of you, and that you will be sorry for what you do so impetuously.

However, I shall not have to see it. No, indeed. I am going to London, and by the time you read this, I expect I will be the new Marchioness of Saterly. How surprised and delighted Jeremy will be! You know he has adored me for years, and *he*, at least, values me as I deserve.

I quite agree with you that it would be best if we do not meet. I do not think I could stop myself from telling Miss Lancaster exactly what I think of her for coming between us, and poisoning both your mind and Tiny's against me. As for Tiny, since she has become so *thick* with Miss Lancaster, she may live with her. I wash my hands of her, ungrateful daughter that she is. And I hope you will not rue the day you give your permission for her marriage to Jason Willoughby. No doubt he will treat her as rudely as his father treated his mother, but that is not my concern anymore.

Darling boy, how sad it is that our love for each other must end this way in bitterness and estrangement. Remember I will always love you, with a love stronger than you will ever have from *her*.

Your grieving *Maman*

The viscount crumpled the letter between his hands in disgust. His face was grim as he took it to the empty hearth and set it afire. How typical of his mother that missive had been, how revealing! She still refused to accept any blame for what had happened, placing it all on Merry instead. And how quick she had been to cast her beloved daughter aside! He was glad his sister would never know what her mother had written about her. And it was not only Jane she had decided to abandon. By going to London and cajoling the marquess into marrying her immediately, she had conveniently forgotten her sister's death. So much for her *shame* when he had refused to spend a full year in mourning!

As the paper became ashes and the brief flame went out, he nodded in satisfaction and dusted his hands. As he quit the room, he realized that burning those false words had put a most effective period to his mother's influence on him . . . forever.

In a hurry now, he only paused for a moment to speak to his butler and make sure Merry's bouquet was ready, the champagne iced, and the wedding repast prepared. Then he ran lightly upstairs to his rooms.

Jane was already in the hall when he came down again an hour later, now wearing impeccable morning dress. He thought she looked very lovely in her new blue silk gown and matching bonnet, and he knew Jason would think so too when they met him at the church. But the compliment he had thought to utter died in his throat when he looked up the stairs and saw Merry coming down to join him. In her simple yet elegant ivory silk gown, she was more than beautiful, she was all women on their wedding day: lovely, serene, a little tremulous, and yet so very trusting. He made a silent vow that he would never do anything to extinguish that trust as he bowed low to her, his eyes full of his love and admiration.

Next he turned, to take the large bouquet of creamy roses that Durfee was holding out. As she accepted them, Merry smiled at him. "Are you ready, my love?" Edward asked.

"For any eventuality," she told him, her dimple in full display.

As he watched, bemused, she reached into the tiny reticule that hung from her gloved wrist and took out the silver needle and pin case he had given her all those weeks ago in Bath. And when she pointed to her train, he began to chuckle.

"But how very foresighted of you, my dear," he said.

Then his handsome face grew serious as he held out his hand to her. "And now, shall we go to church, hand in hand, as you wished, love?" he asked, his voice a caress.

The old butler's eyes were wet as he watched Miss Lancaster put her hand in his master's, with such a confident gesture of love and faith. But as soon as the wedding party had left the hall, he wiped his tears away. He knew he had a great deal to do, for in just a short time now he had to have the entire staff assembled in the hall to welcome the *new* Viscountess Trumbull home.

SIGNET REGENCY ROMANCE
COMING IN SEPTEMBER 1988

Sandra Heath
An Impossible Confession

Laura Matthews
Miss Ryder's Memoirs

Caroline Brooks
Regency Rose

The New Super Regency
Mary Jo Putney
Lady of Fortune

There's an epidemic with 27 million victims. And no visible symptoms.

It's an epidemic of people who can't read.

Believe it or not, 27 million Americans are functionally illiterate, about one adult in five.

The solution to this problem is you... when you join the fight against illiteracy. So call the Coalition for Literacy at toll-free **1-800-228-8813** and volunteer.

Volunteer Against Illiteracy. The only degree you need is a degree of caring.